A Cold Harbour

MARTIN KEABLE

First published in Great Britain in 2012 by Martin Keable

ISBN 978-1481051965

For Nikki, my soulmate.

ACKNOWLEDGMENTS

Enormous thanks go to Aidy, Jim, Jim and Jim for their contributions on police procedures, Nicky, Bryon, Debs, Kez, Wendy Rob and Fi for constructive criticism and especially to Nikki for her unending support.

CHAPTER 1

Simon Hearst lay shivering on a hard surface. A cold draught scuttled over his bare feet. Trussed up and gagged with an oily rag, he heard his captor's footsteps padding around the room. Dried tear stains had laid tracks past the blindfold on his dusty cheeks. The last hour had flashed by in a blur. A thud on the back of his head and a jolting, rolling journey in the back of a van. His muffled yells had grown quieter until all he could manage now were brief, whining snorts that covered the makeshift gag with snot.

He felt warm breath on his cheek and smelt stale tobacco. 'You got too close,' the heavily accented whisper trickled into his ear. He frantically tried to place the voice.

'What have I done?' he thought. 'Who are you?'

He heard a large door scrape shut, cutting out the breeze but giving him no comfort.

'You have caused great difficulty in my business,' the voice continued from across the room. 'And you will answer for that.'

Hearst desperately searched his memory for a reason why he could be lying here. Then, in his mind, the voice matched up to a face and he froze. Why had he been so greedy? He shook his head and tried to speak through the gag.

'Please, no.' His incomprehensible plea was ignored.

'But what of the money?' The voice had moved to another corner of the room. A stifled squeal filled the air. 'Hmm. The girl might pay off your debt. If she lives long enough.'

Hearst writhed in his bonds, desperate to escape.

'No!' He wanted to shout, but instead choked on

1

his own saliva. 'Leave her, she's mine,' he begged silently.

'You should not play games with men you are not equal to.'

The whirr of machinery drowned out Hearst's coughed attempts to beg for mercy. Fresh tears traced lines over his cheeks and ran into his ears as the whining closed in.

Detective Constable Chris Raine walked down the bank-side footpath in yesterday's clothes. Wet grass brushed against the legs of his trousers, his shoes already sodden. Damp and slightly hung over, he was beginning to regret agreeing to the call of 'just one more pint, then a curry'.

He'd been called off of his mate's sofa an hour ago to a spot on the river Nene, near the market town of Oundle. Up ahead the outline of a narrowboat emerged from the morning mist, a uniformed officer standing at the tiller.

'Morning,' Chris said, the word rasping from his dry mouth. He showed his badge and made to step aboard. 'Anyone else been here, yet?'

'Not yet,' the constable replied, blocking his path. 'SOCO's are on their way. You'll have to wait until they clear you.'

Chris baulked at the refusal. He looked up at a low, milky sun trying to burn off the early mist. The Scene Of Crime Officers would take ages, photographing, measuring and picking fibres. A cold wait beckoned.

He coughed to cleared his throat. 'Who reported it in?'

'Old fella walking his dog. Said he walks this stretch of the river every morning.'

'How did he know there was a problem?'

'Said he'd seen the cabin doors open and thought it was unusual because the morning was so fresh. I know what he means,' the officer rubbed his pale hands together.

Chris took his own hands out of his pockets and cupped his eyes against a window at the side of the boat. He briefly saw the outline of a body in the dimly lit cabin before recoiling from the glass.

'Not squeamish are you?' the constable laughed.

'No. The boat just moved – I nearly fell in.'

'You don't want to get trapped between the bank and this thing,' the PC said. 'they weigh Tons. You'd be squashed flat before you had a chance to drown.'

'Yeah, cheers for that,' Chris said. He ran a hand through his damp, sandy coloured hair. He'd barely seen the body before his balance had shifted as the boat strained against its mooring ropes. There had been no time to be squeamish.

He took a look at the boat. It was around sixty feet long, had a black painted hull with red upper, and flowers painted around the brass rimmed windows. On the roof he could see a chimney, flower baskets and a couple of boat hooks. The boat's name, 'Mathilda Way', was painted in gold near the stern. Chris took a note of the number stencilled underneath one of the windows. The Water Authorities would tell him who its owner was.

He looked around at the river and the field he'd crossed to get here. He couldn't see far before mist enveloped his view. A short way down the river a few men sat on collapsible chairs, huddled into their jackets, fishing. He wandered over to one of them.

'Anything biting?' he asked.

The man simply grunted at him. Lost in his own world, reluctant to engage.

'Did you see anything happen over on that narrowboat this morning?'

The man didn't even look up. 'Nope,' he said.

A moorhen gave a sharp call. The sound pierced the air over the river and was quickly muted by the dense atmosphere.

Chris stood for a moment, wondering whether to dip into his pocket for his badge again, but decided to leave it. For now he'd wait until the SOCO's had finished and have a good look at the crime scene, come back later if need be.

His phone beeped, rewarding him a scowl from the angler. He moved off and took the call.

'Are you at the scene yet?' Detective Inspector Paul Crighton's voice barked into his ear.

'Yes, Sir,' he said. 'But it's going to be a while before I get to take a close look'.

'Never mind that for now, so long as you're there. I've got a meeting at HQ and won't be able to get over to you this morning.'

'OK.'

'DS Whitelock is off sick, so you'll have to manage on your own for now. Think you can handle it?'

'No problem, Sir. I've got it covered. I'll forward my initial report to you later today.'

Chris ended the call and swallowed hard. He'd been with Kettering's Criminal Investigations Unit barely six months and was still finding his feet. The Army had always made sure he had plenty of backup during the ten years he'd served, the latter part in Afghanistan, Seconded to the Intelligence Corps, where he'd assisted with target assessments for special forces raids.

He made another attempt at looking through the barge's windows, wishing he had the freedom of access afforded to him in the desert. No waiting for SOCO's in a war zone.

Being careful not to lose his balance, he spied a dusty pair of jeans and a bloodied, pale blue shirt, but his view of the upper part of the body was blocked by a cupboard. He shifted along to the next window and craned his neck further to reveal the corpse's face. There wasn't one. Chris fought the urge to heave as he realised the head was missing. The collar and shoulders of the shirt were dark with blood and the body's neck ended in a ragged hem of skin, gristle and bone.

Chris bent over on the bank and took a few deep breaths in an attempt to clear his head.

You might have warned me, he thought, scowling

at the PC grinning down at him.

He looked over to see the pathologist arrive. The tall figure of Dr. Beckman strode across the field adjoining the river, the gaunt beak of his nose aiming at Chris. His mac, hat and scarf fitted the weather better than Chris's attire and his trousers were tucked into wellingtons. Chris made a mental note to stash some outdoor clothes in his car as he wriggled his toes in their wet socks.

'Good morning Dr. Beckman,' Chris said, standing straight. 'SOCOs should be here soon'.

'Yes,' replied the pathologist, his curt reply matching his demeanour. 'I've just left them at the layby, unloading their kit. They'll have to bring it over here before preparing so as not to contaminate their suits.'

Beckman looked down his nose and continued to describe the procedure the SOCO's would take to secure the scene. Mid-sentence he stopped, stared at Chris for a moment, then asked, 'You're Crighton's new DC, aren't you? Where is he?' He looked around as if expecting the DI to appear from nowhere.

'DI Crighton's not able to make it. Something at HQ prevented him from leaving,' Chris replied.

'Well there must at least be a DS here. What's going on?'

Chris cursed inwardly but calmly replied. 'DI Crighton will be able to fill you in on the details but we're short staffed so he's authorised me to proceed without him.'

'This is most irregular,' huffed the doctor. 'Let's hope Crighton has staff enough to debrief you, eh?'

'Yes, Doctor.'

'Ah, here they come,' Beckman announced. 'Time to get started.'

'Can I come inside, Doctor?' Chris asked.

Beckman stared again, then nodded. 'You may. I will of course be sending a full report to your DI, but despite your rank I think it's worth you attending, to gain experience.'

They suited up with the SOCOs, the white paper suits displaying a ghostly pantomime to the nearby anglers. 'There's little room aboard one of these craft so try to keep out of the way,' Beckman warned Chris.

The team squeezed into the thin passageway of the narrowboat. A SOCO stopped them. 'Wait a second, this isn't going to work. There's no room for everyone to go in from this end. Split the team and enter from both ends of the boat.'

Chris joined two of the SOCOs at the front of the boat and they checked the lock. It was open. One of the men raised his eyebrows at the lack of security.

'Bloody hell, he's a mess,' the lead SOCO commented.

The crowded cabin made it difficult for Chris to see what was going on and he soon became hot from his oversuit. Beckman was speaking into a Dictaphone:

'Confirm one deceased. Subject, male. Unable to estimate age as is headless. Body seated in wicker easy chair. Blood soaked through shirt but none evident on carpet or surrounding areas. '

Beckman stuck his head out of the door for a moment, then continued speaking.

'Blood trail was noted during entry, suggesting deceased did not die here but was transferred from scene of death. Further analysis needed to confirm this estimate. Serrated edge used for decapitation.' He paused, looking closer. 'Direction of serration is all one way. Unusual.' He looked up, 'Take a look into all cupboards and alcoves – see if the head's anywhere aboard.'

They took to the task. Chris lifted cushions from the seats running down the sides of the main cabin area, revealing covered storage areas but no sign of the unfortunate victim's head. He looked over the cabin. A bench seat ran down one side whilst a cabinet-come-galley formed the other. On top of this sat a small portable television, a lead snaking to a rooftop antenna. At one end of the living area sat a small wood-burning stove with a chimney that poked through the roof. He gently placed a hand on its surface. Cold. He continued on his hands and knees, searching the multitude of small storage areas, but came up blank. He caught glimpses of the corpse between the legs of the SOCOs. It's jeans and bare white feet were covered in a light brown dust. His stomach was still turning over at the sight of the headless torso.

'Who are you, fella?' he whispered to himself, 'and who did you piss off so much they had to chop your head off?'

'Nothing at this end,' he called to the pathologist.

'It's clear here too,' came a voice from the other end of the boat.

'OK - erm, Raine, isn't it?' Beckman asked. 'you can go now. Tell DI Crighton the scene will be secure for the rest of the day if he deigns to bestow his company upon us.'

'Can you tell me if he had a wallet or drivers licence on him, please?' Chris asked.

'Wait a second,' one of the SOCO's said. He carefully went through the corpse's pockets. 'No ID,' he confirmed. 'Don't know what these were doing in there.' He held out his hand. On the latex-clad palm sat a thin red elasticated hair band, a packet of sweets and a small, munchkin-faced, plastic kitten.

'Strange things for a bloke to have in his pocket,' Chris said.

'He might have had long hair,' the SOCO replied. 'Won't know for sure until the head's found.'

'Doesn't explain the toy and the sweets, though,' Chris said. The men shared a look.

'We need to be getting on,' Dr. Beckman said. 'If you don't mind.' He ushered Chris from the boat.

Having been dismissed by the pathologist, Chris stood on the bank for a minute staring out over the river and the bare trees while the Pathologist and SOCOs continued their work.

What could this man have done that deserved

this kind of treatment? Chris thought. He looked over the scene again, trying to visualise what had happened here. There didn't seem to be enough blood inside the cabin for the decapitation to have happened there. The grass surrounding the boat was also untainted. Was he taken away to be killed and then the corpse returned to the boat? And why did he have a kids toy with him? A kidnapper's bait?

Since completing his two years in uniform, then joining the Kettering force, Chris had been lucky that no child abduction cases had crossed his path. Walking over the field to his car he was reminded of an incident a couple of years previously. A dad had blown a fuse and suffocated his wife and two children. But Chris had been a fresh-faced bobby then, barely on the periphery of the investigation. His phone rang again, disturbing his thought process. It was the emergency switchboard at Kettering.

'DC Raine, we've got an incident at Brownford nature park,' said the officer at the end of the line. 'I've been informed that you're in the area. Can you attend?'

'Sure, what is it?' he replied.

'Got a panicked call from the park warden over there. Something about a body in one of his bird hides.'

Chris's pulse quickened. 'I'm on my way,' he replied and with a churning sickness in his stomach he hurried down the footpath to the nearby park.

The warden was waiting at the entrance to the nature reserve, doing his best to discourage anyone from entering the car park and ushering the few remaining visitors away.

'I'm DC Chris Raine, Northants Police,' Chris said, showing his badge.

'Thank God you're here,' the warden replied. 'I'm having a hell of a job clearing the place out.'

Although it was still early in the day, there were a good number of visitors at the park. He directed Chris towards the hide and continued to usher traffic out of the park entrance.

Chris walked down a well beaten path at the edge of a small lake that was no more than a filled in gravel pit. For a park to be so close to a road it was surprisingly quiet. Even bereft of leaves, the trees occluded almost all traffic noise and he could hear the ducks out on the water. A brilliant white tern dove into the lake and emerged with a silvery fish in its beak.

He approached the hide, dreading what he might find. The image of the plastic toy kitten swam across his thoughts. The hide was built from sturdy timber giving it a rustic log cabin aura and was surrounded on it's front face by a tall wicker fence that stretched about ten meters ahead. Three wooden steps covered with a high grip surface led to the entrance. It was designed for ordinary people - those who'd bring a packed lunch and a flask to pass the time in this contrived idea of a sanctuary.

Chris's thoughts were interrupted by the hurried arrival of the park warden.

'Have you seen it yet? It's ghastly,' he stammered, out of breath.

'Not yet,' Chris said tersely. He'd hoped to be able to examine the scene uninterrupted. To have this nervous busybody around would only get in his way. 'Have you managed to close the park?'

'I'll never be able to clear it totally, I've just done the best I can to stop the gawpers,' said the warden. 'The hide is well protected but you can still see into the viewing slits from across the way. I just tried to minimise the fuss.'

Chris eyed the hasp on the door. There were fresh marks scraped on its surface.

'Is this hide normally locked overnight?' he asked.

'Yes, of course, but the padlock's been broken off,' the warden seemed proud to have detected something. 'I found it lying in the grass.' He reached into his pocket and took out the lock, offering it up to Chris.

Chris didn't want to handle the lock. 'Sir, can you just place it on the floor, please? It will have to be checked by forensics.'

The warden started to argue but did as he was asked and stepped back.

Chris took a deep breath and pulled the door open. A viewing slit had been pegged open with a wooden toggle, permitting a limited amount of light to spill inside onto empty floorboards. Chris looked around, confused.

'Where was the body?' he demanded of the warden.

'There,' the man pointed to the open viewing slit. Chris looked up and saw the silhouette of a head facing out towards the nature area. It was perched on a thick book and leaning on the window frame, as if looking out onto the wildlife area.

Chris was taken aback by the grisly sight. He'd seen worse than this in Afghanistan but in this idyllic rural retreat the severed head seemed alien and menacing. Standing at the door, Chris's eyes roved the interior. Plenty of room to decapitate a victim, he thought, but no blood on the floor. Plastic sheet used, perhaps? Posters were pinned to the walls depicting woodland birds and wildlife, in stark contrast to the macabre scene at the window. In one corner a chalkboard was screwed to the wall with a note asking visitors to write down what wildlife they'd seen recently. There was no chalk.

'I thought you said body. I thought there'd be...' he couldn't bring himself to say what he'd feared to discover in the cabin.

'Well of course there's no body, but, well, what was I supposed to say on the phone?' the warden bleated.

Chris brushed roughly past the warden and allowed the door to close on it's spring. 'A PC is on his way to secure the hide. I'll wait here for him.'

'What else can we do?'

'The best thing you can do is go back to the gate and control public access.'

'Are you sure I can't do anything more for you? I could get some sack cloth to cover the head,' the warden stuttered.

'No. We can't disturb it,' explained Chris. 'We'll have to take your prints too, and a DNA swab at some point,' he began

'You can't think it was me!' exclaimed the warden. 'I couldn't do such a thing as, as this.' His shaking finger stabbed toward the door.

'Calm down, sir, it's just a precaution,' Chris's own voice was raising. 'We have to take your details to help eliminate you from any suspect matter that may be in the hide. It's standard procedure. You've already handled the padlock, which you shouldn't have done by the way. And I don't know what else you've touched in there.'

Chris was still arguing with the warden as PC Taylor arrived. The officer's uniform seemed to subdue the warden. Still shaking with anger at the warden's poor choice of words, Chris left him in Taylor's care and called the station back to arrange another team of SOCOs to attend the hide.

Chris returned to Kettering CID by mid-afternoon. The office was bustling with people assembling the incident room. The overhead projector had been loaned out to another department so someone had been sent to retrieve it, and a search for flip charts and marker pens was being orchestrated. This was no high-tech metropolitan set-up that Hendon training centre and his former Intelligence Corps briefing rooms could afford. Chris had needed to get used to some older technology pretty quickly. There were no electronic whiteboards here.

'Alright, Rainey Day', Joe 'Soap' Alden called. 'Things getting ahead of you are they?' he quipped, earning a half hearted chuckle from his colleagues.

'Soap,' Chris replied, nodding at Alden and wishing he could lose his own nickname.

'Anything I can do to help?' he asked.

11

'No, we can manage, cheers. You need to get your report done for the Guv. Glad I didn't get that call – last thing I'd need to wake me up in the morning.'

Chris reached his desk and logged on to his computer. He started going over the details on the case. The boat would need its number checking against the Environment Agency records. He also had his reports on both crime scenes to write up for his DI, so he let the others carry on.

He had a bad feeling in his gut. Rural murders generally fell into one of two categories. Those committed by family or someone close to the victim and those unfortunate acts of brutality, when a robbery on a farm or other desolate dwelling went wrong. But this didn't appear to follow any of those patterns. Why place the head and body in different locations like that?

He was so engrossed in his work that he didn't notice until he heard her voice behind him. 'Caught yourself a big one this morning, DC Raine,' DS Sally Whitelock said.

'Oh, hello Sarge,' he said calmly, though she'd caught him off guard. 'Didn't think you'd be in until tomorrow.' He swivelled his chair to face her.

'Couldn't let this one go, Raine. Needs a proper eye on it,' she replied with authority, looking slightly put out that she'd not been able to surprise him. She didn't look like she had a sickness bug, although she was wearing a thick layer of foundation and had applied dark eye make-up. Probably trying not to look too pale so as to hide her sickness, Chris thought.

'Glad to see you up and about. How did you hear of it?'

'Got a call from a friend on the switchboard,' she said, loftily. 'She keeps me up to speed if anything serious happens. Not that it should matter to you. What are you doing now?'

'I'm working on the crime scene report for the Guv.'

'Make sure I get a copy of it first. I don't want him

having to read any unnecessary tripe.'

'No problem.'

'You should have called me when the Guv told you he couldn't make it.'

'But you were off sick.'

'Doesn't matter, I need to be kept informed.' She moved away, 'Hi Joe, how's the incident room going? Are we going to be ready for the Guv this evening?'

'Yeah, we're nearly there. Just a few odds and sods to sort out.'

'Great.' She turned back to Chris. 'We'll be running late tonight. If you've got a date, Raine, you'll have to let her down.' She paused, her fingernails tapping a staccato beat on his desk.

'No date,' Chris said, shrugging.

Satisfied, she walked off to organise his other colleagues.

She's completely different with anyone else in the team, he thought. What's it going to take with her to get accepted?

'Don't let it get to you Chris,' he told himself. 'Carry on as normal, deal with her as you do anyone else and maybe she'll come around.'

CHAPTER 2

Crighton leaned against the edge of a desk and addressed his team for the evening's briefing. 'This is a serious situation,' he looked around the room. 'A violent killer is on the loose and there's currently no reason to think he won't kill again. Until we catch him, this takes priority over whatever cases you are working on.'

'He, sir?' asked Joe Alden.

'I believe we are looking at a man, yes,' Crighton said. 'With all due consideration,' he glanced at Sally Whitelock 'we're looking at a fourteen stone corpse. It's not an easy lift.'

Whitelock nodded in agreement. 'Do we have an identity yet?' She asked

'Not yet. His pockets were empty so we don't even have a drivers licence to go on.'

'Not empty, Sir,' Chris said.

'True,' Crighton acknowledged. 'Child's toy, hairband, sweets. What do you make of those?'

'Paedophile?' Soap suggested. 'Could be someone's caught a kiddie fiddler and executed summary justice.'

'Possible,' Crighton nodded, looking around the room. Alden's suggestion wasn't generating much support. 'As yet, we've not received any reports of missing children.'

'Could simply be someone's dad,' Whitelock said. They all looked at her. 'Pocket full of stuff his kid's not allowed to take into school.'

'A hairband wouldn't be banned from school premises,' Chris said. Whitelock met his gaze and cocked her head as though waiting for a better answer. She laughed.

'You don't have kids, do you, Raine?'

14

'Neither do you.'

'My sister does,' Whitelock said. 'You should see the junk she ends up carrying for them.'

'But this is a man,' Chris countered.

Whitelock laughed again. 'So dads are banned from taking their kids to school, now?'

Chris, caught in her mocking stare, glared back.

Crighton intervened, 'Lets leave this until we get an ID on the corpse or we find positive evidence that someone else is involved. I take it he wasn't the owner of the boat. Any news on that?'

'A Mr. Alec Cartwright. We're trying to locate him,' Chris said.

Alden chipped in, 'So, we've got a murderer who cuts of a bloke's head then carries the body to a boat and dumps it. How far is the river from the road?'

'Not too far,' Chris said. 'I'm pretty fit, but I wouldn't want to carry a body over a field.'

The others looked at him. He stood six feet with broad shoulders and though not bulky, he was clearly athletic. Whitelock's eyes seemed to remain on him longer than the others. Was she scrutinizing him, weighing up whether his claim was viable?

'It's a good point, Raine,' Crighton offered.

'Sir, it could have happened another way,' Chris said. 'The killer could have taken the body by another boat to the narrowboat.'

'Go on.'

'It is rare to have any activity on the river at night and it would probably be noticed by people moored on the river.'

'And your point is?'

'If we check out the residents of the static moorings up and down river we might pick up a sighting. That way we might get an idea where the killer entered the river.'

'You're becoming a real old mariner, Raine,' Whitelock said, bringing a chuckle from the others. 'Thought you were ex-Army, not Navy. Who's to say the body wasn't wheeled down there in a barrow? I think we'd be wasting time traipsing up and down the banks, Guv. We should concentrate on finding the boat's owner.'

Chris reddened. Here we go again, running me down in front of everyone.

'I think it's worth checking out, that's all,' he said.

'OK,' Crighton said. 'We're still waiting for forensics reports but I want you all to keep an open mind. We could be looking for a vigilante killer taking revenge on a paedophile, or there could be any number of reasons someone might want this man dead. I want you Sally, and Raine, to go back there first thing tomorrow and have another look around. If we locate the owner while you're out we can call it through to follow up.'

Chris looked at Whitelock and she smiled back at him, an unfathomable look on her face.

The meeting began winding down at half past six.

'Pub, Rainey?' asked Joe.

'Might see you in there a bit later, Soap. I want to catch the Guv before he leaves,' he said.

'No probs, don't forget to take an apple for Teach,' grinned Joe.

'Sod off,' Chris laughed.

Sally Whitelock wandered over. 'See you at the pub, Raine?'

'Maybe, Sarge. Got to clear a few things up with the Guv, first.'

'Oh? Anything I should be dealing with? Don't want to bother him needlessly, remember.'

'No, it's personal, that's all.'

She frowned but let it go. 'Well if we don't see you in the pub I'll pick you up tomorrow. Seven thirty, OK?'

'Sure thing,' Chris said.

Chris waited whilst DI Crighton finished off a call. The room grew quiet as the noisy team cleared out. He tried formulating what he wanted to say to his boss but was immediately put off guard by the DI.

'So Raine, you wanted to speak with me. But first you need to tell me why you didn't question the fishermen more thoroughly this morning.'

'Er,' Chris stalled. 'I guess I didn't expect them to leave so soon after I arrived - I think.'

'Chris, you've got to take the opportunities when you see them. I bet you had nothing else to do before the SOCO's arrived did you?'

'Um, no. I'm sorry Guv. I didn't even get any names before the Doctor took over. By the time we'd finished, they'd all left.'

'OK, don't worry too much about it.'

Chris sighed, relieved.

'I'm sure they're creatures of habit and will be back tomorrow. Make sure you and DS Whitelock arrive before seven tomorrow and quiz the first ones you see.'

'OK, sir.'

'I'm not sure about your idea of transporting the corpse by boat, but you can check that out after you've spoken to the anglers.' His tone eased. 'You wanted to ask me something?'

'Yes Guv, although I'm a bit reluctant to raise it now. I know I've made mistakes today and I think I need to put those right first.'

'It's OK, Chris, I won't bite.'

Chris shifted on his feet. It seemed petty to bring up his issues with Sally Whitelock but it was grating on his nerves.

'It's just that DS Whitelock is a hard nut to crack.'

'How do you mean?'

'I don't know. I can't seem to fit in with her. She's different towards the other DC's than me. I'm hoping it'll resolve itself in time. Do you know if a replacement to Sergeant James is on its way?'

Crighton flinched at the mention of the name.

'You don't get to choose who you work under, Raine,' he growled. 'Sally is a good DS. She's been through some tough times, and takes her time to trust someone. You never knew James, did you?'

Chris shook his head. He'd heard the story. Six months previously, Sergeant Aiden James had been working on a drugs case, in liaison with the Metropolitan Police. Slovakian drug dealers had established a foothold in the East of the country and several cells emerged in the Norwich, Peterborough and Kettering areas. James had met his demise during a botched police raid on a suspected drugs base.

'Aiden and Sally are – were – similar in their approach,' Crighton corrected himself, screwing up his eyes to shake off the error. 'You wouldn't have it any easier under him.'

'No, Sir,' Chris said, regretting bringing the subject up. 'I just wondered if there was anything I could do to make things easier.'

'Don't worry lad,' Crighton patted Chris on the shoulder. 'She's said some good things about you. I'm sure it'll get better.'

Chris's eyes widened. 'Oh. Thanks for letting me know Guv, I didn't know. Are you going to the pub?'

'No. I've a few things to finish off here so I won't have time. Speak to you tomorrow.'

Chris moved off, collecting his jacket from the back of a chair and checked his watch. Could he be bothered to join the others in the pub? His clothes were dirty and he was sure there was the smell of something dead on them. Maybe a pint would help him shake off the sights he'd experienced that morning. The head's dead eyes still came easily to him if he closed his own.

He turned right and wandered down the alley that ran parallel to the side of the station building, past the churchyard and into the High Street.

The Three Crowns was busy for a week night. Not much more than a converted end of terrace house, the long bar squeezed its patrons, mostly off-duty police, into a narrow room. A few reporters from the local paper were in, looking for details on the day's big story.

Joe Alden waved Chris over and passed him a pint. Chris savoured a mouthful of lager and tried to close his nostrils to the smell of sweat, stale beer and deep fried food. He almost longed for a return of smoking in pubs. A few lungfuls of secondary smoke would have been tolerable if only to help suppress the odour in the Three Crowns.

'You're in high demand tonight, mate,' Alden said.

'Eh?'

'Half the hacks in town are looking to grill you, and Sally keeps asking after you. Seems she's got the hots for you, eh?' he said with a wink.

'Yeah, good one Soap,' Chris said, shaking his head. 'You've seen the way she treats me. I'm like a dog that's pissed in the corner half the time.'

'Classic diversion tactics mate, mark my words.' Joe nodded to the woman arriving at Chris's shoulder. 'Looks like another admirer. See you later.'

Chris turned to the woman. Straight red hair, freckled face and intense green eyes. The chief reporter from the Kettering Gazette, Hazel Moran, smiled through orange lipstick.

'You look like you've been dragged through a hedge backwards,' she commented, looking him up and down. Her Irish lilt was almost hidden by the Northants accent.

'Flattery won't get you anywhere,' he answered.

'Obviously you were down at the river today,' she said. 'Can I get you a drink?'

'No, thanks. I'm only stopping for this,' he waved his glass in the air.

'Early start tomorrow then? Have you worked out the significance of the book, yet?'

'How do you know about the book? That info wasn't released in the police statement.'

'I have my sources,' she replied, coyly.

The park warden, thought Chris. He must have had a snoop around before we arrived and couldn't keep his mouth shut when the papers questioned him.

'Well, I'm afraid you'll have to wait until we release a further statement to hear about it officially,' he said, trying to divert attention from his omission.

'Well now, never mind,' Moran said, her hand was raised to her face and a straight glass of gin and tonic rested against her cheek. 'I did my own research. It looks like a revenge killing to me.'

'Jumping to conclusions a bit early, aren't you?'

'The book – The Count of Monte Cristo – classic tale of treachery and revenge. Stands to reason it's a message.'

'And what message would that be?'

'Fuck around with me and this is what you get,' she said, her tongue flicking over her teeth, challenging him to deny it.

'Shame our victim couldn't read it then, isn't it?' Chris said, annoyed at himself. Again, he'd missed a clue by not taking a note of the book title.

'Okay,' she drawled. 'You're touchy, aren't you.' Deciding there was no more information to glean, she left him at the bar.

Chris excused himself to Joe and looked for Sally Whitelock, hoping to mend some of the friction between them. He found her slouching on a stool at the other end of the bar. 'DS Whitelock, we'll have to leave earlier than half seven tomorrow.'

'Whoah,' she replied. 'Who's giving the orders here?' She prodded a finger at his chest.

'The Guv wants us to get there early to question the fishermen.'

'It's Sally, Chris. Relax,' she screwed up her face and flapped the same hand she'd poked him with, as though swatting at a fly. In her other hand, white wine made a bid for freedom from a wavering glass.

'Yeah, OK. Sorry. Anyway, I'm off. I'm knackered and I've got to get out of these stinking clothes.'

'I'll give you a hand', she said, leaning forwards. She saved herself from falling off the stool by clapping her free hand on his chest.

'I'm sure I can manage,' he said. He helped her back onto her seat and looked anxiously around for someone to save him.

'Pfff, We're off duty. What's the matter? Am I not your type?' she sulked.

He ignored the question. She's attractive he thought, when she's sober perhaps. But also married, so in my eyes, off limits. 'We'll have to leave Kettering by half six. I'll see you tomorrow,' he said, edging away from her.

'Oh, right. See you tomorrow.' She turned sulkily back to the bar.

The cell that contained Molly Gowland was nothing more than an under-stairs cupboard. There was barely enough room for her to sit, tied and cramped amongst the brooms and mop and the lemony smell of cleaning liquid, the same type as her mum used. Angry voices filtered through the door. The first was unfamiliar but she would never forget the second, the man with the strange voice. The man who'd killed her father.

'Why did you have take her as well?' the first man was saying.

'She wasn't supposed to be there.' The second man spat the words out.

No. I was supposed to be on holiday with mum, Molly thought.

'You'd better not kill her,' the first man warned. 'What you did to Hearst was bad enough.'

'I do what I want,' came the growled reply. The girl shivered. In her mind she could still hear her father's strangled scream abruptly cutting off. The memory made her whimper and she scrunched her body up tight, crying into her blindfold.

'She can't stay here.' He sounded kinder, the first man, as though he wanted to help her.

'I know. I have contacts. She will be out of this country before the end of the week.'

Please let me go,' the girl begged silently.

'I don't like it,' the first man sounded reluctant. 'You're going too far.'

He's not strong enough, she thought, hope leaving her.

'It is not your concern. We will deal with it.'

The voices faded as the men left the room, leaving the girl sobbing in her dark cell.

The following morning, Sally Whitelock's car picked its way along the row of small terraced town houses in Princes Street. It squeezed along the narrow road between the tightly packed cars, not an inch of space to park this early in the day.

Chris was watching from his living room window and left the house, carrying a holdall with a spare pair of boots in it. He wore a winter coat, determined not to get caught out today.

He lifted the remains of a fast food breakfast from the car's passenger seat and eased himself gingerly into Sally's old Peugeot. Scraps of paper, empty biro tubes, sweet wrappers and soft drinks bottles were scattered around.

'You don't have a maid, then' he joked, his foot nudging a bottle.

'I may order you to clean it up' she replied, tartly.

'Look, can we get something sorted, please?' he started. 'Why are you always on my case?'

'I'm your DS, I have to keep you in line.'

'It's not like I'm out of line. I was only kidding just then but at work it doesn't seem to matter what I suggest, you don't like it.'

Sally looked taken aback. 'Calm down. I'm usually only testing you, making sure you can back up what you say.'

'It's affecting how some of the other DCs are with me.' He stared out of the side window, dawn's light beginning to emerge on the horizon. 'A lot of them are less experienced than me but they see you pulling me down all the time and think it's OK for them to do the same.'

'Maybe you need a bit more backbone.'

'No, it's not that.' he sighed. 'I can deal with them, but I'd prefer not to have to.'

'Don't take yourself so seriously,' she said. 'What about in the pub last night? 'DS Whitelock, we need to leave early'' she mimicked. 'We were off duty.'

'Well, that's because I don't know how to take you. And you were drunk last night . . . .'

'I was not drunk,' she protested.

'It looked it to me.'

'Let's just get on with the job,' she sounded embarrassed but her cheeks failing to redden. They were again covered with thick foundation, although her eyes were free from eye-liner today. He looked over but couldn't see her properly. Her dark, almost black, hair was framed closely around her face in an outgrowing bob.

'OK, maybe I have been a bit hard on you,' she eventually said, reaching out and turning the heater from screen to cabin. 'Look, I used to go out with a squaddie and he turned out to be a complete shit. Maybe I've tarred you with the same brush. Truce?'

He nodded.

'Just don't let me down,' she said.

They drove a while without speaking, Chris beginning to sweat in his heavy coat.

'It's unusual there aren't any missing persons reports on file at the moment,' Sally said, breaking the silence.

'There are, but they're all either young adults or women,' Chris said.

'Oh, took a look did you?'

'Yeah. I double checked to make sure. None of them fit the age and sex of our victim.'

'I wonder if there's anything in that. I mean if he was a married man, expected home for his tea, someone would have missed him,' she mused.

'Maybe he was a lorry driver out on a long haul.

Or a business rep not due home for a few days,' Chris suggested.

'True, and if he lived alone it could be days before anyone misses him and reports it in.'

'I can't get my mind off the stuff he had in his pocket. If there's a kid involved, and we don't pick up on it in time. . .'

Sally shook her head. 'If you speculate too much, it'll tear you apart,' she said. 'Like the Guv said, until we get his ID we can't do anything about that.'

Sally pulled into the layby where Chris had parked the day before. They climbed a wooden stile into the field adjoining the river. Chris shivered, despite his coat. The thin layer of perspiration he'd accumulated in the car absorbed the chill of the morning.

A small herd of cattle rested at one edge of the field and one of the beasts lifted it's head, watching them walk along the well beaten footpath. A white tent had been erected next to the moored up narrowboat

'Those aren't bulls, are they?' Sally asked.

'Bullocks,' Chris answered.

'I only asked.'

Chris laughed. 'No. They're bullocks. No udders, see? I think we'll be safe so long as we keep to the path and don't disturb them.'

They continued over the field, keeping a wary eye on the cattle. A uniform sat inside the tent nursing a lukewarm mug of tea.

'Any of that going spare?' Sally asked.

The officer reluctantly poured a cup from a Thermos and scowled at Chris, daring him not to ask for some. 'There aren't any more cups,' he said.

'That's all right,' Chris replied, opening his holdall and taking out his own flask. Sally took a look at the bag.

'Bringing your own supplies, eh?' she curled a finger around the holdall's zipper, tweaking it open for a better look. 'We'll have to check for sandwiches and crisps later,' she said, sipping her tea.

'So, what made you think our killer dropped the

corpse off by boat then, Chris?'

This took him by surprise. First name terms?

'It's just one way of doing it.' He said. 'He could have put a small boat in the water further up river, nearer to where the nature park is, closer to the road. He wouldn't be exposed on land for long then.'

'And if he'd dragged it across the field, even on a barrow, he'd be more obvious?'

'Pretty much, yeah.'

'So the sound of an outboard motor on the river in the middle of the night isn't obvious?'

'Hmm, got me there.'

'Exactly. That's why I think we're wasting our time.'

'The Guv has given us time to ask around, so we should make the most of it. After we've caught hold of these anglers, of course.'

They left the relative warmth of the tent and walked along the bank. The same man was fishing in the spot that Chris had seen him the previous day.

This time Chris watched as Sally spoke to the man; cajoling a few names out of him and alternating between sweet talking girlie and hard nosed DS to find out that he really didn't know anything about the incident on the boat.

They spoke to a few other anglers and after a while they had no more solid information. These men were only interested in fishing and the natural world about them.

'OK, where do you want to waste your time, first?' Sally asked Chris, accepting they'd come up short.

'Well, we should take a look around the bank by the barge,' he suggested. 'Then let's go south. We'll find a static mooring area near where we parked.' his pointed finger traced the route he described. 'From there the river flows south-east, then around a large arc and north until it meets up with the main road again. Brownford park is located within that arc and most of the river is accessible from the road.'

Before they left, they took a good look at the bank near the the narrowboat. The dried blood trail remained on the boat but it wasn't obvious where its source could be on the grass. 'Maybe whatever the corpse was carried in split, as it was taken aboard,' Chris guessed.

'Forensics will have been over the grass. They'll give us a better idea if there's any trace on the ground,' Sally replied.

They made their way to the static moorings. After about ten minutes walk six boats came into view, moored up to their left. On the bank, each boat had an area cleared between the river and a row of trees, for its owner's use. A couple of vans were parked along the tree line, along with a motorcycle and a push bike.

A thin-faced young man emerged from the first boat and looked them up and down. 'What do you want - officers?', he asked, scratching his straggly beard, a smug look on his face.

'We're investigating a suspected murder on a narrowboat just down the way,' Sally began.

'Thought so,' said the man. 'I heard it on the news. I can't help you. Not been off my boat for three days.'

'Do you know who owns that boat?'

'No. Try the marina.'

'No matter. We're checking out how the body could have been taken to the boat.'

'It wasn't the owner then.'

'No.'

'Who was it?'

'We can't tell you right now.'

'You don't know, do you,' he sneered.

'That's not what we're here for,' Sally's voice hardened. 'Did you hear any boats come past any time the night before last?'

The man stretched out a gaping yawn, exposing a row of uneven, brown teeth.

Sally looked at the rusty white van parked next to

the boat and started walking over to it. 'Is this your van?'

'Yeah, why?' His voice lost a bit of his cockiness.

'You've got an MOT for it, I hope. Not in the best condition is it?'

'It's all legal.'

Sally turned back to the man. 'Listen, we're not bothered what you might or might not have wrong with your van. We're looking for a killer and at the moment that's the only priority we have,' she said. 'Can you help?'

'Well, I'll try', he said, lighting a cigarette. 'What do you want to know?'

'Would you have heard a boat come by in the night?'

'Probably.' He was blinking rapidly, cigarette smoke stinging his eyes. 'Depends on how big it was. I'd either hear it or feel the wake bump against my hull. But I didn't hear anything that night.'

'Depending how big it is?'

'Well, if it's a barge, it might rock my boat about a bit, but not a small outboard. I'd hear it though.'

'Where can someone launch a small boat nearby?'

'Well, Barnwell lock is upriver,' he said, warming to his subject. 'So you'd probably launch from one of the portage points between there and downstream at Ashton lock.' The two officers looked at each other, both wondering what a portage point was.

'We're interested in someone who'd be trying to avoid contact with anyone,' Chris added.

The man nodded. 'There's an inlet that joins the main river near Barnwell. You could get a boat in there if you tried.'

'Are there more static moorings around?' asked Sally.

'There's a bigger one upstream, past the Barnwell locks but I doubt anyone would launch a boat that far up. They wouldn't want to go through the lock at night. There aren't any more moorings downstream until

Yarwell and Wansford, about three locks down. You won't get any luck from anyone that far down.' He flicked his cigarette stub into the river.

'So, if you didn't hear anything then he probably launched downstream at Ashton,' Sally said, her voice suggesting she was losing interest.

'There are temporary moorings down there, yeah,' he admitted. 'I've just had a thought! He could have used an electric motor.' he said. 'Yeah, they're virtually silent. And a small boat wouldn't cause enough wake to affect a barge like this.'

'An electric motor?'

'Yeah, some people use them as emergency backup for a bigger boat.'

Sally's phone rang. She took the call and held the phone to her chest a moment.

'Get his name and some numbers,' she told Chris, nodding to the van and the boat.

Chris turned his attention to the man and lead him away from Sally.

'Name?'

'Jim Cook.'

'And do you have a phone on the boat, Mr. Cook?'

'Mobile,' Cook replied, reciting his number. Chris also took down Cook's van and boat registration numbers.

'C'mon Chris,' Sally called from the footpath. 'That was the Guv. The boat owners have been found.'

Chris nodded goodbye to Cook, who smirked and sloped back to his boat.

'Call the station please, Chris,' Sally said, on their way back to her car. 'Get someone over here with a warrant to search that van,' she said.

'OK, Sarge. I think I know why.'

'You saw how his attitude changed when I mentioned his van, didn't you?'

'Yeah, he couldn't help us more if we'd paid him. And he was too nervous to be worried about his MOT, or insurance.'

'That's right. There's a lot of mud on that van's wheel arches, and it's sitting low on its springs. The track from his mooring to the road isn't muddy. He's either got suspension trouble or there's something in the back of the van he doesn't want us to see.'

'Where are we going?'

'A village called Ashton, a couple of miles away. Guv took a call last night', she explained. 'The owners tried to return to their boat yesterday.'

'Wonder why the uniform didn't tell us,' Chris commented, observing the incident tent from the edge of the field they were skirting.

Sally shrugged. 'Don't know. The owners were taken to Oundle station. Guv interviewed and released them.'

'What's he done that for?'

Sally re-mounted the stile that led to her car. She looked down at Chris. 'Doesn't think they're suspects. They were at the pub in Ashton the night of the murder, leaving the boat empty. Crighton wants us to check their story out.'

CHAPTER 3

Chris stood at the bar in the Chequered Skipper, Ashton's only pub. He was amazed to see the huge array of butterflies, pinned in cases that hung on a side wall. All species were on show including some the size of a small bird. He wandered over and looked at the title. 'Humming Bird Hawk Moth', it read. It was hard for him to imagine them being real, they looked so unusual.

'Your drinks.' The barman's call drew him away from the display.

Chris carried his cola and Sally's house white to their table.

'The landlord is writing up a list of anyone he can remember being in the pub the night of the murder,' he said.

Sally took a long gulp of her wine, surprising Chris with the speed at which she was draining the glass.

'Why?'

'I think it had to be someone who was in here the night the body was dumped. Who else would know that the narrowboat would be empty?'

'Apart from the owners, you mean?'

Chris was beginning to accept Sally's often contrary arguments to any idea he had. They were a good test to the credibility of his thoughts.

'You think the owners might have double-bluffed us? Guv said they weren't suspects. He should know.'

'They told the Guv they stayed overnight with friends,' she looked at her notes. 'Diane and Geoff Ellis. They live in the village. Who knows what the four of them got up to.'

'I suppose so,' he agreed. 'Maybe we can call on them while we're here.' He picked at a beer mat while they waited for the landlord to complete his list.

'So, why did you leave the Army?' Sally asked,

breaking him out of his daydream.

'Hmm? Oh, my last tour of Afghanistan finished off my Army aspirations,' he said. 'I thought it was time for me to do something closer to home.'

'You settled down with a local girl?'

'Not yet. Thought I'd get more time to myself out of the Army, but you know what it's like, work swallows your up and you end up with a dull social life.'

'You're not dull,' she argued. 'The local girls don't know what they're missing.'

'Right,' he said, reddening.

'C'mon, you've got a lot going for you. Good looks, an Afghanistan hero. Not like my ex. He was a waste of space. You could have your pick of girls.'

'And you?' Chris asked.

'Mmm, maybe,' she said, leaning over to him.

'I meant what about your relationship?'

'I'd rather talk about you.'

'You're married though aren't you?' Chris asked. He'd briefly met Tony Whitelock, at the station's Christmas party, shortly after joining the Kettering force.

'In name,' she snorted, sitting back, a scowl on her brow.

'How do you mean?'

Sally changed the subject. 'Let's go down down to the lock and see what Jim Cook was talking about,' she said, getting unsteadily to her feet. She'd sunk her wine too quickly and was looking tipsy.

Chris settled the bill and asked the barman for directions. The man scrawled a map onto a paper napkin, outlining the route.

'It's about a half hour walk,' he said, handing over the napkin and the list of patrons from the night of the murder. 'A bit muddy, mind.'

Probably why the Cartwrights didn't want to return to their boat in the dark, Chris thought.

The two detectives followed the map, walking along a footpath past an old mill. The building's wooden cladding was rotting and peeling away from aged bricks.

Sally slipped in a muddy patch and stumbled into Chris, pushing him against the wall. White crumbing cement brushed onto his coat.

'Easy,' he said, standing her back up straight.

'Oops, sorry. Good catch,' she smiled.

'I can see why the owners didn't go back to their boat after dark,' Chris commented. 'Did the Guv say they stayed at the pub?'

'No. Apparently they have friends in the village. Stayed with them.'

'This is where the temporary moorings are that Cook spoke about,' Chris said as they neared the lock. 'There's no-one moored here today.'

'What's that over there?' Asked Sally.

'Looks like a weir. It's in the way of the footpath though.' Chris's mind started racing. 'The Cartwrights said they'd walked to the pub, didn't they?'

'Yes. Let's go over,' Sally suggested. 'We'll soon see if their alibi stands up.'

They climbed the footbridge over the lock and walked towards the weir.

Were the Cartwrights pulling the wool over their eyes? How did they get past this obstacle?

The weir was about twenty feet long, made of stone, with an eighteen inch wide lip at the top. A shallow slope split off to the right, down which water cascaded. It carried along a branch of the river and met up again with the main body past the lock. A length of rope secured a number of red and white plastic floats along the weir's length, to warn boaters and canoeists of the danger.

'The water's only about three inches deep,' murmured Sally, pointing to the ledge. She leaned over the edge of the footpath to get a look downstream. 'I'll bet they wore wellies and walked across.' She was swaying slightly. The sight of the smooth, slick water rushing over the weir's edge was captivating, mesmerising and making her already light head spin.

'Careful!' Chris tried to alert her but he was too

late, her feet had already slipped. The wet mud bordering the weir gave no grip and he failed to catch her pin-wheeling arms. She screamed and fell, legs scraping down the slope towards the churning water at the base of the weir. A hand desperately grabbed for the safety rope and a wake of icy cold water fanned out from her head as she was dunked underneath. She clung to the rope, her legs scrabbling to catch a grip on the algae covered slope.

In an instant Chris flung himself to his stomach, stretching out as far as he dared to catch a hold of her flailing handbag. It had slipped down from her shoulder and she'd caught the strap with her hand. He gasped as the water's chill knocked the wind from him and he strained to get a grip on the wet leather. He reached her hand and pulled, but she wasn't coming to him. Her panicked grip was too strong on the rope.

'Let go of the rope!' he shouted. 'I've got you.'

'What?' she spluttered as she lifted her head free of the water.

'Let go!' he repeated. 'I can't pull you out unless you let go of the rope!'

She released her hold and grabbed the rope again further along. Slowly she edged along the parapet and ashore, coughing and gasping in shock.

She cut a bedraggled figure sitting in the damp grass. Her hair was plastered to her scalp, sodden clothes dripped water. Low moans escaped from her mouth every now and then as she panted.

Chris quickly took off his overcoat and crouched down. He wrapped it around her, holding her close to him to transfer some of his body heat. She leaned her head onto in his chest. He rubbed her head with the coat to help dry her, feeling her shiver underneath. She looked up and he frowned at the sight. The friction had cleared her wet face of make-up, revealing an ugly black bruise over her left eye. He sat back, stunned.

'What's wrong?' she stuttered through chattering teeth.

'Your face,' he answered. 'You don't get a bruise that black so quick.'

She stared at him for a moment 'Oh, shit,' she cursed, quietly. Her eyes betrayed shame and she buried her head deep into his chest.

Chris held her, shivering and confused. He felt her deep sobs wrack through him, her hand gripping his shoulder, kneading into the muscle. Eventually her sobs subsided, replaced by occasional sniffs and coughs, her hot breath warming his chest through his wet shirt. They both smelled of the river.

Sally took a deep breath. 'Thanks for saving me,' she said in a level voice, and pulled away from him. She rose, her face tight and stony. Composing herself, she collected her bag from the ground and began walking to the footpath, back to her car.

Chris sat and wondered after her. After all of that, she's back to her normal self. Calm, assured, confident. He had to hand it to her, she could be cold when she needed to be.

Chris waited a while to give her some distance between them, some time to recover her dignity. She's in trouble, he thought. That bruise had to be from a fist; her expression had told him enough. He'd seen plenty of bruises in the past to know that a whack from a door handle, or whatever excuse people gave to cover up abuse, wouldn't provide the same shaped mark.

And look at the rate she drinks, he thought, that's got to be a sign of stress. But why was she coming on to me today? Is she looking for protection? A way out? Or does she do that to all the new DCs?

When he arrived at her car she was standing at the driver's door looking into the distance. Her chin jutted out in defiance to her exposure. Chris's coat hung loosely from her shoulders like a cape, her arms folded around herself. A piece of twig stuck out from her hair.

'Are you OK?' Chris asked.

'I need to dry out somewhere,' she sniffed.

'We're supposed to check out the Cartwrights'

alibi. The Guv said they stayed over with friends in Ashton, remember?'

'I can't go like this.' Sally shivered as if to prove the point.

'Sure. Home then? You'll have a change of close there.'

'I'm not going back there today,' she snarled through gritted teeth, her brown eyes flashing with a mixture of anger and shame.

'OK. Lets at least sit in the car and work something out. You'll only get colder standing out here.'

She handed him the keys and he unlocked the car. They both sat in silence for a few minutes. The extra moisture they'd brought in with them misted the up windows and the fan worked overtime to clear the car.

'Here, drink this.' Chris handed over a cup of coffee he'd produced from the flask in his bag. It was barely lukewarm but she seemed appreciate it, gulping it down quickly. Handing back the cup, she sniffed.

'Thanks, Chris. I'm sorry. Look, can we go back to yours? I need to shower and get some dry clothes on.'

'OK. I've got no women's clothes at home but I'm sure I can dig out something.'

'Thanks. I've got a change of clothes in my locker at the station but I'll need to fix this first.' She pointed to her face. The deep blue/black bruise stuck out vividly against her clammy white skin.

He put the car in gear, not wanting to bring the subject up, yet. He needed to work out how to approach it, and Sally was in no state to give him a rational account yet.

They passed each other at the bottom of Chris's steep stairs. Sally looked refreshed with a towel around her head and was drowning in the baggy clothes Chris had loaned her. She carried her own clothes in a thin plastic bag.

'I'll be down soon,' Chris called as he bounded up the stairs for his own shower. 'There's a fresh coffee on the table and toast if you want it.'

He returned a few minutes later to find Sally looking in his living room mirror. She'd salvaged some make-up from her sodden bag and was re-applying foundation from a squeezy tube.

Chris hoped she hadn't noticed his hastily tidied room. Newspapers and magazines were stuffed down the side of the settee and last night's Chinese carton was poking out of the kitchen bin. The room still smelled of king prawn curry. Sally shifted her focus, studying a picture on the wall of Chris and his troop on deployment in Iraq. He still didn't know how to raise the subject of her bruising.

'I'm gonna have to visit the dry cleaners before the week's out,' he said awkwardly, sitting down and lifting his coffee mug. 'This is my last clean suit and I'm out of dry cleaning vouchers. D'you suppose I can put the cost through expenses?'

'So long as you fill your 241 form out properly, I won't object.'

'Thanks.' He took a deep breath. 'There's no easy way to say this, so,' he hesitated, 'How did it happen? Have you got problems at home?'

'Spare me the third degree, Raine,' she answered loftily. 'You don't have to worry about me. I can look after myself.'

'Sally, I know it's hard to talk to me about this. We've not worked together much,' he sighed, trying to get his approach right. Things were going to go wrong quickly if he didn't take this gently. 'Is there anyone else you can speak to?'

'There's nothing to say. And it's Sarge to you.'

His mug banged on the coffee table. 'Look, I've just dragged you out of a stinking river and cleaned you up, sparing you a trip home - a place you are clearly frightened of returning to,' his voice was rising but he couldn't stop himself. 'Here you stand, in my clothes, in my house telling me to butt out. Something's wrong and you need to start opening up before it gets worse.' He held her gaze, heart pumping, fighting to reclaim control of his voice. 'Sarge,' he finished, quietly.

Sally sank on the settee, arms resting on her knees, cradling her empty coffee cup. She tucked her feet under the bottom edge of the sofa. The towel to release itself from her lowered head and a corner dangled loosely. She didn't attempt to tuck it back up.

'You don't know me, Chris,' she whispered, looking at the floor. 'You don't know my husband. For all you know we both fight all the time.' her chin rose defiantly but it trembled slightly.

'I'm not stupid, Sally,' he said gently, wishing he'd handled this better. 'You can front it up at work OK, no problem, but as soon as your husband is mentioned you shrink into yourself. We know how to spot this type of behaviour, remember? You can't see yourself displaying it.'

She looked at him, a tear rolling down one cheek. Or was it water from her hair? 'Your right, I suppose,' she sniffed in resignation. 'It started about three months ago. Tony's been promoted at the factory,' she shrugged. 'He gets stressed with the extra responsibility and brings it home. Makes him near impossible to live with.' She gave a short laugh. 'Listen to me, 'impossible to live with'. He can be overbearing and we bicker about it all the time. I could let it lie, really, so I'm probably asking for it.'

It saddened Chris to hear the confession and the stark echoes of so many other abused women escaping from her lips. This was his sergeant, who so recently had been playing hardball with him to keep him on his toes. At the same time it made a kind of sense. He could see she was a vulnerable person hiding behind a steely mask, forging a career in a highly charged organization and unable to deal with her personal situation. Why put up with it, though? She was fearful of her husband, that was obvious.

Why had she made a pass at him earlier? Was she trying to prove that she was still in control of her own self esteem? Convince someone else that she was worth having feelings for?

'First, and most importantly, no-one should be knocked about like you have,' he said. 'You don't 'ask for it'. If your husband's answer in an argument is the fist then that's his problem, not yours.'

Sally scowled, staring back at the carpet. 'You don't know what it's like,' she said whispered, shaking her head.

Chris collected up their cups and dropped them off in the kitchen. Typical of me, he thought. Always looking for a solution. I'm in way over my depth here.

On the way back he made a decision.

'I'm sorry, Sally, you know I'm not the best person to help you here. I can offer you support, but you need to speak with someone who can help you deal with this.' He felt bad about cracking her shield, then letting go of her. He realised he should have thought about it more before wading in, that there was no way he could fully understand what she was going through.

'I won't mention it to the Guv or any of the team but you need to do something. Is there anyone else you can talk to?'

'I understand, Chris. I'm still your Sergeant, and we need to work together. I'll deal with it.'

'Just let me know if you need a hand with anything,' he tried to reassure her.

'Yeah, sure,' she said, unconvincingly. 'Let's get back to the station. We've still got a job to do. I want to see if the team have unearthed anything new.'

Chris and Sally walked through Kettering station's rear doors and along the corridor to the locker room. Sally turned into the doorway to get changed.

'I'll meet you upstairs in a while,' Chris started, spotting Joe Alden chatting to a couple of officers, slouched on a sofa in front of the lockers. Joe raised an eyebrow at Chris when he noticed Sally's attire and quickly jumped up to follow him out of the room.

'You're a fast mover aren't you,' he gave a low

whistle. 'That's your gear she's wearing isn't it? I recognise the sweatshirt.'

'Knock it off, Joe,' Chris replied. 'She managed to fall in the river, that's all.'

Alden laughed. 'Priceless,' he chuckled as he followed Chris up the stairs and behind the reception counter. 'And she couldn't come back here to get changed?' He dug further. 'You only live a couple of minutes away.'

'Just leave it, Joe,' Chris spat.

'OK, mate. Just kidding,' but Joe wasn't finished. 'By the way, uniform followed that lead up on the van by the canal.'

'Really? Anything come of it?'

'You tell me yours and I'll tell you mine,' Joe smirked.

'Joe, there's nothing in it,' Chris insisted, his voice raising.

'Nothing in what?' a new voice said. They'd reached the main offices and DI Crighton had arrived at their shoulders. He stood with a questioning look.

'Oh, nothing Guv,' Chris said. 'Just a disagreement between us.' He glowered at Joe who radiated innocence.

'Hmm. What did you find out at Oundle?'

Chris brought them both up to speed on the morning's events up until Sally's dip in the river, carefully omitting his discovery of her black eye. Joe, thankfully, didn't press the matter of the visit to Chris's house.

Sally entered the CID area in as he was finishing. Her hair was dry and shone under the fluorescent lights. Once more it hooded her face slightly, casting natural shadows over her eyes. She slipped easily into the conversation, offering her thoughts on Cooks information. The earlier episode with Chris had been dismissed from her behaviour as though nothing had happened.

'Cocky git, but knows his stretch of the river,' she said of Cook. 'Raine's guess that the body was dropped off by boat is plausible. Did you go to the autopsy, Guv?'

Crighton looked up from a sheaf of papers on his lap, startled.

'I've been wrapped up with this drugs cartel investigation,' he indicated the papers he'd been studying. He coughed. 'It's safe to assume the cause of death, though, don't you think?'

'No, Guv, I don't. He could've been beheaded after death.' She slapped a hand on the large blank space on one of the flip charts. 'C'mon Guv, look at the board. We're scratching around in the dark. We need all the info we can get and don't even have an ID yet. Isn't this case as important as your drugs one?'

'They're both very high priority,' Crighton countered, his voice gruff. He turned to Alden. 'Is there any news back from the mortuary yet?'

'Nothing so far,' Joe had to admit.

'I've got a mate who works in forensics,' Chris suggested. 'He could ask around at the mortuary, see if anything has come up.'

'Thanks, Raine but I can't really condone cutting corners like that,' He looked at the flip charts. 'Although we are behind. OK, do it. See what you can come up with - but be discreet.'

Crighton stood and returned to his office. Sally followed the DI, slamming the door behind her.

'Wonder what's going on in there,' Joe mused, nodding to the Guv's closed door.

'Do you have to have your nose in everything, Joe?' Chris turned to his desk.

'Got to keep your ear to the ground, mate. It's the only way to find anything out around here,' Joe replied, grinning. 'Such as who's in line for the Sergeants board or what was in the back of that van by the river.'

'That's right, you still haven't told me,' Chris spun around on his seat to face Joe. 'C'mon Soap, spit it out.'

'Eight industrial lawnmowers. We think they were stolen from a tool hire shop,' Joe shrugged. 'Nothing major, but a collar is a collar, eh? Well done, by the way.'

'It was Whitelock's shout, really,' Chris admitted. He'd had the same thoughts as Sally about the van but it was she who suggested calling it in.

'I mean well done for the making the Sergeants board,' Joe was still smiling as he revealed his last morsel of news.

Chris sat stunned for a moment, still absorbing what Joe had said. He shook his head.

'What?'

'Gen up, mate. That's what I'm hearing on the grapevine,' Joe said. 'You've got to keep it under your hat, though,' he urged. 'There's nothing official out there, but I've heard your name mentioned in high places.' He flicked a rubber band at Chris. 'Good luck, Rainey, remember us minions when you make DCI.'

Chris turned back to his computer, his head swam and his brain buzzed with excitement. Promotion? already? It took him a few minutes to calm down and focus on what he was supposed to be doing.

Raised voices leaked from Crighton's office and the two young men shared puzzled looks. Suddenly, Sally Whitelock wrenched the door open and stomped out, a scowl creasing her face.

The junior detectives kept their eyes down and focussed on their work as DI Crighton raised himself from his chair and softly closed the door.

CHAPTER 4

Chris looked up his contact in forensics. Jed Chambers was an old friend and colleague. They'd both gone through Hendon together and had shared a shift in Northampton during Chris's days in uniform. Jed had nearly lost his career, and his life, one night after a call out to a nightclub fight. The violent altercation had left him with a badly injured leg which had downgraded him from active duties. Heading for a medical discharge, his career was saved by a transfer into forensics. Now in his second year in the post he was quickly becoming an expert in the field.

'Hi Rainey,' Chambers answered his phone.

'Hello Jed, Sorry to bother you about this but could you check something with the Mortuary, please? I need to see if they're anywhere near identifying a body.'

'I can give it a go, Chris, but they might not like it. Are they dragging their heels, then?'

'No, not really. We're just a bit keen to get moving on the case. There's not much else to go on, so we could do with all the help we can get.'

'I know the coroner down at the hospital, and he owes me a favour. He'll be able to tell me if there's any hold up.'

'Thanks Jed.' Chris gave his friend the details of the case.

'I'll call you back as soon as I have anything, Chris. Take it easy, mate.'

'Cheers, Jed. Speak to you soon.' Chris hung up, drumming his fingers on the table. What was up with Sally Whitelock? Why had she stormed out of the Guv's office? He thought about following her but held back. The morning's revelation had been bad enough to discourage seeking more friction with her. He looked over to Joe's desk to find it empty. His colleague's nosiness meant that he'd find out soon enough, anyway.

Chris began to run his list of pub regulars through his computer to organize the names and addresses. He added them to a mapping program to calculate the best route to start the rounds.

'Door knocking tomorrow,' he sighed.

A few minutes later Joe sidled back to his desk.

Chris leaned back in his chair. 'Go on then, give me the scoop.'

'Oh, so you want the gossip when it's not about you, eh?' Joe smirked.

'Do I have to beat it out of you?'

Alden raised his arms in mock surrender. 'Sally's fuming because the Guv's tied up with his drugs case. She says he's been obsessed with it since Sergeant James was killed. Blames himself for letting James go out on the bust.'

'Yeah, but we're hardly racing ahead with clues on this case. Why shouldn't he work on the other?'

'Sally thinks he needs to be more hands on. That he should've been going through his informants more thoroughly, or banging on Beckman's door for an ID.'

'The Guv isn't daft enough to ignore those,' Chris said. 'He'll have weighed up whether his snouts have any knowledge around the river.'

'That's not what Sally thinks. I wonder whether she's getting giddy about this morning's collar. As if everyone who lives on the river is a criminal.'

'As if. Just because they choose a different lifestyle doesn't make them all murderers,' .

'She's got a point about the Guv, though,' Joe admitted. 'He does seem distant. Normally when a fresh body turns up he's the first to remind us it's someone's relative lying on the slab, and that we should be putting all our efforts in relieving their pain.'

'It's been nearly two days and no-one's come forward to claim him.'

'Doesn't mean he's not gonna be missed, though.'

'So there is a compassionate streak in that tiny

brain of yours. Look, I'm sure the Guv knows what he's doing.'

Joe didn't appear convinced.

'You noticed anything funny, recently, about Sal?' he asked, changing the subject and surprising Chris.

'Um, not really,' Chris lied. 'Why?'

Joe scooted his chair over the carpet on its casters, closing in on Chris until they collided.

'She keeps taking time off. Odd days here and there,' he leaned forward and, though they were the only two in the room, lowered his voice for effect. 'Every time it's a sickness bug.'

'There's a lot of it about.' Chris didn't like where this was heading.

'Nah, mate. She's up the duff,' Joe leaned back and opened his eyes wide. Joe's assumptions were normally pretty accurate, but he was missing the vital piece of evidence on this. The one fact that only Chris knew about, and couldn't share.

'Sod off. Where are you getting your bullshit from? One minute you think I'm having a fling with her, the next she's pregnant.' He stopped, realisation dawning. 'Forget it, Joe,' he snarled, wiping the knowing look from Alden's face. Joe began shuffling his chair back. 'You're way off the mark. Whatever Sally has going on, it's not that. And it's definitely not with me.'

'You seem pretty sure of it,' Joe conceded. 'Care to share?'

Chris rose from his desk and grasped the arms of Joe's chair, pushing him hard the rest of the way back to his post. 'I said back off,' he growled.

'All right mate, calm down.' Joe chuckled nervously. 'S'just, last night you said she was on your back all the time. Today you're all protective of her.'

Chris forced himself to calm down, unclenching his grip on Joe's chair and holding his hands palm up. 'There's nothing going on, Joe,' he reiterated, avoiding eye contact and turning back to the mapping software on his computer. The office fell into an uneasy silence, broken only by the occasional mouse click and printer whirr. Doubtful that he'd been able to allay Alden's suspicions, Chris felt ashamed of his behaviour. How long Joe would stay quiet about his ridiculous idea, Chris couldn't tell, but he hoped Sally would sort out her problems before the gossip became too damaging.

Paul Crighton sat in the quiet of his own office. It was late. The station deserted and he was alone, reviewing the notes on his drugs case and ruminating over that afternoon's altercation with Sally Whitelock. She was right to have pulled him up about out his lack of attention. He knew that, yet he knew that the joint drugs investigation needed him.

She has a fiery temperament, he thought. If she knew what I'm going through she'd understand.

The loss of DS James preyed heavily on his mind and he'd made a personal pledge to see justice done for the officer. He could also see the damage that was being done by the influx of cheap drugs to the citizens in his part of the country.

The Fens were a good place to hide hardened East European criminals. Many farms in the area were employing cheap labour from Poland, Hungary and the Czech Republic, and that influx brought crime with it. Although by far the largest group, the Poles weren't the issue. Slovakian and Czech Republic gangs with sources in Vietnam were importing drugs into the UK using various channels, including foreign workers. Money laundering, drug dealing and the associated crime that went with them was spreading through the towns. Increasingly, guns were being used in spats between rival gangs and the fear they brought was filtering into the local communities. A joint operation between police forces was closing in on the ringleaders and James had been sent along with a raid on one of their bases. Crighton recalled the notes on the operation and imagined James's role in it.

James had arrived at a large detached house in

Barton Seagrave, on the outskirts of Kettering at four a.m. accompanying a team of firearms officers from Northants police. James had assisted with the planning of the raid. Sixteen gas-masked officers surrounded the house dressed in assault gear and carrying Heckler and Koch MP7 automatic weapons. They moved in. 'Flashbang' stun grenades were clipped to each of their backs - this allowed easy access to a grenade for an officer behind the one opening a breach. One of the officers was armed with the 'master key' - a Remington 870 shotgun loaded with Hatton breaching rounds. These were normal shotgun shells filled with material designed to destroy a door lock or bolt then disintegrate, without following through into the room behind and potentially injuring a civilian.

Unarmed, but wearing protective body armour, James had accompanied the raid with instructions to keep a wide berth on the action.

'This is the bit I hate,' whispered one of the officers to James. 'Why we have to go calling out into the night before an assault, I don't know. It's supposed to give them a chance to surrender, but all it does is warn them to arm themselves'.

'Armed police!' shouted the team leader.

A battering ram swung towards the solid front door, smashing through the lock within two strikes. The team seethed into the hall. Another team could be heard coming through the back door into the kitchen. Further shouts of 'armed police' rang out through the house. Four men from the first team disappeared up the stairs to the right and the remainder stacked up against the living room door on the left. 'Clear' came a call, and four from the rear team ploughed through the adjoining door between the kitchen to the hall and followed their colleagues upstairs. The remaining four would be making their way through the downstairs areas to join the first lot in the living room.

Aiden James had watched all this, fascinated at the co-ordination and discipline of the firearms officers and no doubt thinking of how to apply for a transfer as he leaned against the stair banister. Suddenly, a door behind him had opened from beneath the stairs. Before he'd had a chance to turn, a knife was at his throat, it's blade biting deep through his carotid artery, releasing a spray of blood that, in his dying moments, he watched paint a messy arc on the pale wall opposite. The assailant ran towards the front door but within seconds he was lying at the welcome mat, taken down by a bullet to the thigh.

The killer, a man who'd moved silently from the kitchen into the understairs cupboard on the first sound of the police, had apparently been in the kitchen looking for a drink having been unable to sleep. He'd taken the knife from a wooden block on the kitchen worktop and hidden himself away. It was pure chance that James had been in the way. The worst thing about it was that no evidence could be found on the site that could help with the case. Seemingly the gang had received a tip-off and had cleared the house out of incriminating evidence. The case of James's murder was still being investigated by the IPCC.

Crighton shook himself to clear his mind of the incident. He picked up an email from DC Raine. Attached to it was the list of pub regulars at the Chequered Skipper. Those who'd been in the night of the murder. He picked out one, no, two, names from the list, cross-referencing them with another list on his desk.

CHAPTER 5

Chris opened his front door to the smell of a spicy lamb hotpot. He inhaled deeply and sent silent thanks to his neighbour for saving him the trawl of fast food outlets in town. The lady next door had gently impressed herself upon him as substitute mother over recent months. Occasionally bringing him food, she had also persuaded him to lend her a key and allow her in to do a bit of tidying. She missed her own son, a soldier serving abroad. Chris had met him a couple of times whilst he was visiting on leave. The picture the lad painted of Army life was a world away from his own time serving and it surprised him to note that five years had passed since he'd last been to Afghanistan.

The lamb dish was sitting in his oven keeping warm and a note was stuck to the oven door. 'Hope this is enough for two of you,' it read. He let out a wry chuckle.

'Nothing gets past you, Ida,' he said to the empty kitchen.

His phone gave a muffled beep from his coat pocket in the living room, signalling a text.

Reaching into the fridge he plucked out a can of beer and set it on a tray with a plate of steaming food. He carried it through to the living room and retrieved his phone, noticing he still had white cement dust from the old mill on the back of his coat. He was reminded of the dusty, pallid feet of the corpse he'd seen the other day.

'Call soonest, got answers,' the text from Jed Chambers read. Chris looked longingly at a slice of green pepper lying in the middle of the meal, wondering whether he could ignore the message and tuck into it. Duty won out and he called Jed's number.

'That was quick work, Jed.'

'It doesn't feel like it, Chris. I feel as though I've

been waiting at the coroner's door all evening,' Jed sounded tense. 'I've got a name for you but it won't be formally released until tomorrow at the earliest.'

'How's that?' Chris asked.

'Well, the pathologist had to ask for the forensic dentist to come in because the victim had no forms of ID on him.'

'OK, but why can't they say for sure?'

'The dentist has only been able to make a possible identification. He got it from records at an Oundle dentist, but until they get the full records from the other local dental practices they can't declare it a positive one.'

'Right, so we've at least got something we can follow up,' Chris said, interest building.

'I guess so, but go cautiously. It might turn out to be a false lead and it's my head on the chopping block if you make too many waves. We've already had one decapitation. We don't need another.'

'Your neck will be safe, mate, don't worry.'

'The victim's name could be Simon Hearst. I have an address in Oundle for him.'

'Thanks, Jed. I owe you one.'

'That you do, Chris. Go carefully.' Jed gave Chris the details and hung up.

Chris wolfed down a few mouthfuls of dinner, burning his tongue. He looked longingly at the beer can on his way to the kitchen, quenching his mouth with water. He dialled Crighton's number.

'Sir, we've got a possible identity on the body,' he gabbled into the phone.

'Calm down, lad,' Crighton replied, getting straight to the point. 'Only a possible, you say?'

Chris explained the situation.

'OK, it's still worth chasing up. I'll meet you there in half an hour. Don't go knocking before I arrive.'

'OK Guv, see you over there.' He managed a couple more swallows of food before slipping his coat on and fishing his car keys out of a pocket. Closing the front door behind him, he immediately slotted the key back in the lock, stomped through to the kitchen and turned the oven off. Ida wouldn't be back in tonight, having no doubt heard him arrive, and he didn't fancy having the house burned down.

He arrived at the address in Oundle to find Crighton already there, waiting in his blue VW Passat. The house was a large four bedroom place built with large stone blocks. It was newly built and stood at the end of a thirty foot drive. The porch that stood proud of it's fascia was flanked by two thick stone pillars. There were no lights on, yet even though it lay in darkness the dwelling had a presence that was completely at odds with the rest of the street. Crighton looked up and down the road and could see no building similar to this. The neighbouring houses were detached properties, built in the 1930's by the looks of them and displaying none of the opulence of the new intruder.

They strode up the drive and knocked on the door, to no avail.

'Nobody home,' Chris commented. 'Could be our man.'

'Unless he's a heavy sleeper,' agreed Crighton. 'Nine o'clock is a bit early to be in bed though. Let's try next door.'

In contrast to the dark house, the neighbouring one was bathed in security lighting. The door was answered by a man in his carpet slippers. Crighton lifted his warrant card.

'Good evening, Sir. Sorry to trouble you. We're looking for the person who lives next door,' he said.

'Yes?' the man asked.

'Do you know him?'

'Not really. We say hello now and then. He keeps himself to himself.'

'Do you know his name?' Crighton asked.

'Yes, it's Simon Hearst,' the man confirmed. 'He has it written on the side of his van. I wish people wouldn't park trade vehicles around here, it's against the

Council's rules,' he tutted.

'It's not there at the moment,' Chris said. 'Can you remember what else is written on the van?'

'It has Hearst Masonry on the side but I couldn't tell you where they are.'

'Has it been here recently?' Crighton asked.

'No, but he's not often there.'

'He stays away a lot?' Crighton asked.

The man nodded.

'So, he's a Stone Mason?'

'Yes. You can see by that monstrosity of a house.'

'He built it himself?' Crighton guessed.

'Yes. I don't know how he got planning permission. Some of the locals objected but it got through, somehow.'

Chris could believe he was speaking to one of the protesters.

'Thank you, Sir. You've been most helpful,' Crighton said.

'Is he in trouble?'

'Oh, nothing you should worry about. Goodnight, Sir.'

They walked back to the darkened house. 'This has got to be our victim,' Chris said. 'Where do we go next?'

'I want to have a look around the house first, then I guess we'll have to find the stone works.'

'I can look the address up on my phone,' Chris offered.

Crighton looked at him blankly for a few seconds.

'It has an Internet connection.'

'Oh, of course. Amazing devices, aren't they?' Crighton acceded.

Chris tapped on the keypad on his smartphone, finding Hearst Masonry on Google.

'Here, Sir. It's a small quarry North East of Oundle,' he held up the phone to show Crighton a map of the site.

Crighton squinted at the small screen and

retrieved his glasses from his pocket to get a better view. Peering closer, he said,

'I can't see much there, Raine. I'll take your word for it. If it's not far, we could go and have a quick look tonight. Lets have a look around the house first.'

Crighton walked to the back gate of Hearst's house and opened it. No dog barked, no lights illuminated and no alarm cried out. He continued around to the back of the house and dug inside a pocket for his Mini-Maglight torch. It cut a bright beam through the dining room windows, revealing a sparsely furnished abode. The place had a few items of expensive looking furniture on show. No pictures adorned the walls, just a large flatscreen television and surround sound speakers. Moving to the kitchen window he noted the spotless work surfaces and five bottles of red wine stacked in a rack. Aside from that the kitchen was bare. A bachelor's house, he concluded. That could explain the lack of a missing persons report, but what about the man's work colleagues. Surely they would notice him missing.

They returned to the pavement at the front of the house.

'Not much more to find out here tonight,' Crighton said, getting into his car.

Crighton followed Chris's car out of town and along the A605. A few miles out of town they turned off to an unclassified road that led them to the entrance of a small open-cast quarry. A five-bar gate blocked access to a wide-spread area of stoneworks. A couple of large sheds stood in the foreground and various stone blocks lay about on the ground. A look at Chris's phone revealed the quarry was near the river.

'This could be our man, or we could be pissing in the wind,' Crighton told Chris. 'I can't call a squad out tonight on just a maybe. Get yourself back home and meet me here first thing tomorrow. We'll speak to the staff and find out if we've got the right man.'

'You don't want DC Alden and me to go door knocking then, sir?' Chris reminded him.

'No. We still don't have a firm identity yet. We can the list after we've investigated this place.'

'OK, sir.'

'I'm going to ask Alden to check with the council planning department about Hearst's house. It's out of character with the rest of the street.'

'Are there rules about that, sir?'

'Yes. In some areas, if you're building a new property it has to fit in with the local style of the place. Hearst's is unusual. I suppose he wanted something grand to show off his stonework connection but as the neighbour said, that's going to encourage complaints.'

Chris drove back home to the cold remains of his meal.

They were back the next morning before the quarry opened up. A harried looking man stood fumbling with a large padlock on the gate. Crighton tapped him on the shoulder, making him jump and drop the keys.

'We'd like to speak to Mr. Hearst,' he said.

'Eh?' the man jumped and span around to see Crighton's warrant card in his face. 'Oh, right. He's not here. I'm the first in today.' The man stooped and collected his keys from the muddy ground. He indicated the rusty lock.

'I'm not even sure he'll be in today. We've not seen him for days,' he continued.

'Aren't you concerned your boss has been away for so long?' Chris asked.

'What, him? He's not what you'd call hands-on,' the man said, bitterly. 'The foreman pretty much runs things. We don't see Hearst very often.'

He'd successfully opened the gate and straightened up, expectant. 'I've got to go and open up inside. Get things warmed up,' he said. You can come in and wait for the foreman, if you like.'

'Thanks,' Crighton said, following him into the yard.

A cold breeze whipped its way over the exposed

work yard. At about half an acre in size there was plenty of room for the limited amount of stone laying around. Two large sheds dominated the front area. Off to the rear, past the yard, Chris could just make out the small quarry around twice the size of the yard. A flat-bed truck was parked alongside one of the sheds.

They followed the worker through a large wooden door into a shed. Chris stopped short at the entrance.

'Guv, look,' he called.

Crighton was about ten paces ahead, with the worker. He turned at Chris's call and looked in puzzlement to where Chris was pointing. The interior of the shed was populated with machinery, a fork lift truck parked in the centre of it all. Stone cutting and shaping tools littered bench tables, loaded with large blocks of light coloured stone.

'What?' he asked.

Chris was pointing to a large table saw.

'The saw,' Chris said. 'The cut on Hearst's neck was all in one direction. His head wasn't sawn off with a hand-held blade. This is how he was decapitated.'

'All right, keep it down,' Crighton urged, looking around at the worker. He was at the other end of the shed now and hadn't heard Chris's exclamation. 'We don't want to alarm him. We're still not sure it's Hearst yet.'

'Of course, sir. Sorry,' Chris said.

'We're going to have to check this out,' Crighton acknowledged looking at the large circular blade. 'I'll get some uniforms and a forensics team over.' He took his phone out. 'Get that man to set aside some space for the workers to wait, then go and watch the gate for when they arrive. Oh, and tell him to make us a brew, will you?'

Ten minutes later the shed bustled with voices. A group of workers sat in the corner talking excitedly amongst themselves. Chris stood watching over them. He overheard DI Crighton on the phone:

'I know, Eric, we should have waited,' he was

54

saying to Dr. Beckman.

'Yes but we're here now. What are the odds it isn't our man?' he waited.

'Well come on, then. Let's get this thing moving. Never mind how I found out. Can you get someone over here? OK, thanks,' He hung up, looking over to Chris.

'Beckman's on the war path,' he said. 'I've kept your mate out of it for now. I just hope we find something.'

Chris nodded, hoping he was right. Crighton called the foreman over and asked him to prepare a room for interviews. He was directed to the managers office, a small partitioned area in one corner of the shed. A topless woman gave him a brilliant white smile through the green fronds of a palm tree. Her raised arm leaned against its trunk. She sported a necklace of shells, and tiny grains of white sand stuck to her taut bronzed skin. An immaculate blue sea filled the background. Crighton lifted the calendar that showed the tropical scene from the wall. He laid it face down among the plans and stone samples littering the desk. In contrast to the idyllic image, the grubby office housed nothing of comfort aside from a small fan heater. The device coughed out a meagre aura of warmth that barely penetrated the room.

While they waited for the uniforms to arrive Chris asked the foreman what work they did at the quarry. The man explained the quarry had been going for nearly five years.

'We've been getting work in the last eighteen months or so from the Council, providing restoration stone to some local stately homes via English Heritage and the like,' he said. 'We don't have the quality of stone for large batches, so we concentrate on smaller features,' he continued. 'We started off selling garden ornaments and slabs to the domestic market through our own marketing and through DIY stores. If we can expand the quarry we'll do better with the maintenance work.'

'You need to expand?'

'There's more stone under the adjoining field, but the owner doesn't want to sell.'

The uniforms arrived. Crighton and Raine took the workers one by one into the interview room and grilled them of what they knew about Hearst and his movements.

After hours of questioning and bad coffee the two detectives had a pile of paper and an assessment of Hearst as an employer.

He wasn't well liked and was rarely at the quarry. Some of his men saw him at the Chequered Skipper pub occasionally. As it was their local, Chris was unsurprised to recall seeing some of them on his list from the previous day. He was able to make notes on their movements the night the body was disposed.

The workers had a darts team who played there against other local craftsmen's teams. The boat builders at the marina nearby were leading the league and their skill was a common complaint in the interviews when the pub was mentioned.

Hearst was described as a bit flash. Always passing on cheesy chat-up lines to the women in the pub. It caused a bit of consternation among some of the workers who thought their partners should be off-limits to their boss, even though they were out of working hours. The foreman hovered outside the room, eager to get the factory back up and running.

Crighton called DS Whitelock to bring her up to date.

'Sally, I want you to gain access to Hearst's house and get a good look around. Pick up anything you find useful,' he ordered. The chief Scene of Crimes Officer knocked on the office door, rattling its single pane of glass and shaking the partition.

'The place is clean, Paul,' he said. 'We've been over all the tools and can't find a thing.'

'That's a shame,' Crighton replied. 'Our lad here was convinced Hearst was cut up in his factory.'

Chris felt stupid. He frowned and asked, 'Did you

check whether they've changed the blades on the cutting machines?'

'Yes son,' The SOCO said sympathetically. 'They did it a couple of days ago. They keep the old blades in a bucket before disposing of them and the bloke who made the change was able to point out the last blade.'

Chris's shoulders dropped.

'Maybe they took it off site?'

'The blades cost £500 each,' the foreman answered. 'My men have to sign them out of the stores. I'd know if one was missing.'

'Aside from that, the surfaces have all come up clean,' the SOCO continued. 'Believe me, if he was killed here, we'd know. There's so much dust and debris it would be impossible to clear the whole place out. Sorry.'

Chris wandered out into the shed. He looked out over the factory floor. The low sunlight streamed through the windows and caught the myriad motes of dust disturbed during the search. He felt as small as one of those particles. He'd been certain the stonemason had been finished off here.

What was it he'd been taught in training? Follow the evidence, not your hunches. He didn't believe the saying but it seemed to be mocking him. You strip out all the uncertainties and what you're left with is the truth, no matter how difficult it is to accept.

OK, if that's right, why did DI Crighton let him pursue this? He must think there was a possibility in the theory. Or was this another lesson? No, he thought, as he watched the SOCOs clearing up their equipment, too costly to be a lesson.

He turned back and caught the DI's eye. Crighton excused himself from the SOCO's attention and came out into the cold shed.

'I know what you're thinking, Chris,' he said, 'and it is a good theory in the absence of any other facts.'

Chris stared at the floor. 'Didn't pay off though, did it.'

'We'll just have to keep our powder dry for a

while,' Crighton continued. 'Let forensics finish their investigation and let us work with what we've got. We took a lot of information from these workmen.'

'OK, Guv Those interviews haven't brought up anything which moves us on, though. All we know is Hearst was a bit of an arsehole who could hardly be bothered to keep his eye on his business and had more of an eye for his workers wives than he did them.'

'All important information, Chris,' Crighton said. 'We're building a picture of what Hearst was like. This way we have a chance of finding out why someone might want him killed.'

The Foreman still lingered at the office door.

'Can we get back to work now?' he called across the shed.

Crighton returned to the office to gather his papers, hanging the calendar back up on the wall as he went.

'Didn't want that being a distraction during the interviews,' he indicated the scantily clad woman.

'That's a point,' the foreman said, noticing the calendar. 'I wonder where his daughter went.'

Crighton and Chris looked from the foreman to the calendar then to each other. Chris's heart flipped and a surge of panic coursed through him. What had they missed? The kid's items they'd found in Hearst's pocket. They must be relevant, after all. But what had triggered the foreman to connect the woman on the calendar with Simon Hearst's daughter?

'What daughter?' Crighton demanded.

The foreman returned their stares. 'His ex-partner came in here last Friday. She was going on holiday. That picture reminded me,' the foreman pointed to the beach on the calendar by way of explanation. 'Said it was time he took some parental responsibility for the girl and left her with him.'

'Just like that?' Crighton hunted through his coat pocket for his phone.

'Yes. It certainly put Simon's nose out of joint,'

the foreman confirmed.

'And you didn't think of telling us this before?'

'Didn't think it was important. Knowing Simon I expect He'd offload her onto family if he could.'

'Does he have family living nearby?'

'No idea.'

Crighton waved for Chris to continue while he made a call on his mobile phone.

'How old is the girl?' Chris asked.

'Dunno. About ten, maybe,' the foreman said.

'Can you give me a description of her?'

The foreman did his best with the description. While he wrote, Chris eavesdropped on Crighton's calls. He was organizing family and schools checks via the station's emergency switchboard. The urgency in his boss's voice worried Chris. They were two days behind in tracing the girl's whereabouts. Already two thirds of the way through 'The Golden Hour', the window of opportunity after which the odds of successfully locating a person or solving a suspicious death rose drastically. He hoped for her sake the girl was staying with a granny or an aunt.

'Get back to the station,' Crighton told Chris, hanging up his latest call. 'I've just asked Sally to look out for evidence of the daughter's presence at Hearst's house. You,' he pointed to the foreman. 'Come with me.'

'But,' the foreman jumped at Crighton's order. 'I've got to supervise the men.'

'Then delegate,' Crighton growled. 'We've got a body to identify.'

CHAPTER 6

A low hum of muted conversations filled the incident room. Joe Alden stood at the centre of it, coordinating a team of uniforms manning the phones. He and Chris had populated the incident board with an extra layer of information by the time Crighton arrived from the mortuary.

'Good work,' Crighton nodded, spotting the updates. He collected a fax from his office and asked Joe to run off some photocopies.

'Schools have been helpful,' Chris said, pointing to a list of children on term-time holiday grants and other absentees. 'No 'Hearst' on the list yet.'

'Hearst wasn't married,' Crighton reminded him. 'Her surname won't be the same.'

Chris looked at the list of children's names. The Guv was right, of course it wouldn't be the same. He stared down the black hole of possibilities and the huge task ahead of them. How the hell could they discover where the girl was when wasn't even apparent who they were looking for?

'We've got the schools helping us account for the whereabouts of all the absent children,' Joe said as he returned with the photocopies. 'But it's going to take a while.'

'Why's that?' Crighton asked.

'Some parents won't be answering their phones. Maybe they're abroad. Some might be in hospital with a sick child.'

Chris chipped in, 'There's also the chance a school doesn't have up to date contact details for a parent. And then there's Hearst's ex. I mean, what kind of mother drops their kid off with an estranged partner then buggers off on holiday?'

'We'll worry about their parenting skills when we've found the girl,' Crighton said. A number of faces turned towards him. 'And we will find her,' he barked, shooing the staff back to their work. 'Chris, Joe, in here.'

Crighton led the DC's into his office and motioned for Chris to shut the door.

'I think we can rule out a vigilante killing,' Crighton started. 'Let's concentrate on Hearst for a minute.'

He handed out copies of the the fax he'd received. The pathologist's report. 'The forensic dentist's investigation is a formality thanks to the quarry foreman's identification of the body. Also, we don't think Hearst was a paedophile. His daughter was supposed to have been with him when he died. However we can't rule out the possibility that he arranged for someone to look after her before he met his end.'

'No surprises on cause of death,' Joe said, reading through his copy of the report.

'And I'm right about the cutting motion on his neck,' Chris confirmed. 'Toxicology report shows no foreign substances,' he noted. 'Suggests he knew his killer and didn't need to be drugged to be subdued.'

'No, the whack on the head did that for him,' Crighton said.

'Doesn't mean to say he didn't meet his killer face to face before he was hit.'

'Hmm, good point. Deceased for around twelve to fourteen hours when the pathologist examined him at the scene,' Crighton said. 'So if our killer was in that pub, he was either in an unsettled state or a very cool customer.'

'The dust on the corpse's jeans confirmed as Limestone,' Joe noted. 'That's the stone they use at his quarry isn't it?' Joe asked.

'That's what the foreman told us.'

Chris sat quietly as the others ran through the rest of the report. He felt an itch at the back of his head. He leaned back in his chair. He was convinced he had the murder method correct. But how?

He closed his eyes and imagined himself as Hearst.

I'm lying on a saw table. I've been dragged around barefoot, hence the cuts on my feet and they're covered with brick dust. I'm crying, feeling pathetic about how I got into this mess. I know why I'm here. I see the saw start up. Do I beg for mercy?

Chris opened his eyes and checked the forensics report. 'Compressions on forehead show evidence of blindfold used.' He looked further down the page to see that Hearst had been bound and gagged too. He closed his eyes again.

So, I don't know it's a saw table. I don't know where I am and I can't plead with my captor. I hear the saw start up – some machinery at least. Would I recognize the sound? I don't visit the quarry very often, but I know how the stone is cut so I probably would. Who has the capability to do this? Somebody in the business perhaps? A rival? An employee with a workshop at home? A timber merchant even? They use machine saws. He felt the draught of a spinning blade at his neck and jolted at the thought of it biting into his flesh. Heart pounding, he looked around him. The others were intent on their work. Through the window of Crighton's office he spotted his coat hanging on the back of a chair, the white cement from the mill still ingrained in the wool. He looked down at his shoes, caked in mud and dark brown dust from the quarry yard. More on his trousers. He looked up again at his coat, then back down.

Something wrong? Different shades of dust. So? Come on, think! It wasn't the coat catching his attention. What was it?

'Did Hearst have a workshop at home?' Chris asked out loud.

'No. Why do you ask?' Crighton looked up. Chris was staring across the room, fingers rubbing the hem of his trousers.

His brain trickled the information to his mouth,

'He was coated in light coloured dust when we found him.'

Crighton looked over the top of his glasses at Chris.

'He works at a quarry,' Joe prompted.

'What are you saying, Raine?' Crighton said, knocking Chris from his trance.

'Hmm? I'm not sure. It probably doesn't matter,' he said. He wasn't willing to open up to them right now. He'd already screwed up again today.

'Try to stay awake, lad. What did you find out about the planning permission on Hearst's house, Alden?'

'The application forms were all filled in correctly, Guv. It was stamped and signed. The protests were noted but didn't warrant a re-inspection. They didn't seem bothered by it but they're sending copies of the documentation over anyway.'

'OK. What about these other points we're finding out about Hearst. The neighbouring farmer. He wouldn't sell land to Hearst to let him expand his quarry. Raine, get yourself down to that farmer and see what that's all about will you?'

'Yes, Sir.'

'We'll have to re-interview the boat owners, the Cartwrights, now we have an ID. They may have known him. Also the pub regulars. We've captured some of those today in our interviews at the quarry but there are more. I recognize a couple of them and I'll be speaking with them as part of my other investigation.'

They all looked up at the sound of the office door banging. The handle fought against the latch for a second until, released from its catch, the door flung open. Sally staggered in under the weight of a large box. Her handbag, swinging from her elbow, did its best to tangle itself around her legs.

'You're right, Guv,' she said over the lid as she passed the threshold. 'He had a girl at the house.' She dumped the box onto Crighton's desk.

63

'Was she still there?' Chris asked, immediately regretting his words as he caught her scornful look.

'D'you think I'd have kept it quiet if I'd found her?' She turned to Crighton. SOCO's have removed a suitcase and some clothes for tests, but they let me have a look before taking them.'

'Anything? Crighton asked.

'Molly Gowland,' Sally replied. The others stared at her open mouthed. She frowned back. 'Found her name on a school exercise book.'

The team burst into life and Chris led the race to the incident board, the others scrabbling close behind. He traced a finger down the the list of names.

'Got her,' he shouted, stabbing a finger at the list. 'Forest Gate C. of E. Junior school in Corby.'

'Get onto it,' Crighton instructed Alden. Joe jumped into action, grabbing a phone from one of the uniforms and commandeering his desk in order to begin tracing Molly Gowland's mother. Once she was found they'd have a better idea of what family or friends she may have gone to. 'Anything else, Sally?' Crighton asked.

'He did live alone,' Sally confirmed. 'The house is very sparse. Little in the way of furniture and only men's clothes in the wardrobe. Seems Molly was staying temporarily. Hardly any food in the house and her room isn't even decorated. None of the rooms were for that matter.'

'I'll have to organize a press conference with DCI Ashton this afternoon,' Crighton said. 'And we'll have to launch a search appeal.' The mood in the incident room had stepped up a gear and officers were working with renewed vigour. 'I'll have to catch up with the drugs case at some point today, too.'

'What's happening with that?' Sally asked, annoyed at the interruption.

'It's with the Met., mostly. Serious Organised Crime Agency have their eye on it too. There are some local connections that I still have to chase up. One of them is the owner of the house where DS James was killed. I believe he's a local property developer, buying then letting out houses. Another is a Magistrate who we have our eye on. He's been criticised for handing down lenient sentences to local drug dealers.'

'I didn't know SOCA were involved,' she said. 'Big stuff.'

Crighton gave a grim, thin-lipped smile. 'Big stuff,' he agreed, hands in his pockets. He turned Chris, the lines on his face suddenly deeper.

'Would you rather I stay and help out here, Guv?' Chris asked, unsure of where his skills would be best used.

'No, we'll cover things here. Chase up that farmer, would you, son?'

Chris excused himself, lifted his coat and left the station. Every time the drugs case raised it's head Crighton seemed to age another year and Chris felt sorry for the man. The weight of losing his Sergeant must be hard for him to carry. During Chris's tours of Afghanistan, in the early years of the conflict, fewer than ten of his Forces colleagues were killed, none of whom had been known to him. He had little to compare with his boss's loss, nothing to help empathise with the situation. Sally knew Sergeant James too, but she didn't seem affected by it as Crighton was. Maybe, as Joe had said, he did feel responsible for James's death after authorising his participation in the raid. Where does that put the rest of them? It's an odd team, he thought, and he didn't really fit in yet. Sally had thawed slightly since her revalation, but she still made him nervous around her. The Guv was distant and unfocussed, worrying Chris about his leadership capabilities. Even Joe had proved to be untrustworthy. What was he thinking pointing the finger at Chris over some fantasised affair?

Although due at the farm next door to Hearst's quarry, Chris chose first to visit the one person he knew he could trust. Instead of following the A14 towards Oundle he turned onto the A43 to Northampton and into Forensic Science.

65

He poked his head around Jed Chambers' office door thirty minutes later. 'Hi Jed. Can you spare a few minutes, mate?'

'Come in, Chris' Jed gestured Chris into his shared lab. 'What's up?'

Chris sat down in a spare chair. 'I had to come and see you Jed. I can't get this out of my mind.'

'I heard you had a crew of white-suits out again this morning,' Jed said. 'Came up blank, didn't they?'

'Yeah. That's why I'm here. I can't afford to go shooting my mouth off every time I get a hunch but this time I think I'm onto something.'

'OK, shoot,' Jed grinned.

'We found Hearst covered in limestone dust, yeah?'

'Yeah.'

'His quarry works limestone. But look at the dust on my trousers. That's from Hearst's quarry. I don't remember the stuff on his jeans being this dark.'

'Hard to say without a direct comparison.'

'That's what got me thinking. If we can compare this with the evidence on Hearst's clothing it might point us in the right direction.'

'Which is?'

'Hey, I've already let my instincts get in the way of the evidence already today. I'll tell you if you can prove I'm right.'

'But you want this off the record?'

'For the time being, if you can, mate,' Chris said.

'Let's take a look at it then,' Jed reached over his desk for a scraper and microscope slide.

He carefully scooped a sample from Chris's trousers onto the slide and placed it under the microscope.

Chris chewed on a fingernail. He was going to be late questioning the farmer. He hoped the bollocking coming his way would be worth the risk.

A few minutes later Jed stood and walked over to an evidence cupboard, returning with a tray containing more slides. Time slipped by, with Jed alternately squinting through the microscope's eyepiece, consulting a scientific database on his computer and jotting down notes.

Chris looked over Jed's shoulder at the computer monitor and saw geological descriptions of stone formations. It was all way above his head so he sat back, content to watch his friend working.

Jed's really come into his own here, he thought, looking around the lab. He recalled Jed always having some kind of technical anecdote or other when they'd shared long nights on foot patrol. That injury was probably the making of him. Chris wondered how he'd have taken life as a career bobby. Would he have moved into Criminal Investigations with Chris, or taken another speciality? Would he have taken a winding course through the force to forensics, hitting it at forty and wondering how it had taken so long to get there?

'I'll make a brew,' he suggested, earning a positive grunt from Jed, engrossed in his work.

Chris thought of his own choice as he wandered to the tea machine. He hadn't been forced into it as Jed virtually had. Why had he decided on CID? All coppers wanted to put the bad guys away and he was no different in that sense. He guessed he took things more personally. Needed to know the motivation behind criminals actions. It wasn't good enough to collar them, book 'em and move onto the next adrenaline fix. The complex layers of serious crime called for all levels of policing, from detectives, uniform, scientists and psychologists. He felt lucky to be at the centre, pulling in specialities when needed.

He returned to Jed with refreshments, waiting patiently for him to finish.

'So genius, do you want the good news or the bad?' Jed said eventually, picking up his tea.

'Just give it to me straight, doc,' Chris joked.

'You're right, the evidence you so expertly gathered on your trousers is a different type of limestone to that found on Hearst's jeans,' Jed said.

'And the bad news?' Chris asked, waiting for the gotcha.

'It's not bad news as such,' Jed reassured him. 'Let me explain.' He pointed to the scientific journal on his computer screen. 'Most of the limestone in this area of the country comes from a seam of stone called Lincolnshire Limestone. Imagine the country 165 million years ago in the Jurassic period. Much of it was a warm, almost tropical sea seething with life. As the sea life died, their shells and skeletons sank to the bottom of the sea creating a thick sediment. Over time the seas dried up. Ice ages came and went and a whole bunch more geology and land covered these deposits, squashing them under enormous pressure to form limestone. Take a look.' He indicated the microscope.

Chris peered into the eyeglass and instantly spotted the outline of a tiny shell in the specimen under the scope.

He looked up, blankly. 'I still don't understand,' he said.

'The Lincolnshire Limestone is formed by two distinct layers separated by a layer of the fossilised shells of Acanthothris crossi, that's what you can see in the microscope. The lower layer has a finer grain and appears darker than the upper layer, which is made from cross-bedded oolite limestone and has a lighter colour and a more coarse, shell-like texture.'

'OK,' Chris said, beginning to get the idea.

'The whole seam thins out around Rutland and Kettering. The lower layer gives way to sandstone, which is plentiful further South. There are still some very small pockets of both layers around Kettering, Peterborough and as far south as Oundle. I'm willing to bet your man has been quarrying the lower layer, hence the darker construction.'

'And the lighter debris on his jeans has come from another quarry that's been cutting into the upper layer,' Chris finished triumphantly.

'That's where the bad news raises it's head,' Jed said bringing Chris back down to earth.

'What? I thought you said Hearst was cutting the lower darker layer,' he said.

'It's not as bad as you think,' Jed consoled. 'First things first. You've brought me dustings from your trousers We can't use that as evidence. We have to wait for the official forensics reports from the samples taken at the quarry to quantify it.'

'Of course, yes,' Chris agreed.

'That's not so bad. Secondly, and more difficult to ignore is that Hearst's clothing does have traces of both kinds of stone in it, and at different levels.'

'Oh?' Chris said.

'Yeah. From what I can see, the freshest coating on Hearst is the lighter upper layer. That's on both his skin and his clothes. Then we have traces of the dark dust in the fabric of his clothes and yet deeper into the fabric are traces of the upper layer. Work that out, Einstein,' Jed finished.

'I dunno. I'll have to think about that,' Chris said, scribbling in his notebook. 'I still reckon we've got a lead. He could have been offed in another quarry upstream of Hearst's.'

'Not upstream, Chris,' Jed admonished. 'North.'

'You said the stone was made skeletons of marine life. I thought you meant the riverbed.'

'I can see you're not a scientist, mate,' Jed laughed.

'I know the river isn't salt water now. You said all those millions of years ago it was a sea.'

'That's right, a sea. The rivers Nene, Ouse, Trent, you name it, they weren't here, so you have to disassociate today's geography from where this stone is. Also, glacier activity long after the Jurassic period has pushed the geography around to where it is now.'

'Right,' Chris said, still a little confused.

'I think you're correct. Hearst would have his own stone on his clothes, but crucially he only has the light coloured dust is on his hands and feet. That suggests his last port of call was at a place that works that stone. He may have visited it days or weeks before, hence traces deep in the fibres of his clothing, or he may even have been working the light stone at his own quarry.'

'Wait, what are you saying?' Chris interrupted.

'He may have both kinds of stone at his quarry. The two layers are interconnected after all. You might find he found both in his dig.'

'Maybe. I'll have to ask at the quarry again,' Chris said, aiming to quiz Hearst's foreman further. 'Cheers for this, Jed. I owe you one,' Chris said.

'No Chris. You owe me two, now,' Jed grinned. 'And a beer sometime?'

'Yeah, definitely. Come over at the weekend, we'll have a pint and a curry.'

'I may do. Catch up with you soon, mate.'

CHAPTER 7

Chris arrived at the farm next to Hearst's quarry late, as he'd expected. He found the farmer, Jack Polson, working in an open fronted barn, segmented into six animal pens. Young bullocks peered over the barriers with inquisitive eyes and dripping noses. Polson was scooping food pellets into a bucket from a box stationed on a forklift truck. The sound of shuffling bodies, animal snuffles and occasional moos mixed in the air with the smelly fug of a hundred bovine bodies.

'Yes, I know Hearst,' Polson answered Chris's opening question, spitting on the ground. 'He came to me a few weeks ago. Barefaced cheek he's got.' Polson threw feed into a trough in the pen, then vigorously shovelled the bucket around in the box for more. 'Virtually bankrupted my brother and has the cheek to push himself onto me!'

'Sorry, Sir. You'll have to slow down.'

'Can't slow down, lad,' the bucket scrabbled about in the box once more. 'Cattle have to be fed.'

'No, I meant you're getting ahead of me,' Chris explained. 'What do you mean he bankrupted your brother?'

Polson stopped, stretched his back and looked steadily into Chris's eyes. 'Son, I've got 700 animals to feed this evening. I haven't got time to stand about chopsing. If you want to ask your questions, you'll just have to try and keep up.' He hefted another bucketful of feed over the fence.

Chris paused. The 'we can do this down at the station' routine wasn't going to work here. How would Crighton handle it. With respect, he supposed. The bloke's got a job to do and I am late after all.

'OK, so how did your brother know Hearst?' he asked.

'John owned the field where the quarry is. Hearst

71

came along and persuaded him to sell. Then he got the money back by persuading John to re-invest in the business. Well, the quarry only produced half what Hearst expected. He'd worded the partnership to virtually write my brother out of any profits if it didn't deliver.'

'I see.'

'Now he's got the balls to come after me because he knows that seam of rock runs through my land,' the bucket dug again into the box. 'Well, hell will freeze over before I give way.'

'I don't think you need to worry about that, Sir. Hearst is dead.'

Polson didn't pause in his work. 'That's good,' he said.

'A man has lost his life, sir. That doesn't bother you?'

'No,' Polson said. 'The bloke was a swindler. Maybe my brother will get some of the money he's owed, now.'

'I see. Just bear with me a minute will you, please?'

'Do what you like son but I can't stop this,' he indicated the feed.

Chris began to walk around the farmyard, finding some distance from Polson. He took his phone out and called DI Crighton.

'We'll have to get him and his brother in to provide a statement,' Crighton said after Chris had filled him in. 'Ask them to come to the station on Monday morning at eleven, would you?'

'You don't want to bring them in now? There's a possible motive here, Sir,' Chris said.

'We can't arrest everyone who shows a dislike for Hearst, Raine. We'll look into it, though, don't worry.'

'What about Molly Gowland? There must be a hundred hiding places at a place like this.'

'Listen son, the girl isn't even officially missing,' Crighton said to Chris's surprise. 'When we've been in touch with the mother we can pass her details onto the Missing Person's Bureau, but until then we have to follow procedure. I'm not about to start ripping up every farm or workshop that you have a hunch about.'

Chris mumbled a meek, 'OK, Guv,' and hung up. Crighton's attitude confused him. One minute he was cut up about his officer's death the next he didn't seem bothered about a missing child.

Not missing, he mocked himself. She could be safe yet, at her gran's house or somewhere similar. He continued around the farmyard past more cattle pens, enthusiastic calves and bullocks greeting him on the way with expectant eyes. His stomach grumbled and reminded him that time was getting on. He looked through the doors of an enclosed barn in a half hearted attempt at a search. The barn provided a parking place for farm machinery and a workshop area. A workbench was home to a vice, pillar drill and workman's tools. In one corner stood a vertical band-saw. Alerted to the potential connection in the way Hearst had been murdered, Chris eased through the entrance and drew closer. He noticed sawdust scattered around saw's base and a pile of logs stacked along one wall.

In the gloom he felt detached from the muffled clanking and clanging of cattle pens outside. A cloying aroma of wood and diesel permeated the air. He bent down to look closely at the saw. The debris on the ground could have been used to soak up blood, he thought, but where's the spatter on the wall? And there's no sign of blood on the saw itself.

A scraping sound jerked him upright, banging his head on the saw's support. The barn door opened and light flooded inside.

'What are you doing in here?' Polson called out.

'Just having a look around,' Chris replied, his hand on his head. 'I had to make a phone call.'

'I can't have you wandering around unsupervised,' Polson scolded. 'If you have an accident, I'm liable. What's up with your head?'

Chris looked at the sticky blood on his fingers.

'I banged my head. It's just a scrape,' he said, feeling for the lump beginning to rise under his hair.

'See what I mean? Come out of there.'

Feeling sheepish, Chris left the barn. He passed on Crighton's request and asked for the brother's phone number. He returned to his car and called Polson's brother to arrange his statement,

then joined the road from the farm track. As he passed the quarry next door, he noticed lights gleaming from the sheds. The clock on his dashboard showed that he had time to question the foreman again, using the information Jed had given him.

The foreman was in the process of shutting down the machinery in the quarry and locking up the sheds.

'I won't keep you long,' Chris told him. 'Just a few questions.'

They sat down in the managers office again. The calendar was back in place. The white smile and bare breasts distracting Chris from the lifeless office. He concentrated on his notes.

'Can you just run me through what stone you quarry here again, please?' he asked.

The foreman looked depressed. Identifying his boss in the morgue had clearly got to him. picked up two stone samples from the desk. Each had been cut into a small ashlar shape and had a distinct hue.

'We've been quarrying this stone for three years,' he explained in a flat tone, handing a smooth dark brown stone to Chris. 'We cut it into decorative features for gardens and the like. The other,' he said, hefting a light coloured ashlar in his hand. 'is fairly new to us. We've been able to sell limited quantities through the English Heritage agreements and some local stately homes over the last year and a half. They use it to maintain their buildings.'

'Why can't you use this?' Chris asked, looking at his sample.

'Too dark, and too smooth' the foreman replied,

his voice picking up slightly as his interest grew,. 'If you fitted that in a limestone wall it would stick out like a sore thumb.'

Chris was getting a better picture of Jed's geological summary.

'Do you alternate much between the stone two?'

'Only when we have to. When we started we only had the dark stone to dig. The light stone was revealed as we expanded the quarry. We were getting a better price for that so concentrated on it until we reached the land boundary. Now we've gone back back to our original market until Simon negotiates an extension,' he fell silent. His words echoing in the deserted shed. 'What are we going to do now?'

'I can't help you there. Are there any other stonemasons that might buy the place?'

'Funny you should say that' the foreman said. 'There are about ten stone companies in the county.'

'What's funny about that?'

'Without a green light on expanding into the field next door they won't be interested. They can't get at the quality stone.'

Chris began to get the picture.

'Has the Polson been in touch?'

'Yes, and his brother. Polson next door came to me first, shortly after Hearst tried sweet talking him in to selling.'

'What did he want?'

'He asked lots of questions about the contracts we have for that kind of stone, then offered me a job to manage the place if he started up a quarry.'

'What did you say?'

'I told him I'd think about it. I guess I'll have no choice but to work for him now.'

'Or his brother at any rate,' Chris said.

He left the foreman contemplating his future. At least that explained both grades of stone dust on Hearst's jeans, he thought. But the foreman had admitted to reverting back to the dark stone recently, which left the question; why were the hands and feet on Heart's corpse covered with a fresh coating of light coloured limestone dust?

The second that Chris opened his front door he could sense something was amiss.

'Ida?' he called.

No answer. He could feel someone was in the house. Doors were closed where he'd left them open that morning and a shift in the atmosphere had set his senses on edge. He bunched a fist around his keyring, leaving the longest key poking out between two fingers. It made a pretty inadequate weaon.

'It'll have to do, Rainey,' he said to himself, wondering why he'd just called himself by his nickname. Nerves taut, and navigating with smooth efficient movements, he began a sweep of the long, narrow house. Hallway clear and into the living room. His eyes scoured the room. He didn't recognize the box resting on the coffee table. A shadow moved behind the kitchen door. Chris crept up to it, ears alert to every sound.

The door opened and he leapt forward jabbing out his fist. He halted suddenly, stumbling and catching the door frame at the sound of a scream and the crash of breaking crockery. Sally Whitelock stood frozen in the doorway, shattered plate and ruined toast at her feet.

'Jesus Christ, Chris!' she gasped. 'You scared me.'

'Butter side down,' he noted, relaxing his hand and dropping the keys into his pocket. He didn't let on how close she'd been to receiving a perforated face. 'How did you get in?'

'I'm sorry, Chris,' she sighed. 'I had nowhere else to go.' She stooped to scoop up the remains of her snack. 'I spoke to your neighbour. She'd seen us together yesterday and I persuaded her to let me in. I hope it's all right?'

'She shouldn't have done that,' Chris answered. He liked his privacy and didn't appreciate his colleagues having the run of the place. He'd have to speak with Ida later. 'Anyway, why are you here?'

'I couldn't go to my friend's. I stayed at home last night because Tony was on nights. He's at home tonight. I couldn't . . .' she tailed off.

'You didn't speak to your friend?' Chris asked, hoping she was going to tell him she'd begun facing up to her problem.

'I couldn't, Chris,' she answered. 'I can't bring myself to tell her. You're the only one who knows about this. I think you know how I feel.'

'I really don't,' he admitted. 'I tried to put myself in your shoes last night but it didn't work. How can I really know what you're going through.'

'I think you do understand. It'll be OK in a few days. He'll calm down and we'll talk it through.'

'Blokes like him don't stay calm for long, Sally,' Chris said. 'You know that.'

'It'll be OK,' she repeated.

'What's he going to do when he finds out you're here?'

'I'll tell him I stayed at a hotel.'

'Maybe that's what you should do.'

'Can't I stay here, Chris, please?' she begged. 'Just for a few days?'

'I don't know, Sally. It's awkward. You're asking me to be a part of it.'

'I'll sort it out, Chris. I promise. I'll report him if it happens again.'

He wrestled with the choice. He didn't believe her promise but didn't want to let her down. They were supposed to be working together on the murder case yet this was getting in the way. He imagined the possibilities that might emerge if she stayed over. He wasn't ready to deal with them and hoped this wasn't going to be a mistake.

'You can stay on the sofa tonight but I'm not sure about any longer,' he agreed.

'Thanks, Chris. You won't know I'm here,' she said.

'What's in the box?' he asked.

'It's some of Hearst's documentation. I was going to go through it tonight. Paul dragged me around Kettering today, interviewing the magistrate and a few others involved in his drugs case. I didn't get time to make headway on this earlier.'

'I won't know you're here, eh?' he chuckled. 'You won't be wanting any help with that then?' He pointed at the box.

'Only if you're at a loose end,' she teased, in an instant at ease and relaxed.

'I'll get the coffee on.'

Chris dug out some bedding for Sally and made coffee.

'Did you get anywhere with Molly Gowland this afternoon?' He called through from the kitchen.

'Joe managed to contact her mother in Spain.' Sally knelt on the floor, organizing the documents into a chronological order. 'She doesn't know of anyone local that Hearst could have used to look after the girl. Strange, Joe said she seemed more bothered about cutting her holiday short than the fact her daughter was missing.'

'Some people, eh?' Chris leaned through the door to emphasise the point.

Sally nodded in agreement. 'She's on the first available flight back, but won't be here until Sunday.'

'It'll be five days since Molly went missing by then. I can't believe we're not doing anything more to find her.' Chris set the cups down and sank into his sofa. He felt inept, powerless. Sally reached up from her position on the floor and rested a hand on his knee

'There's not much more we can do, Chris. Missing Person's Bureau have been notified and there's an appeal going out on TV tonight. At the moment the best thing we can do to help her is find whoever killed Hearst. That'll link us to Molly.'

He found it hard to resist the urge to rush out and bang on doors, demanding answers. But who's doors?

What answers? He heard the sense in her words. Hearst's murder was the key to finding his daughter. They had to understand Hearst's work, his patterns of behaviour. This would bring them closer to answering why someone would want him dead. Was the girl their goal or just an unfortunate coincidence?

'That's it.' Chris sat up straight. 'He was supposed to be alone.'

'What are you talking about?'

'Hearst was executed. The blindfold, a circular saw of some kind. All used to raise fear in him. Someone wanted to put the shits up him before killing him.'

'That makes sense,' Sally agreed, although there was hesitance in her voice. 'But getting to the girl could still be the reason behind his death. The torture was just the final humiliation for him.'

'When they planned to take Hearst, they didn't expect her to be with him.' Chris leaned forward, his brain spinning. How could he be sure?

'Because she landed in his lap at the last minute,' Sally voiced Chris's thoughts.

He nodded. 'They'd have planned Hearst's abduction in advance. But Molly's mum dropped her off on Friday without notice. They didn't kill Hearst to get to her, I'm sure.'

'You keep saying they.'

'Has to be the work of more than one person,' Chris said.

'And now there's someone with an unwanted hostage. Probably wondering what the hell to do with her. She's a risk to them, but would they be so cold hearted to kill a child?'

'I hope not, but you're right. At the moment, finding out why Hearst had to die is the only way we'll get close to locating his daughter.'

They settled down amongst the jumble of documents. Sally had brought the most recent contracts and diaries, those that she'd thought to be the most relevant. The rest would be delivered to the station by the SOCO team.

'His spelling is atrocious. Handwriting's even worse,' Sally murmured, leafing through the paperwork.

They were making no real headway after half an hour when the doorbell rang.

'That'll be Ida,' Chris said. 'She sometimes brings me some dinner. If it's not her we'll get pizza or something later.' He rose from the mess of strewn paperwork and moved into the hall.

But it wasn't Ida at the door when he opened it. DI Crighton stood in the cold night air and Chris stared back in mild panic, wondering how he was going to explain Sally's presence.

'I know it's Friday night and a bit short notice, Raine. I'm on my way to question someone and could do with the backup. Are you busy?'

'I, er, I. . .' Chris started.

Sally's head poked around the doorway into the hall. 'Hello, Guv,' she said.

'Sally?' Crighton said, his surprised eyes alternating between her and Chris.

'Chris and I are working through Hearst's documentation. I didn't get chance earlier and he agreed to give me a hand.'

'Good to see you both working well together,' Crighton coughed, raising his eyebrows at Chris. 'I was just asking Raine to accompany me to question someone about the Hearst case.'

'OK Guv. I'll get out of your hair, see if I can find something to eat in town. Unless you need me to tag along, Guv?'

'I think we'll be able to manage Sally. Get yourself some dinner.'

'I'll pick these up tomorrow if that's OK, Chris?' Sally winked at him and collected her coat, leaving the documents spread out over the coffee table. 'Tell the Guv about your theory.'

In a half daze, Chris put his coat on and followed Crighton out to his car.

CHAPTER 8

Crighton drove them to Elton village, north of Oundle. 'Reeks of money eh, Chris?' Crighton growled as they passed the well-to-do houses in the village.

'Yeah,' Chris responded, engrossed on his phone's screen. 'I've been looking up this John Stoke on the internet. He's hard to track down. You say he's in property development?'

'Yes, among other ventures. We haven't got a full view of his business dealings yet.'

'Looks like he likes his privacy. I can't find much at all on here'

'Hmm,' Crighton said.

'So, why are we going to question him?'

'He was in the pub the night the Cartwrights left their boat unattended,' Crighton explained. 'I've got uniform questioning as many people as possible but I want to speak to a few myself.'

Chris was about to mention something when his phone beeped with a text.

'Sri bout earlier. gone 2 travelodge C U 2mrw. Sal x'

That's a relief, he thought. Takes temptation, trouble and work away in one quick bite. 'x'? Does she end all her texts like that? He thought back to when Sally had slipped and pressed her body against him at the mill, wondering if there had been anything intentional in her move. It wasn't an unwelcome feeling. No. Concentrate on the job, Chris.

The house they arrived at was set in its own grounds. Chris couldn't see much in the darkness. He made out the silhouette of a horse in a half acre paddock flanking the drive.

'Why do you need backup, Guv? The house looks pretty posh. Are we likely to meet trouble?'

'Not necessarily. Don't want to run into anything unexpected, though.'

Crighton rang the bell.

An elegantly dressed woman opened the door. Chris guessed her age as mid-thirties. Her blonde hair and expertly applied make-up created a visage he had trouble tearing his eyes from. Expensive looking jewellery adorned her neck, ears and wrists and her tantalizing perfume crept into his subconscious.

She spoke, breaking the spell.

'Good evening, gentlemen. How can I help you?' she said.

Chris noticed Crighton regaining control of his gaping mouth. He'd been as stunned as Chris at the appearance before them.

'Er, good evening, ma'am,' Crighton managed. 'Does a Mr. John Stoke live here?'

'Yes. I'm his wife, Gemma,' she replied. 'Who shall I say is calling?'

'Detective Inspector Crighton, ma'am. Northamptonshire Police. This is Detective Constable Raine.'

'Just a moment please, gentlemen. I'll see if John's available.' Mrs Stoke closed the door on them.

Crighton and Chris shared a look.

'See if he's available? I'll knock the bloody door down if he's not.' Crighton coughed, shaking some sense back into himself.

Chris thought the DI was more rankled about how easily he'd been overcome by Mrs. Stoke's looks than any perceived disrespect for authority. He didn't blame his boss. He'd been caught off guard too.

Gemma Stoke returned to the door and ushered the detectives in.

'He's through here,' she said, leading them a short distance into the house to a large study with a bay window at the front of the house. Stoke would have had a view of them standing at the doorway if he'd ventured a peek through the curtains.

'Should I get the gentlemen a drink, John?' she offered.

'No, thank you, Gemma,' her husband said. 'I'm sure we won't be long,' he waved a hand over the paperwork on an oak desk, both to dismiss his wife and indicate to the detectives they'd caught him at a busy time.

Gemma backed slowly out of the room as if reluctant to miss the conversation. Stoke's large frame dominated the desk space.

'So officers,' he began in a low, calm voice. 'Care to let me know why you're disturbing me at such a late hour?'

'Oh, eight o'clock is not so late,' Crighton said, casually looking at the clock nestling between two original oil paintings on the study wall. They depicted hunting scenes; men dressed in red coats on elongated horses with all four hooves off the ground. Dogs ran ahead chasing down a red brush that disappeared into long grass. 'DI Crighton and DC Raine,' he pointed at Chris. 'Mind if I sit?'

Stoke nodded. Crighton sat in the only available chair. Chris stood to one side.

Stoke carried on working. He shuffled some papers, scrawling a few notes on one or two with a Mont Blanc pen.

'Well?'

'Hmm?' Crighton said.

'Come along, officer. I don't have all night.'

'When you're ready to give us your full attention, sir,' Crighton said, an edge to his voice.

Stoke dropped the heavy pen onto the paperwork, steepled his large, calloused fingers and touched their tips to his pursed lips. 'I'm all ears,' he said.

'I appreciate you might not be used to being disturbed in your own home, Mr. Stoke. If you'd rather speak to us at the station, I assure you it can be arranged.'

Stoke contemplated the threat, and relaxed his

arms, laying them gently on the desk top.

Chris let the battle of wills continue in front of him. He'd seen something on Stoke's desk, pulled his phone out and was busy searching the internet.

'Mr. Stoke, do you frequent the Chequered Skipper pub in Ashton, at all?' Crighton asked.

'Occasionally. Why?'

'We're following up a number of leads on a case we're working on. We need to clarify the movements of as many people as possible who use that pub.' Crighton explained. 'You don't prefer the local here, the Crown?'

'I meet an old friend every now and then at the Skipper. It's convenient for both of us,' Stoke said.

'Who would that be?'

'Graham Yarwood. The Skipper is about half way between here and his place at Thurning.'

There was a soft knock on the door and Gemma Stoke re-entered carrying a chair for Chris.

'Ah yes, Mr Yarwood. A magistrate. We've found ourselves speaking to him a lot recently. He's been letting off some of the local scumbags that appear before him somewhat easily. They're seeping back into my patch in Kettering. Drugs, Mr. Stoke.'

Gemma Stoke's head twitched at the mention of Yarwood's name and Stoke threw her a stern look. He waited while she left the room before continuing.

'I'm not aware of anything he might be doing with your 'patch' Mr. Crighton,' Stoke said. 'That has nothing to do with me.'

Chris sat down and got Crighton's attention. He showed him the phone's screen.

Crighton looked at the web page, his eyes flickering in recognition 'You know I can't see a thing on those things, Raine,' he said. 'Turn it off.'

Chris jumped at the rebuke and stuffed the phone back in his pocket. Stoke snorted. He was about the same age as the DI and Chris guessed he probably had the same attitude towards technology.

'I didn't say it was connected to you, Mr. Stoke,'

Crighton said. 'Were you at the pub three nights ago?'

'Let me see,' Stoke said, leafing through his desk diary. 'I was in London that day searching for properties. It was a late finish. Yes, I think I did drop in quite late for a quick one.'

'Did you meet Yarwood there?'

'No. I thought he might be in but in the end I was alone. I didn't stay long.'

'And then you came straight home?'

'Yes. Don't worry Mr. Crighton, I only had the one. I'm not a drink driver.'

Crighton smiled, as if sharing the joke. 'So, you're a property developer, Mr. Stoke?'

Stoke nodded.

'A lot of money to be made there,' Crighton's looked around the room, illustrating his appreciation of the expensive décor.

'I've made some money in my time,' Stoke acknowledged. 'I sold a lot of properties just before house prices dipped in 2007 so I have to confess it's part luck and part judgement.'

'You have some properties in Kettering, don't you?'

'Yes.'

'Wasn't one of your houses the scene of a serious incident last September? A gang was holed up there and killed a policeman.'

'You're well informed Inspector,' Stoke said. 'I did hear something about it but you'll have to speak to the letting agency for more details,' he looked down his nose. 'I don't choose the tenants.'

'I will, sir,' Crighton said, smiling again. 'Could I have their number, please?'

Stoke sifted through a pile of business cards in his desk drawer and tossed one over to Crighton. He also lifted a packet of cigarettes out and lit one, not asking if the others minded nor offering them one.

'Have you had any dealings with a Mr. Simon Hearst?' Crighton asked.

85

Stoke frowned and looked at the wall for a moment. 'I've heard the name. I don't recall doing business with him. I have management teams working for me so if he has done work for me then one of those will have dealt with him. Why?'

'Mr Hearst was murdered earlier this week,' Crighton said.

'Oh?' Stoke said, a blank look on his face.

'Yes. Terrible mess he made. Had his head cut off.'

'Nasty,' agreed Stoke.

'You didn't see Hearst in the Chequered Skipper?' Says Crighton.

'I wouldn't know. As I said, I've never met him,' Stoke repeated. 'Is this going anywhere, Inspector? Anyone else you think I may or may not know?'

Crighton shook his head. 'Not for now, Mr. Stoke.' he stood. 'I'll let you get back to your work.'

The detectives let themselves out of Stoke's study. Gemma Stoke was waiting in the entrance hall, hovering conveniently close to Stoke's study door. She let them out of the house.

'Guv, don't you want to know what I found?' Chris said when they were in Crighton's car, annoyed that he'd been silenced so sharply by his boss. 'You saw the stone ashlars on his desk, didn't you?'

'I saw the screen too, Chris,' Crighton confirmed, turning the ignition on. 'I wasn't about to go shouting off in there before checking properly first.' He drove down the gravel drive, looking at the line of garages and workshops to his left, and pulled out onto the main street.

Chris's internet search had revealed Stoke as being a director of Superior Masonry & Stone, a stonework specialist company based in Peterborough. Chris couldn't work out why Crighton hadn't quizzed Stoke on his involvement with the company.

'Look Guv, I spoke to my mate in Forensics today,' Chris said. 'He's as good as said that Hearst was at another quarry on the day he was killed. We should be locking down this Superior Masonry & Stone and checking it out as thoroughly and as soon as possible. Stoke could be involved in his murder.'

'Hold on Son,' Crighton said. 'Sometimes you've got to look at the long view. I've had Stoke on my radar for months now. That's why we've come out tonight rather than send uniform. I wanted to see him for myself.'

Chris bit his lip. He was keen to get to the bottom of Hearst's murder and was having trouble understanding Crighton's methods.

'Stoke is involved with the international drugs ring we've been investigating, I'm sure of it,' Crighton said. 'Hearst's death may be connected but we won't find out by tearing Stoke's place apart and stomping around. We have to take things carefully.'

Crighton dropped Chris off at home and gave him orders for the next week.

'I want you to go through Hearst's documents on Monday and see if you can find any connection with John Stoke. Let me know as soon as possible if you find anything. Leave the rest of it to me.'

Chris aimed his key at the front door, scowling at Crighton's departing car. His scowl changed to a frown when he felt no resistance. The door swung inwards before he could insert the key. Someone had been here. He thought back to Sally. Has she returned and asked Ida to let her in again? Why would she leave the door open? Then he noticed the splintered wood around the Yale lock and realised that Sally wasn't the culprit.

'Damn,' he cursed.

Alert again, he eased his way back into his house. Darkness pervaded every room. Chris's ears strained for any hint of sound. All he could hear was a siren off in the distance on the dual carriageway. He flicked his living room light on and let out a groan. The place had been turned over, resembling the aftermath of an earthquake. A bookshelf lay at a crazy angle, leaning against the sofa with all books thrown to the floor. The TV had been pushed off of its stand. Mercifully the LCD screen didn't appear to be damaged. Chris quickly searched the rest of the house to find that only the living room had been disturbed.

Doesn't look right, he thought. Nothing really damaged, aside from the door jamb. Nothing appeared to be missing. Had he disturbed the intruder? He checked the back door. Locked. No broken windows either. What's wrong here, Chris?

He put the kettle on. He felt anger at his privacy being violated. Again. Sally's unexpected visit earlier still ate at him. He sat down with a coffee wondering whether it was worth reporting the break-in.

Then it hit him. Shit! Where's Sally's box? Hearst's documents. Chris grabbed his phone and dialled her number. Did she come back and take them before the break-in? Could she help? The line went straight to answerphone.

'Sally, it's Chris. Call me back as soon as you get this. I'm back home and the box of documents you brought over is missing.'

He hung up and slouched on the sofa, tossing the phone onto the coffee table. Gingerly, he traced his fingers over the bump he'd received after the altercation with the band saw.

Crighton was probably right about not chasing Stoke's tenuous link to Hearst. Chris reluctantly retrieved his phone and dialled his boss' number. Preparing for a bollocking, he informed him of the break-in.

'When is the next lorry coming?' the man asked. 'I don't want her here any longer than necessary.' The accent made his second language sound clipped anyway. With stress edging his words they came out more curt than usual. He listened for a moment to the excuses streaming out of the earpiece on his phone.

'I don't care. That is too long. Bring it forward. Wednesday, no later.' he cut the call, throwing the phone onto a table where it skittered off of the polished oak and bounced on the tile floor. The back cover flew off and the battery slid under a door.

The man stomped over to retrieve the bits, cursing at the phone's build quality. He opened the cupboard door and glared at Molly, still tied up inside. She hadn't eaten properly for four days and her skin had sunk around her face. Chocolate wrappers and a small bottle of water lay strewn around her. She stared back with wide, fearful eyes brimmed with tears. The cupboard stank of stale urine and when the man bent to retrieve the battery his hand came back wet. He reached back in the doorway and flicked a smack on the girl's cheek. Tears sprang and she squealed behind her gag. The man noticed a bottle cap on the floor and relented when he realised the liquid had come from an open bottle. He lifted the girl to her feet and marched her to the toilet, pulled down her soiled knickers and planted her on the seat. He stood by the door while she relieved herself, then roughly re-dressed her.

She started to struggle as he returned her to the cupboard and he rewarded her with another cuff to the head.

'Soon, little one,' he growled. 'You will begin your new life. Soon.'

CHAPTER 9

Chris sensed the smell of Sally's damp hair in his nostrils. He'd carried her from a warm tropical sea and they lay on clean white sand, her head resting on a driftwood branch. She lay naked but for a necklace of shells. Her white smile teasing, encouraging, taunting. Chris leant forward and kissed her, tasting salt-water and holding her eyes with a searching gaze. 'Is this what you want?' he said. Tiny grains of sand dropped from her eyelashes as she closed them, offering her body to him. A surge of excitement coursed through his being when she pushed against his chest and he felt her taking hold of him, leading him to his desire.

'Caught myself a big one this morning,' she chuckled and he watched her drift away from him. Her face changed to a mask of bruises and her bright smile twisted into an unintelligible screamed warning, then faded from sight into darkness.

Chris woke with a start and looked around the prison cell, feeling his erection receding and the white heat of desire quickly dissipating.

'Dreaming about her now, Chris,' he chastised himself. 'That's not a good sign, mate.' He tried to recapture her last words in the dream but came up with nothing. He sat up, rubbing his face and yawning, then scrabbled on the floor for his shoes.

He'd only scrounged a few meagre hours sleep, having commandeered a spare cell at Kettering police station. The Friday drunks had kept him awake most of the night, only handing him respite in the early hours when their inebriation had passed into full effect. He thought of his house, cordoned off until forensics performed their routine. He knew he shouldn't be bothered. There was nothing at home that could get him into trouble. It was the thought of people tramping around his home and sifting through his possessions that made his skin itch. For the third time in twenty four hours he found his privacy being held up to the light of strangers.

It had taken him long enough to trust Ida to understand how he felt about his home. Having spent so long in the Army, being pulled all over the world every six months, his life packed away in a cardboard box, he found an almost primal appreciation of the permanence and security of his home.

Each violation edged him closer back to the nomadic mindset of the squaddie. The acceptance of being nothing more than a resource, a white painted number on a rifle butt shuffled from armoury to armoury, dulled his sense of being and rearranged his id.

He looked around at the bland cell walls and up to the small barred window. It reminded him of the times he'd spent on guard at some barracks or other. He'd often chosen to sleep in a free cell in the guard house, to find some peace from the snoring of sleeping comrades and the movement of his squad when they came in from patrol.

Today's cell was a cold harbour. No doubt he was in trouble for allowing the box to go missing. His co-accused had taken herself off the radar, probably distancing herself from the security breach. His boss had all but told him to butt out of the investigation, too. Some priority this case was taking. Sally was right on that at least. Crighton did seem to be focussing more on revenge for DS James than finding Molly Gowland. Sure, Hearst didn't appear to have had many supporters in life, but that shouldn't stop them from doing their best to rescue his daughter.

Chris left the station. The desk sergeant waved a copy of the Saturday paper at him as he left. 'CANAL BOAT MURDER: GIRL ABDUCTED', the headline screamed. 'Police still in the dark,' the sub-heading mocked, and below a stock school photo of Molly Hearst. Freckle-faced, hair in braids and a smile showing a tooth missing. The gap suggested the shot had been taken a couple of years ago, when the girl's adult teeth would have been coming through.

Chris found a café in the High Street and settled down with his own copy of the paper. He read Hazel Moran's piece with a growing sense of dread, waiting to read some other titbit that his team might have missed. It seemed the press were having no better luck than him in ferreting out pieces of the case. They were still following the line that Hearst had got in the way of the abduction of his daughter.

Chris drank his tea and watched a teenage girl miming along absent-mindedly to the tune playing on the radio. 'A singer in a smoky room, A smell of wine and cheap perfume.' Another girl tapped her pen in time to the beat on her university book. The song had been celebrating a fresh release on the airwaves thanks to a TV show, but he knew the original was even older than him. The girl caught him staring and threw a condescending look back. He didn't feel old enough to be classed a dirty old man, yet her attitude suggested it. Maybe it was the crumpled suit, red eyes and unshaven face. What was Molly Gowland thinking right now? Was she still alive, even?

He decided to return to the station and get stuck into the documentation from Hearst's home office. He had nothing to gain by dwelling on the trouble he was in and there was no point trying to go back home yet. With breakfast inside him, he tried to shake off the veils of that morning's dream and his depression, and returned to the office.

Two hours later he was leafing through a desk diary from two years previous, noting that the letters D.E. appeared in the corner of some pages. Wait a minute. Didn't he see the same in a diary at home the day before? No, not the same. What was it? His vision swam over the initials. Not D.E. What then? He looked back through his notebook. Did he write it down? Yes, there it was. J.S.

J.S. - John Stoke. It had to be, didn't it? Of course, his notebook wouldn't stand up as evidence on its own but it at least gave them an angle to work on. He wished he still had the diary to refer back to. Which one was it? He checked his notes. This year's. 'How did we let that box get away from us?' he cursed.

The burglary didn't make sense to him. The only thing he could think of that was missing from home was the box. The break-in was co-ordinated somehow. Did Stoke arrange it, checking him out after his visit last night? He'd have had to work at incredible speed to identify Chris, find out where he lived and arrange the theft in what, twenty five minutes? No chance. Not only that, Stoke would need to have known the box was at Chris's house and that its contents implicated him. Too many variables.

Did someone else who'd known Hearst take it? The neighbouring farmer, Polson, and his brother, maybe? They'd had more time to track him down but again, they wouldn't know he had the box at home.

Chris also remembered the seemingly endless queue of employees who'd lost no love over Hearst's death. You're clutching at straws, Chris. At least you've got something to go on with the initials.

Thankfully he'd listed the dates on which they appeared in the diary.

His phone beeped. 'still on for curry tonight?' Jed's text read.

'Rain check, mate. Got burgled last night' he tapped out his reply. He didn't fancy having to put Jed up in his ransacked house.

Two minutes later his phone rang. Jed.

'Hi Jed,' he said.

'Rainey. What's up?'

'Sorry about tonight mate, my house will be a mess. Someone broke in last night. Forensics are over there now.'

'You're getting a bit familiar with my boys, aren't you? Why are they out for a domestic burglary?'

'I had some of the evidence in our murder case taken.'

'Oh, right. Bugger. Look, they're bound to be finished by this evening and I've seen the state of your place at the best of times. Don't let it put you off.'

'Cheeky sod. OK, lets do it. See you about eight?'

'Yeah, first one's on me. You sound like you need cheering up.'

Chris spent the rest of the day searching through the contents of Hearst's business documentation for clues of his working life. Knowing that the most important information wasn't there didn't help his motivation but he stuck at it. He checked his phone regularly to see if Sally had been in touch and rang her number a few times. No answer.

His phone rang mid afternoon with a message from forensics to say they'd finished at his house. They couldn't tell him if they'd found anything significant, only that there hadn't been much evidence to lift.

Before leaving the station Chris phoned DI Crighton. He updated the DI with the forensics news, then said:

'Guv, I'm still at the station. I've found something in the documentation that might be worth chasing up.'

'Go on,' Crighton said.

'Well, I made some notes when we still had the box. Hearst had different sets of initials written in the corners in some of his diaries. He had D.E in there a couple of years ago, and J.S in this years diary. It's possible he and Stoke had several meetings.' Chris said.

'Hmm, possible,' Crighton agreed. 'Let me have those dates. I'll be sure to ask Stoke about them the next time we meet.'

This was news to Chris. He'd thought his boss hadn't taken Stoke's relevance to the case very seriously.

'Hearst had also begun to win some new contracts on the back of the new stone he was quarrying,' Chris continued. 'It's all through the Council and English Heritage. This backs up his foreman's information. I'd love to be able to see how that progressed through the year.'

'You could always follow it up with English Heritage, Chris. They'll hold records too,' Crighton said.

'I'll do that. I'll also see what notes Sally made from last year's documents when I hear from her. I'm sorry I lost that box, Sir.'

'Me too, Chris. Don't take all the blame, son. Sally shouldn't have taken it out of the station in the first place.'

'Thanks, Guv.'

'See if you can find who D.E is too,' Crighton suggested.

'OK. Speak to you later,' Chris finished the call, thankful that Crighton wasn't blaming him entirely for the loss of evidence.

Chris looked through his notebook again, trying to match up the initials D.E. There was a possibility. Diane Ellis. This was the friend who'd played host to the Cartwrights the night the killer had disposed of Hearst's corpse on their boat.

'I suppose there could be a connection,' he said to himself. He flicked his notebook closed and decided to pay the Ellis's a visit. He couldn't face going straight home yet anyway.

Half an hour later Chris knocked on the door of a thatched, ironstone cottage in Ashton. Mrs. Ellis answered, dressed in casual slacks and a knitted jumper. She looked to be late forties, thickening up at the hips and around the face maybe, but still an attractive woman.

He introduced himself and was led into a small lounge where Mrs. Ellis invited him to sit whilst she made tea.

Chris sat uncomfortably on an overstuffed chair that dominated the room, banishing all other furniture to the edges and corners.

'How can I help you, officer?' Mrs. Ellis asked, returning with a small teacup resting on a saucer. She placed them on an occasional table, relegated to the far wall, just out of Chris's reach.

'Mrs. Ellis, we're following up a case in the local area. I was wondering if you could confirm your relationship with Alec and Maureen Cartwright.'

'We're old friends,' Mrs. Ellis said. 'I've known Maureen twenty years or more. She phoned me on Wednesday to say what had happened.'

'It is about that, ma'am. Did Mrs. Cartwright ask you whether you noticed anyone eavesdropping on you in the pub on Tuesday?' Chris asked.

'Yes, she did. I couldn't think, though,' Mrs. Ellis said, pausing and blushing. She patted her auburn hair, fixed in a pony tail. 'We were all quite merry by then, you know,' she gave a short, high pitched giggle. 'It was late and we were in the bar, I remember that much.'

'Do you know a Simon Hearst, Ma'am?' Chris asked.

She jumped at the name. 'Yes,' she said. 'Why do you ask? You don't suppose he could have done it, do you?'

'I'm afraid he was the victim, Mrs. Ellis.'

Her hand jumped to her mouth. 'Oh!' she cried. 'Oh, no. Not Simon.'

'I'm very sorry Ma'am,' Chris said, regretting his timing. 'did you know him well?'

The door burst open and a large man stomped in. 'Yes, she knew him well enough,' he snarled.

Chris immediately stood, ready to defend himself. The man's fat red face wobbled when he spoke.

'Who are you, anyway?'

'I'm Detective Constable Raine – Sir,' Chris answered.

The man bristled with indignation. 'What about him then, the bastard? What's he a victim of?' he asked, his head turning from one to the other.

'It was him on the narrowboat, Geoff,' Diane said.

'What? Oh. Ha! got his comeuppance then, did he?'

'You know him, Mr. Ellis?' Chris asked, guessing he was speaking to Geoff Ellis.

'Not that I want to. That little shit's been tupping half the women around this place,' Ellis replied.

'Don't use such coarse language, Geoff,' Diane Ellis objected. 'And don't speak ill of the dead.'

Chris looked at Mrs. Ellis. Her cheeks had reddened further and tears spilled down them. He guessed there was history between these two and Hearst.

'Mr Ellis, could we speak outside, please?' He stepped forward in the cramped room giving Ellis no choice but to turn and leave or stand chin to chin with Raine.

'Ma'am, I'll come back and speak with you again in a minute, if I could, please?'

'Oh. OK,' she said, her eyes distant, thoughts elsewhere.

Ellis led Chris through the house to the back garden. Tools lay on the lawn and by the sweat stains on his check shirt, Ellis had been out here digging beds for spring planting when Chris called. He must have crept into the house and listened-in at the door. Not much trust in this relationship, Chris thought.

'So why don't you tell me about your little outburst in there?' Chris asked.

Ellis's face twitched, sending more wobbles through the loose skin at his throat.

'They had an affair, didn't they,' he said as though it were obvious.

'When?'

'Three years ago. She said she broke it up after a few months but I've always thought they never did.'

'What makes you think that?'

'Well, you're here aren't you. Why else do you need to speak to her unless it was still going on?'

'I'm here because you both know the Cartwrights,' he lied. His suspicions had been roused as soon as Diane Ellis's initials matched up back at the station. 'That's all.'

'Right,' Ellis said, caught off-guard. 'Well yes, we do.'

'Yes.' Chris left the word hanging.

'He did her as well, you know,' Ellis blurted out.

'Who, Mrs. Cartwright?'

Ellis nodded, unable to voice his disgust.

'I'm sure we don't need to go into that, Sir,' Chris said and watched the tension ease slightly on Ellis's face.

'I don't know what they all saw in him,' he said.

Quick to put Hearst into the past tense, Chris thought. 'Did you stay with your wife and friends all evening on Tuesday, Mr. Ellis?'

'What? Are you suggesting. . .' Ellis's said, mouth agape.

'I'm not suggesting anything, sir,' Chris's neck tingled. Something was up.

'Good.'

'Well, did you?'

'I, I had to come back a little earlier to set the fire and get some extra bedding out,' Ellis began, seeing the trouble he was digging for himself. 'I couldn't have got over to that narrowboat and back in time.' Ellis visibly squirmed under Chris's scrutiny.

But Ellis was probably being honest. Even if he'd been driving he would have trouble laying out the corpse parts and returning to his chores back at home without raising alarm.

'I'll let myself out, Sir,' Chris said. 'I won't disturb your wife on the way through. Tell her I said thanks for the tea.'

Chris trod softly past the lounge on his way through the house. Photos of the couple in younger, happier times hung on the hallway wall. He felt sorry for Geoff Ellis in a way. He seemed to be a broken man trying to trust his wife and having a hard job of it.

What goes through a man's mind when he finds out he's been cheated? What would you do, Chris? Have to find a long term partner first, mate, he told himself.

Then gotta make sure it doesn't happen, he thought. A wry smile passed over his mouth and vanished as he thought of the anguish a man must go through, finding out his deepest love and trust has been squandered. Ellis had a reason for wanting Hearst dead. Did he have the means? Did Alec Cartwright know about Hearst and his wife and if so, could Ellis and Cartwright have worked together?

CHAPTER 10

Chris knew he needed to try and relax. The image of Hearst's cold dead stare lingered too often in his mind and although his colleagues in uniform were doing all they could to locate the man's daughter, he felt responsible for her. In the absence of a solid lead, Crighton and Sally seemed to have given up on her. He checked the clock on his car's dashboard and saw there was still time before Jed arrived at his house in Kettering.

Five miles North of Ashton lay Fotheringhay village and two miles further out along a narrow country road was Superior Masonry and Stone. To find a stone quarry here reminded Chris of Jed's remark about limestone being more prevalent further North. Here, he was downstream of Oundle, yet North of it too.

The octagonal tower of Fotheringhay church stood proud in the distance, lit bright by spotlight in the approaching dusk. Mary Queen of Scots had been incarcerated at the old motte and bailey castle at Fotheringhay, then beheaded on Queen Elizabeth I's orders. Nothing remained of the castle these days but a large mound by the riverside.

The church was built from limestone. Chris shook his head, bemused. He had the notion that he was seeing more and more of the stone since Jed's lecture. It was the same observation he'd had the previous year, when he'd thought about trading in his old Ford Focus for a VW Golf. Prior to that he barely noticed them, but as soon as the car came onto his shopping list every third car on the roads appeared to be a Golf.

Chris didn't want to announce his arrival at the quarry, so he parked up in a layby and walked along the road to a turn-off for the quarry entrance. He took his phone out and sent a text to Jed, apologising and cancelling their curry night again. He switched the phone to silent mode and modified the camera's settings on it to use no flash.

The quarry had a similar layout as Hearst's, with the addition of a number of old farm buildings. A tall chain-link fence and a double padlocked gate barred his way and a CCTV camera stared out from the top of a tall pole behind it. Chris could make out a dark coloured Ford Transit van in one corner of the yard.

A search of the perimeter fence to the right of the farm buildings revealed a loose patch of earth at its base. Chris squeezed underneath and into the property. The cold night sent a shiver through him and he cursed himself for coming out with no coat. He edged along the wall of a farm building. The night was drawing in quickly and a biting breeze had picked up, whipping his fogged breath away.

Chris could see the outline of one of the work sheds across the yard towards the back of the property. He had just broken from cover to cross the yard when a large door scraped open in the work shed. Light spilled out, framing the figure of a man. Chris eased himself back into the shadows and watched the man walk across the yard and enter the Transit. The van reversed to the shed and the man opened its rear doors into the building's doorway. Chris couldn't make out much in the gloom but he thought he'd seen a weapon slung on the man's back.

Guns? he thought. In a rural, backwater? What have you got yourself into, Chris? He deliberated for a minute whether to stay or get away. He finally made his mind up and took the width of the yard at a crouching run.

The shed's corrugated iron wall would not surrender a single gap to look through and the windows were too high to reach. He crept along the outside of the shed and rounded a corner. There he found a lower window which offered a view the length of the shed. The Transit stood unattended at the far end, about thirty feet away, with what looked like brown cement sacks loaded on board. Chris couldn't read any labels on them but at this distance he couldn't see much of anything. He tried to see a way of getting closer. The man suddenly appeared from a hole in the floor, carrying another sack over his shoulder. He loaded the sack in the van, turned and stretched. Chris shrank from the window. The man's eyes seemed to bore straight into him. Had he been seen?

The man moved. Adrenalin surged through Chris's body, snapping synapses and triggering his limbs into action.

Shit! Get out of here, Chris, he told himself. No time to find a safe exit, just move.

Stumbling legs took him further away from the yard, down a slope towards the quarry proper.

He leaped a couple of feet into a patch of long grass and dropped to his stomach. Light from a torch flickered up and down on the other side of the shed and Chris could hear running feet crunching on gravel. Old army training kicked in, telling him to shuffle diagonally away from the swaying grass that betrayed his entry point. He tried to see an escape route. The flashlight appeared at the shed's corner and began sweeping the area ahead.

Come on! find a route, he shouted to himself.

His heart beat in his ears, blocking out sound. Keep calm, lie still, his brain contradicted itself.

He backed away from the torch beam until he felt concrete on his shins. He'd hit a storm drain. The U-shaped channel disappeared underground to his right. He slid into it, eyes still following the source of the torch. He inched along the drain, disturbing the freezing, stinking muddy water at its base. The torch's search path continued down the side of the shed. Maybe the man thought he'd seen a trick of the light and was giving up. Maybe he was going to call for reinforcements. Chris hoped for the former.

Where does this tunnel lead? he thought. No time to worry about that, get in there.

He found the concrete pipe gave him enough room, provided he shuffled along on hands and knees. After a few feet he risked switching on his mini-Maglite torch, shielding most of the beam with his hand. The light ahead picked out two red dots. Rats. Suddenly the pipe didn't seem wide enough. He felt the tunnel seem to shrink around him, pressing down on his shoulders and squeezing his heart tight. No choice Chris, he thought, you've got to keep moving.

The tunnel stretched thirty or forty feet ahead. He shuffled along, jarring his knees on the concrete and shivering with cold. The torch's beam scared the rats away ahead. They stopped every now and then, staring curiously at the intruder. They ran on as though guiding him through the stygian depths.

The storm drain ran out to a ditch outside the perimeter of the quarry. Chris dropped into the ditch and up to his shins in water. Both jeans and jumper were soaked from the journey and he could feel the energy sapping from his body, leaving him weak after the adrenalin subsided.

'Not long long before hypothermia sets in,' he spoke out loud through chattering teeth. 'Must find my car. Which way is it?' He orientated himself and began to make his way to the road. 'Got to keep moving, got to keep alert,' he said, trying to keep his brain working over. 'If you go under out here, mate, you're done for.'

The night had grown colder but the wind had mercifully dropped off. A crisp ground frost covered the field he'd been ejected into. The sky was clear with only the slightest sliver of moon cutting into the darkness, faintly illuminating his panting breath. Chris beat his arms across his body to generate some heat and began to make his way to the road. He neared the edge of the field and crept back into the ditch, seeking cover in the darker shadows of the hedge.

On edge, his nerves alert, he peered out into the road. It lay like a silent black snake, daring him to come near, threatening him to stay away. He couldn't see the layby, nor his car. He guessed it was to the right where the road curved and so trailed along the hedgerow to the end of the field. Into the next and along that one, too. The car came into sight through the hedge's sparse foliage, about thirty feet ahead. Chris slowed down then stopped, though he was desperate for the comfort of the car's warmth. His ears strained to detect any movement. Was the man from the quarry waiting here for him?

In the distance an owl hooted. He waited for a few minutes, every sense on alert. The owl was joined by another, further away. Chris counted their alternating twit's and twoo's. After ten counts he was ready to move when he smelled something. Cigarette smoke. Damn, someone was here.

He saw a faint light appear briefly through the hedge, then heard a man speaking into a phone.

'Yeah, I've found a car,' the man said, his accent local. 'Dunno who's it is. Could've been here already.'

The man fell silent, listening to the voice on the other end.

'OK, but I'm not hanging around here all night. It's fucking freezing,' the voice said.

Chris hunched down in the ditch, wondering what to do. They were definitely searching for him but how serious were they? Serious enough to carry guns, he reminded himself. Should he attack the guard? No. Foolish if he's armed. Weariness washed over him and tugged him towards unconsciousness. The inactivity of waiting in the ditch had allowed the cold to finally take effect.

Wake up, idiot. Get moving or you'll die out here anyway.

As carefully as his cold aching joints would let him, Chris retraced his path back along the hedge to the first field. In this one he took the perpendicular route away from both his car and the quarry. The heat he'd generated by moving brought his consciousness back up and he knew he didn't have much time or energy left before he went down for a final time.

A large shape loomed ahead. Giant cylindrical hay bales sat in the next field, protected by thick, black, plastic shrouds. Chris tried to rip the plastic but it was too tough for him in his weakened state. He scrabbled around on the floor for something to cut the shroud with and found a sharp stone. He hacked a couple of squares from one of the covers and stuffed them under his clothes, separating the wet cloth from his body and insulating it against the cold.

Even though the nights temperature had dropped, the bales had stored a meagre amount of heat throughout the day to emit a stinking, lukewarm guff. He squeezed between two of the bales to build himself a musty, uncomfortable nest.

I should call in support, he thought, and dug his phone out from a back pocket. Its cracked screen mocked him. It must have broken in the storm drain, he thought.

Within a few minutes he'd begun to feel drowsy once again. He reflected on the quarry, his discovery and escape. Who were those men? What were loading in the Transit? There hadn't been enough light to grab its registration number. He decided to rest here for a couple of hours before going for his car again. Fatigue dragged him down into a deep, dreamless sleep.

When he woke he could only guess at the time. The phone had been his only timepiece but that was useless now. The inky black sky, still dotted with stars, showed no signs of dawn at its fringes. It could be any time between midnight and five.

He wondered if his car was still under surveillance. If so, he had a long walk to the nearest village and the dubious chance of a working phone box. He contemplated knocking on a farm door. At this time of night he'd probably get a backside full of rock salt from a farmer's shotgun.

He decided on making a break for his car. He traversed the field, in line with the road, then approached the road further up from the car. The tarmac appeared deserted. Chris filled his lungs with air and, bent double, raced across into the field opposite. No shots rang out, no cries of discovery greeted his arrival. This position afforded him a good view over the carriageway, enabling him to evaluate his chances of reaching safety.

The car looked unattended. The mysterious smoker must surely have departed by now, Chris thought. He'd said as much on the phone, hadn't he? Chris steeled himself ready for action and squeezed through a gap in the hedge. He sprinted across the road and shoved the car's key into the lock, twisting it with exaggerated care. If it snapped off in the door he faced instant capture, or worse, were the watcher still present. Chris started the car and drove off unchallenged, stealing a glance into the quarry's entrance as he drew level. There were no lights on and he couldn't see if the Transit was still there. He let out a relieved, guttural sigh, grateful for the familiar feel of his steering wheel, seat, foot-pedals and the gust of warming air entering the cabin.

Thoughts of what to do next jostled for position in his mind. A warm bed and sleep topped the list.

He'd have to tell Crighton.

No, he mustn't say anything yet, not enough evidence.

They had guns, he'd have to say something.

Contradictions ping-ponged across his mind as he drove, his eyes casting frequent glances in the rear-view mirror.

The car's clock indicated it was half past two. Too early to call Crighton. And tell him what? The quarry would be deserted now after he'd alerted the occupants and it was too late to get a squad car out to search for the van. He chose to go home and get some sleep. Come morning he'd work out what to do.

The SOCOs had done a good job of tidying up back home, yet the place still didn't feel like his own.

Books were in the wrong place in the bookcase and the carpet exposed flattened dents, betraying the furnitures layout prior to the break-in.

He scratched under his armpits and groin where the sections of plastic sheeting were chafing. They were consigned to the bin and he tossed the still-damp clothes straight into the washing machine. Naked and exhausted, he climbed the stairs and dropped into bed.

He woke at ten and cursed himself for failing to set an alarm. His limbs ached from the previous night's flight and exposure to the cold. He put the kettle on and took a quick wash whilst it boiled. The red-eyed face that stared back from the bathroom mirror looked weary and confused. He didn't know how he was going to justify his actions to his boss. The only consolation he could think of was the presence of guns at the quarry. Crighton would have to act on that, surely.

Coffee in hand, Chris picked up his home phone. He stared at it blankly and replaced the handset. Only the broken mobile phone, discarded on the coffee table contained Crighton's number. He flopped down on the sofa with thoughts dredging around his head in slow muddy swirls.

'Start sparking, Chris,' he said aloud, slurping his coffee. A few moments passed. The station. Of course they'd hold the DI's number on file. He rang and authenticated himself to the duty sergeant. Within moments he had his boss's number. The sergeant also told him the DI had logged in this morning. He was going to Thurleigh. Probably the magistrate's house, Chris thought. Crighton didn't see the need for backup on that one, did he.

Or maybe he'd tried to get in touch with you after your phone broke, Chris scolded himself.

Chris rang his boss and in the background could hear that Crighton was in his car.

He explained the previous nights events.

'We've got to go in there, Sir,' he implored.

'There's more to Stoke than meets the eye. '

'Are you sure about that, son?' Crighton asked.

'What do you mean?'

'Stoke is only listed as a Director for Superior Masonry & Stone.'

'I don't understand.'

'For all we know he's never set foot in there. You don't know he has anything to do with the goings on at the quarry. You saw how Hearst barely visited his own site, didn't you?'

'Well, yes,' Chris admitted.

'What's the likelihood there's anyone at the quarry now, after they've been spooked?'

'Not much, I suppose.'

'First, we speak to the quarry foreman. Then we get a formal look around the site. Do things properly,' Crighton said.

'OK, Sir. Sorry.'

'I'm glad you got out of there alive, Raine,' Crighton said. 'We'd be in the dark about the weapons if you hadn't spotted them.'

'Thanks, Sir. Do you need a hand with your visit to the Magistrate?'

'How do you know where I'm going?'

'From the locations list at the station, Sir,' Chris confirmed.

'Ah, right. No, I'll be OK with this one Chris. Yarwood isn't a threat and it's just an informal interview. I'll keep the station up to speed. Incidentally, that's what you should have done last night before your little escapade.'

'Sorry Sir, there didn't seem to be time.'

'There has to be time, son. You need to know you're supported. You don't work alone in my team, OK?'

'Yes, Sir.' Chris hung up, not convinced. The DI appeared quite happy to leave him out of the loop when it suited him. Why was he going to see the Magistrate today? Probably as part of the drugs case, he thought.

Was the man being leaned on by a cartel to go easy on their pushers? Didn't mean Crighton had to squeeze me out, though. Chris stretched his aching body and accepted the day off Crighton had given him.

He spent the rest of the day finding a replacement mobile phone and sorting his house out. With his SIM in the new phone he checked his messages. True enough Crighton had left him a voicemail asking if he was free to go on the visit with him. Jed had also left a message asking for a call back to let him know he was safe. Good to know your mates are looking out for you, Chris thought.

No word from Sally, though. This worried him. Was she in more trouble at home? Should he go to see her? He had her address on his old phone but it didn't transfer across onto the new one. The SIM card only contained basic information about his contacts. Another call to the station yielded her address and he drove past her door a couple of times, not daring to knock. He didn't want to escalate an already difficult situation in her private life.

You don't know her well enough, Chris, he told himself. She has friends who look out for her, doesn't she? The woman on the switchboard at work knows her better than you. Yeah but she doesn't know what Sally's been going through. Chris wrestled with the choices, finally coming to the decision that Sally was a grown up and didn't welcome his interference. He reluctantly gave up and drove home.

Sally Whitelock stood in her night-clothes and looked through the net curtain, watching Chris's car drive past her window. Don't stop, she pleaded silently, clutching the dressing gown's collar to her throat. She turned and limped to a chair, sliding into it as gently as possible. A wave of agony coursed through her body and she gritted her teeth against the cry that threatened to escape.

CHAPTER 11

Chris walked to Kettering station on Monday morning clutching a breakfast bap of fried egg and bacon that he'd picked up from the cafe on the High Street. He arrived at the main door and held it open for the hurried figure of Tracey 'Flo' Fenton, the Families Liaison Officer.

'In a rush?' he noted.

'I'll say. Your boss sent out an SOS about half an hour ago.' She sailed past him and into the station. Chris lengthened his stride, trying to keep up with her clicking heels.

'Is it Sally? Is she OK?' Chris asked. No wonder she's been out of touch, he thought. Something must have happened to her. Tracey stopped abruptly and turned back to face him.

'DS Whitelock?' she said, surprised at his question. 'What's about her?'

'Er, I don't know,' Chris blustered, realising he'd said too much. Sally wouldn't appreciate Chris raising her problems with a FLO. 'Just not been able to contact her over the weekend. Thought she might be in trouble.'

Flo Fenton looked at him suspiciously for a moment, then resumed her march through the building.

'Hope you've not been living up to the rumours,' she said, the words trailing behind her like a wake.

Shit, thought Chris. Joe must've been spreading the muck around. 'Look, I don't know what you've heard,' he said, 'but anything coming from Soap Alden isn't true.'

Flo stopped again to open the door to the stairs leading up to CID, and flicked a look over her shoulder that confirmed Chris's fears.

'I'm here to see Sandra Gowland,' she said, changing the subject. At the top of the stairs Chris looked over her shoulder and into DI Crighton's office. The Guv was at his desk looking like a trapped animal. Opposite him and facing away from the window sat a small wiry looking woman. Her dark greasy hair, scraped back in a pony tail, bobbed around as she remonstrated him and large hooped earrings waved from her small ears. Chris could hear her voice barking and watched her waving a thin finger under Crighton's nose.

Flo Fenton knocked on the Guv's door and opened it, without waiting for an answer. Sandra Gowland's smoke cracked voice carried through the open door.

'Don't fob me off,' she was saying. 'I want my Molly back.'

'Miss Gowland, this is Tracey Fenton, our Families Liaison Officer,' Crighton said with evident relief, raising himself from the chair. 'I'm going to leave you with her for a few minutes to cover some essential facts. I need to coordinate my team. I'll be back soon.' He offered his seat to Flo and escaped the room before Sandra Gowland could rev up again for another tirade.

'She got into Stanstead at half-past one this morning,' he explained to Chris. 'It's natural that she's stressed. I'll let Flo calm her down, then I'll have to interview her.' He gave a disgusted glance back into the room. 'God, I hope we find her daughter, but this woman's not fit to look after anyone. Completely self-interested.'

Chris looked closer at the woman in Crighton's office. Thin and tanned, wearing a cheap blouse faded and frayed at the collar from too many hot washes. She caught him looking and returned his gaze with a hard glare, her mouth tightening up as she berated Flo. The dark circles under her eyes betrayed the late night flight. The absence of any redness in them confirmed Chris's earlier assessment of a feckless mother, unconcerned about leaving her offspring with an estranged partner at the drop of a hat.

'Get Alden and meet me in the locker room,' Crighton said aiming for the stairs. 'I don't want her dragging me back in there too soon.'

Chris made his way over to the constable's desk. 'All right, Soap?' he said. 'Good weekend?'

'Quiet, mate. What about you?'

'Guv not told you yet?' Chris paused, surprised that Joe didn't have his nose stuck into the latest news.

'No, he's been in his office since I came in. What's up?'

'Guv wants to see us downstairs. I'll tell you on the way.'

Joe collected a few things and followed.

'I've been run ragged all weekend,' Chris explained on the way down the stairs. 'I was checking out a quarry on Saturday night that I found was protected by armed guards. I spent half the night freezing my nuts off hiding from them.'

'What? Did you call in for support?'

'My phone broke,' He held up the basic phone he'd sourced from a supermarket.

Alden pulled a face. 'Did you go back in later?'

'No, the Guv said they'd have scarpered by the time we could react. He's right, I suppose. We're going over there today to see what we can find.'

'Great. The sheriff's posse rides into Dodge after the bandits have flown.'

'There wasn't much we could do, Soap. Given the time between me being compromised and a firearms team being able to respond, they would have been well away.'

'Guns though. What are they mining there, gold?'

'Dunno, mate. If the Guv's suspicion is anything to go by, there's a drugs link.'

'You think it's tied-in with the case he's running?'

'Could be. We interviewed a bloke on Friday night who part-owns the quarry. Guv reckons he's involved with the drugs case. I think there could be a connection with Hearst's murder too but Crighton seems more interested in the drugs link.'

'Just like Sally said on Friday,' Joe pointed out.

'Yeah.' Chris was beginning to get worried about his boss's priorities again.

'She's not in again today,' Joe said. 'Rang in this morning. Said she's down with a cold after her swim in the river.'

At least she's not missing, along with Hearst's evidence, Chris thought. 'She was at my house on Friday,' he began. Joe's eyebrows shot up.

'Rainey, the smooth operator,' he cocked his fingers as if firing an invisible gun.

'Nothing like that, mate,' Chris dismissed the innuendo. 'And thanks for spreading rumours. Even Flo Fenton had something to say about it.

Joe raised a hand in a conciliatory gesture. 'Sorry mate, I was in the wrong. I'll pass the word on. Why was she there?'

'We were going to go through some of Hearst's stuff. She ended up leaving it there and then I got burgled. They took the lot.'

'You don't get much luck do you, Rainey?'

'Hmm, maybe not,' replied Chris, thinking about the burglary. They had arrived at the officers' changing rooms, and joined Crighton. He slouched in the sofa, knees hooked over the edge higher than his hips, looking drained of energy.

'You OK, Sir?' Chris asked.

Crighton raised his eyes and smiled briefly, acknowledging the concern.

'There are people in this world who have the knack of sapping your motivation without even trying, boys,' he said. 'Can you believe it, all she's interested in is suing us for cutting her holiday short? Like it was our fault the her daughter went missing.' He leaned forward and rested his chin on a hand, elbow balancing on one knee. 'We're the only ones who care about that poor girl.'

We'll find her, Guv,' Chris tried to reassure his boss.

Crighton straightened, then stood, pulling himself

113

back into some semblance of composure.

'Right. Flo's going to help me question Sandra Gowland. We need to make sure she had nothing to do with the abduction and murder. You both remember that Yorkshire woman, jailed for perverting the course of justice, abducted her own daughter?' The men nodded. That girl had been found after several days, safe in the base of a divan bed. Her mother and uncle had conspired to split a £50,000 reward after releasing and then supposedly discovering the girl in the street. 'Who knows what goes through the heads of some people.'

'What do you want us to do, Sir?' Joe asked.

I spoke to that farmer, Polson, on the phone earlier,' Crighton answered. 'He's got an emergency with one of his animals so I've agreed he won't have to come in this morning. I've interviewed him over the phone. I'll take his brother's statement. Chris you sit in that with me at eleven. Alden, I want you to visit these,' he handed the Estate Agents card that Stoke had given him on Friday.

'OK, Sir.'

'They let houses out for a John Stoke. He's a property developer and uses their services. See how they run their business and how much involvement Stoke has with them.'

'Right-oh,' Joe chirped. 'Are you going to get Firearms over to that quarry Chris had a nosey in?'

Crighton looked at Chris then back at Alden.

'He's filled you in, then.' he said. 'They've been on site already.' His attention turned to Chris. 'I called them in yesterday after speaking with you.'

Chris looked incredulously at his boss.

'What changed your mind, Sir?' he asked.

'Procedure and precaution, son,' Crighton answered. He picked an invisible fleck of dust from his jacket. 'I had no doubt there'd be nobody armed on the site and I was right. The Firearms team came up blank. We'll take a drive over there later,' he finished, heading for the locker room exit. 'Let me know when the other

Polson arrives, Raine.'

'See you later, Rainey day,' Soap said, grinning and patting Chris's glum face as he prepared to leave.

Chris wondered why Crighton had organised an armed search after telling him not to bother. Maybe he was doing it to let Chris know he was still the boss of the case. I'm doing a lot of the legwork and coming up with all the leads, he thought. The DI doesn't need to stamp his feet to prove he's leading us.

He pursued Crighton's retreating back. 'Sir, John Polson's not due here until eleven. I've got a couple of hours. Do you mind if I duck out for a while?'

'Anything important?' Crighton asked over his shoulder.

'Could be. I need to speak to DS Whitelock.'

'Oh? I thought she was off sick.'

'Yeah, I want to get hold of her notebook, see what notes she made before Hearst's box was stolen.'

'Okay, but keep your phone on,' Crighton lifted his eyes to Chris. 'Don't be late for Polson.' he warned.

'Sure thing, Guv.'

Chris rang the bell on Sally's front door ten minutes later. He'd commandeered a patrol car and driven south west of Kettering town centre to a modern housing estate off Lake Avenue and parked around the corner from her address. The detached house contrasted to his tight little, two-up two down, terrace on the fringes of town centre.

This street subtly displayed tokens of modest wealth. A Mercedes 'C' Class parked up in a drive. Next door a BMW. Each of them likely belonging to a spouse working from home, or two-car families with disposable income and time to tend the gardens. Daffodils lined the drives and along the borders of neighbouring gardens, their yellow heads nodding in the light cool breeze. Here and there lawns had been shorn at the weekend by keen gardeners in anticipation of spring's arrival. Sally Whitelock's scrubby looking grass awaited its first cut of the year.

Chris pushed the button again, hoping that Sally was in. He bent over and peered through the letterbox. I suppose she could be at the doctors, he thought.

A shadow moved at the far end of the hall.

'Sally!' he called through the gap. 'Is that you?'

He reached up, still looking through the gap, fingers searching the plastic door frame for the bell. It rang once more. No answer. He stood and took out his substitute phone, dialling her mobile. A cheery melody struck up in response, somewhere behind the door. The unfamiliar plastic pressed to his ear announced the call diverting to answerphone.

'Sally,' he yelled again through the letter box. 'It's Chris. I know you're here. Open the door.'

The shade moved again, this time growing and morphing into a human shape, finally revealing a pair of carpet slippers at its base. Sally stood there, head bowed, a hand across her face.

'What do you want, Chris?' came her muffled reply. 'I've already called in sick.'

'I need to see you, Sally. Can't you let me in?' he pleaded.

'I said I'll be back to work later in the week.'

Chris stood and looked up and down the street. He wondered what the neighbours might be thinking, seeing this stranger shouting through the door, pleading for entrance.

Sally came closer to the door but didn't open it.

'What do you want?' she repeated. Her voice, cloaked by the door, sounded as though she was speaking through a pillow.

'Oh, great. It's a séance through the door now, is it?' he said.

'Just spit it out, Raine, and leave me be.'

'Sorry. Look, I came around to ask for your notebook. I managed to write down a few points on Friday. I wondered if you had any notes I could look at.'

'I'll get it. Wait there.'

116

Chris stood at the door, Friday's events turning over in his mind. Sally returned and stuffed her notebook through the slot in the door.

'Here. I'll get it back from you at the station.'

'Sally?'

He could feel her silent presence on the other side of the portal.

'What?'

'He's hit you again, hasn't he.'

Another long pause. Then the latch clicked and the door slowly opened on it's own weight, revealing a plain, magnolia painted hallway and the retreating form of Sally in a woollen dressing gown, limping into the living room. She turned to him at the doorway.

'Jesus, Sally!' Chris breathed through clenched teeth, anger stirring at the pit of his stomach.

A mass of bruises covered Sally's face. One puffed-up eye had been forced closed in a grotesque wink. The other stared back at him, bloodshot and glistening.

'Not exactly model material, am I?' She mumbled through her swollen jaw, leading him into the lounge. She gave a half-smile, which broke a scab on her split lip and fresh blood trickled down her chin. She winced and dabbed at it with a tissue.

Chris stared, dumbfounded. 'Tony?' he managed.

'Tony,' she confirmed, shrugging.

'But, why?' He sat down, stunned at the violence embedded on her face, finding it unbelievable that she'd allowed it to happen to her again.

A frown crossed her forehead and her good eye blinked, releasing a tear. Her gaze flicked around the room, everywhere but on Chris.

'It was him,' she whispered.

'what was?' Chris couldn't work out what she was getting at.

'The break-in at your house.'

Chris stared blankly at her.

'He followed me to your house on Friday.'

He shook his head slowly as the penny dropped.

'Oh.'

'I noticed him waiting outside when I left yours.' She picked nervously at a loose thread on her dressing gown. 'I went back home and confronted him later when he returned. Asked why he was following me.'

'That was pretty stupid.'

'He launched straight on the attack, accusing us of sleeping together. I wasn't expecting it. He laid into me so badly he left me out cold. When I came around I was lying on the kitchen floor. I was in such pain, I thought I'd have to call an ambulance.'

'Where is he now?'

'I've not seen him all weekend. He was on shift and didn't come home Saturday or Sunday. When I picked up your messages and found out the evidence was missing, I realised he must have taken it.'

'Why did you ignore my calls all weekend?'

'I don't know, Chris, I don't know,' she wailed. Her movements were erratic and she fidgeted in the chair.

'You know how much he's set us back, don't you?'

'We'll be able to get around the missing files,' she pleaded. 'We can use the notes we've already made,' she said, pointing to her notebook in his hand.

'Why are you protecting him?' Chris snapped, unaware that he was standing now, looming over her.

'He beat the shit out of me, Chris!' she cried. 'It's a hell of a persuasion.'

'That's no excuse.'

'So you're going to beat me too, are you?'

Chris realised he was losing his cool. His fists were balled and he sensed the aggression in his voice. Sally cowered beneath him. He turned away, breathing deeply, forcing himself to relax.

'I'm sorry. I'm just angry at what he's done to you. And me,' he said, remembering the state of his house. Something didn't ring true though.

'He's a bully but it doesn't normally get as bad as this, Chris, honestly,' she said in a small voice.

Chris paced around the sparsely furnished room.

The absence of plants and pictures gave it a utilitarian atmosphere. A worker's rest place more than a home. A games console sat on the floor, its leads snaking carelessly over the carpet to the TV.

'He thinks we're having an affair,' he thought out loud, staring out of the window. Behind him, Sally winced. 'But when he breaks into my house, he doesn't trash the place like a jealous husband would.'

'What do you mean?' Sally asked.

'Well, not much got damaged. A bookcase and my TV pushed over. Not even broken. A few token acts of vandalism.'

'Maybe he got cold feet. Realised that he was jumping to conclusions about us.'

'I dunno. I get the feeling we weren't the real reason he was there. It looks too staged. A smokescreen for something.'

'For what?'

Chris shrugged. 'Why would he want to steal the box of evidence?'

'I don't know. Jealousy? Spite?'

'Does he know what cases you are working on?'

Sally's eye met his and he could see her beginning to understand his train of thought.

'You know what, he did ask me about that earlier in the week.'

'And you told him about this case?'

'Yeah. He doesn't normally take any interest in my work. You think he was just after the box?'

'It adds up,' he said. 'Does he have any dodgy mates?'

'He doesn't have many mates at all,' she shook her head. ' I don't know. How could he be involved?'

'Maybe somebody knows of his connection with you and they ordered him to get hold of any evidence we had.'

'Who though?' Sally frowned. 'He's never been in trouble before.'

Chris's stopped pacing and his eyes fell on the

only photograph in the room, standing on a shelf. The picture showed Sally and her husband together years ago, on holiday, They toasted the camera from a restaurant table, garishly coloured cocktails in hand and cutlery resting on half eaten meals. The young, happy couple, cheek to reddened cheek, smiled back at him from the past. Sally noticed him scrutinizing the picture.

'It's like looking at strangers now,' she sighed. 'I see that photo and try connect with our old selves. I was twenty-one then, just starting out in the force.'

Chris stayed quiet, waiting for her explanation.

'I remember we spoke about my career, that night at the restaurant.' She took down the photo, studying her husband's shy, uncertain grin. 'Tony was full of support and encouragement for me. He knew his own prospects weren't good - poor results at school put paid to that.'

She lay the picture face down on the coffee table in front of her, stroking it's frame as she drew her hand away.

'My career progressed while Tony stayed stuck in the past,' she looked up at the window tears brimming her eyes. The bloodstained tissue was re-deployed.

'How do you mean?'

'He's always been withdrawn. Finds it difficult to articulate himself. I told you his promotion stresses him out.'

'Everyone has to deal with stress.'

'He can't deal with the staff in the factory, people with similar reticence as him, I suppose. I've tried replaying work scenarios out with him to try and find a method to deal with them. He just loses his temper at me,' she finished, pointing to her battered features.

'Could it be that someone from work put him up to this?' he asked.

'He doesn't have any friends there. Hardly sees anyone outside of it, either,' She stared into space.

'Sally, you've got to tell the Guv about the theft,' he said, his voice calm and quiet. 'Report Tony to

Crighton. Let's get him in a cell and let's get on with the investigation.'

'I want to, Chris. I do. It's just, he's my husband,' her plea petered out.

'He could be a link to the murder.'

'You can't be sure.'

'Come on, he must be. He'll probably be a target now, too. Being in custody will protect him.'

He let the words lie. Sally picked up the photo once more, as if examining it for a reason not to betray her husband.

'I've got to get back to the station, Sally,' he said, checking the the clock on the shelf. 'If you don't tell Crighton before I get there, I'm going to have to.'

He slipped out of the room, leaving Sally staring at her past.

CHAPTER 12

Crighton looked over his spectacles at Chris when he entered the interview room. It was sparsely populated. A basic table screwed to the floor with three straight back chairs surrounded it. A standard issue tape recorder occupied one end. Crighton had already begun to take John Polson's statement. The tapes weren't rolling.

'Sorry I'm late, Sir. Has DS Whitelock phoned you?' he asked.

'I've not heard from her, no. We're in the middle of a statement here, lad,' he scowled at Chris.

'Sorry, Sir. I'll talk to you later about it.'

Crighton turned back to Polson. Chris sat down in the spare chair next to his boss, making sure his new phone was switched to silent.

'So, Mr Polson, you were about to tell me how you came to renew your interest in stone masonry.'

Polson sat opposite, fidgeting in his chair and holding an empty Styrofoam cup. He was pinching lines in the rim at even intervals with coarse, chipped fingernails.

'There's not much to tell, Inspector,' he said, a respectful tone in his voice.

A few years younger than his brother, Chris guessed. Not so many lines on his face. Maybe mid-forties.

'Jack inherited the farm from our dad. He donated a small piece of land to me. I turned down the chance of farming and sold to Simon Hearst.'

'Just a second, Mr. Polson,' Crighton interjected. 'How did you come to know Mr. Hearst?'

'There were a couple of out-buildings on my land. I brought Hearst's stone company in to remove them. He was going to re-deploy them elsewhere. He does renovations and the like and bought the stone. That's when he discovered the limestone.'

'You didn't know it was there before, then?'

'No.' Polson explained slowly, as though to a child. 'It was under the ground.'

'So, Hearst pulled your pants down over the quarry deal,' Crighton retorted.

'I was going to sell anyway the land anyway,' Polson skirted the snipe. 'I'm no farmer.'

'What do you do?'

'I'm a mechanic. I used to fix the tractors for my dad. I was more interested in that than stinking cattle.'

'And you didn't see the scam coming.'

'You could say that. I've no head for business. The contract looked OK to me. He bought the land, then I re-invested in his quarry. I didn't even see the money. Then he wheedled his way out of paying me anything back,' Polson tore at the cup along the lines he'd scored, creating mini crenellations around the rim and tossing scraps of polystyrene in amongst the tea dregs.

'I'd be angry if I'd been taken for a ride like that,' Crighton said.

Polson snorted, sliding the cup out of reach and leaning back, arms folded.

'You learn to live with it,' he said.

'And then you discovered your brother has more of the stone under his neighbouring field,' Chris added.

Polson nodded, his mouth set in a grim line.

'Giving you an ideal opportunity to stick one back at Hearst,' Crighton added. The air between them stayed silent. 'Your brother's not a stone expert is he?'

'No.'

'And nor are you.'

'I've already told you, I'm a mechanic.'

'Hearst's foreman told us you'd been in touch with him. Was he going to front the business?' Chris asked.

'If we could persuade him to come to us, yes.'

'But he was quite happy to work for Hearst,' Chris

revealed. 'He seemed very upset when he found out his boss was dead.'

'You're not suggesting I killed Hearst, are you?' Polson's back straightened as he sat up, his mouth agape. 'Just to get hold of his workers?'

'No, no, of course not, Mr. Polson,' Crighton said, chuckling. 'Only a monster would do that.'

Polson relaxed, unfolding his arms. He reached for the mangled cup, slowly folding out the remaining stubs of styrofoam.

'I didn't like Hearst, that's true,' he said. 'Jack offered me a role in the new quarry venture but I wasn't sure. I didn't want to be reminded of how it failed before.'

Chris watched Polson closely.

'But I put all that behind me. I thought if we could make a go of the business we'd rub Hearst's nose in it. Get a bit of closure, that's all.'

'Hmm,' Crighton said, flicking back a couple of pages in his notes. He nodded to himself and scribbled a note at the bottom of the page.

He looked up and smiled. 'Mr. Polson, is there anything else you'd like to say for your statement?' he asked.

Polson stared back into Crighton's open face.

'No,' he said. 'Can I go, now?'

'Yes, of course,' Crighton said. 'Your statement is entirely voluntary, you know. Mind how you go.'

Chris stood and opened the door for Polson who sidled past and out of the room, dropping the remains of his cup in the bin as he left.

'That threw him a bit, Guv,' Chris said, a bit perplexed himself.

'Well, he didn't given me much more than his brother did, really,' Crighton said. 'One thing they've both omitted from their statements, though.'

'What's that, Sir?'

'Who they're going to sell this stone to,' Crighton said.

'And that's why they targeted Hearst's foreman?' Chris guessed.

'Possibly. With the foreman unwilling to move, though, maybe they had to resort to more drastic measures.'

'It does seem drastic, Sir,' Chris said. 'Is that a strong enough reason to bump Hearst off?'

'Not on it's own, it isn't. When you add the double-crossing that Hearst did to John Polson, it sheds a whole new light on the motive.'

'But what about the girl?'

'That's where things become less certain. They have plenty of hiding places on the farm, but would they risk so much, just for a few contracts?'

'It seems unlikely,' Chris agreed. 'What are we going to do?'

I'll direct the support teams over to Polson's farm. Get a fingertip search over the place.' Crighton fished his phone from a pocket. 'You said something at the weekend about English Heritage,'

'That's right sir,' Chris said, remembering his discovery from Friday. 'I'm sure I saw some contracts in Hearst's files that involved them. Do you think the Polsons wanted information about those?'

'Perhaps. Give them a call, see if you can dig up any more information about them.'

'Sir, I need to speak to you about DS Whitelock,' Chris began.

Crighton put a finger to his lips and his phone to his ear, listening to the voice messages left whilst they were in the interview room.

'I'm not sure you do,' he said once he'd cut the voicemail call. 'That was Sally. I'm going to go and see her. Whatever you two were up to, I'll find out soon enough.'

Crighton left the room. Chris was left wondering what Sally was going to tell the DI. He hoped it would be the truth. She couldn't hide her bruises from the Guv this time.

125

Joe Alden sauntered into the office whilst Chris was on the phone to English Heritage, flicking the back of Chris's ear as he passed by. Chris sat up with a start, kicking his feet off the desk and knocking a pile of paperwork onto the floor. Joe laughed. Chris raised two fingers and was rewarded with a look of mock horror on Soap's face. He waved a piece of paper in Chris's face, taunting him with it. Chris couldn't make out what was written on the sheet.

'Yes, Mr. Duncan,' Chris said to the official at the other end of the phone. 'I appreciate you can't just fax over copies of any agreements. Can you tell me what they contain?'

'I'm afraid, Constable Raine, I'm unable to do that either,' the disembodied voice on the phone replied. Duncan, the English Heritage official stuck to his bureaucratic mantra. 'I do have customer confidentiality to consider. How do I you are who you claim to be?' Chris swore silently.

'Look, we can send a fax from the station with our authorization to disclose information to us, as well as our contact details,' Chris explained, searching for a way through the red tape.

Duncan was quiet for a moment. 'Very well. I'll wait for your fax.'

'Okay. Thanks for your help, Mr. Duncan,' Chris said and hung up, wondering what he was thanking the man for.

'Sound like you're not getting the same luck as me, Rainey,' Joe chirped from across the room.

Chris wheeled his chair over, interested to see what the the Estate Agents had revealed.

'What have you found, Joe?' he asked.

'Well,' Soap whined. 'I'm wondering whether I should keep it quiet till the boss gets in.'

'Don't be daft, lad. Spill.'

'I suppose I could let you in on it,' Alden fingered the sheet of paper protectively. 'The Estate Agent

Crighton sent me to deals with a few of Stoke's houses. He normally leaves everything to them, letting, cleaning, repairing and the likes. Every now and then, though, he interferes.'

'How?'

'They like to vet their tenants, making sure they can pay their way. They don't want them do a runner with half the furniture and leaving a trashed house. Sometimes though, Stoke instructs them to house people without going through the vetting process. He stands as guarantor.'

'And Stoke did this at the house that DS James was killed in?' Chris guessed.

Alden looked deflated. 'Yeah, you got it. He doesn't even give them any names. The rent gets paid by another company, Theodore Black Lettings, Ltd.'

'Who are they?'

'I was just about to look them up, when you stuck your nose in.' Alden looked perturbed.

'Hope you have better luck than me, then,' Chris said, rolling his chair back across the office floor. He turned back to his desk and picked up Sally's notebook.

The office section became quiet as they worked. They were both alerted to the sounds of a commotion rippling through the station. The furore spilled into their area with Crighton and Sally Whitelock at it's head. Sally walked in slowly, head high, eyes straight ahead. Crighton was at her side, fending off the attention from concerned colleagues. The mixed hubbub of sympathetic noise and concerned voices grew louder as colleagues pressed in, eager to know the cause of her bruises. 'Everybody, get back to work, please,' Crighton ordered, following Sally into their section of the office and fending off the attention. 'I'll update you all when we have more information but for the time being let DS Whitelock get on with her job. Please!'

The noisy throng dispersed. Joe Alden jumped to his feet. 'You all right, Sal?' he asked, clearly shaken.

'Yeah, Joe. I'll live,' she said, carefully sitting

down. Crighton drew up a free chair to form a circle, facing away from the desks. Joe mouthed to Chris 'you knew about this?' and was answered by a curt nod. He looked frustrated to have been out of the loop.

They discussed the case, Crighton filling Joe in on the events leading up to Sally's beating. Alden recounted his visit to the estate agent. Chris was relieved to hear that Sally had come clean to the boss. Hiding it from him had been uncomfortable. Chris was glad it was all in the open and he wouldn't have to bear Sally's secret any more.

'We're going to pay Tony Whitelock a visit this afternoon,' Crighton said, summing up the briefing. 'Bringing him in will give us a chance to quiz him on who he's working for, if that is the case,' he looked pointedly at Chris. 'At the very least it will take some pressure off of Sally, and give us a chance to start proceedings against him for the physical abuse.'

Sally's head jerked up. 'No,' she said in alarm. 'I don't want you to charge him.'

'Why not?' Crighton gasped.

'I just - I don't know. It's a bit formal, isn't it? I mean, it's domestic, isn't it. I'll sort it out at home.'

'You'll do no such thing,' Crighton drummed his thigh with the palm of his hand, revealing the stress he was feeling.

'Guv,' she began to protest, then sighed and fell silent.

'Sir, why don't we arrest him for the theft of the box, first,' Chris suggested. 'We can deal with the rest if the Sarge wants to, eh?'

'What? Oh, yes. OK. Whenever you're ready, Sally,' Crighton blustered, standing up. 'We'll pick him up anyway. I'll arrange for some uniform to accompany us.' He disappeared into his office.

Sally turned to her desk. 'Thanks, Chris,' she said, leaning forward to switch her computer on.

Chris smiled at her. 'No problem. The Guv will want Joe and me on the arrest. I've met Tony before so

128

I'll know who we're looking for. Do you want your notebook back?'

'Yes, please. I'll see if I can remember anything from Friday's search.'

'Have a think about what Crighton wants to do. Tony will carry on with this, you know. Even if you don't press charges. A leopard doesn't change its spots. '

'Anything else?' Sally asked, her tone hardening. Back to normal, Chris thought.

'We need to authorize the collection of some of Hearst's agreements with English Heritage,' he handed her a scribbled note with their fax number on it.

'OK, no problem,' Sally was familiar with the procedure so Chris left her to it.

The beverage can manufacturing plant was situated on an industrial estate near Corby, North of Kettering. The giant warehouse-sized factory adjoined a soft drinks facility. Crighton instructed the uniformed officers to wait outside and keep an eye on the exits. The three detectives entered the building by reception and were escorted to the plant manager's office. The room had a window into the main factory area and a low hum of machinery could be heard.

The manager ushered them to sit around a meeting table.

'I'll get a call out to Tony to come to my office,' he told them.

The manager was explaining the ins and outs of can manufacture to the bored detectives when Chris spotted Whitelock through the window, swaggering along a red-painted walkway wearing his factory uniform of trousers, blue polo shirt and a fluorescent yellow vest. Stocky and short haired, Whitelock appeared unconcerned at his call to the office. He noticed the men seated in the office when he got closer and his eyes locked on to Chris in recognition.

'Shit, he's running!' Chris cried, standing and tipping his chair over. He rushed from the room.

'Wait, you need safety gear to go in there,' the plant manager shouted.

Chris ran onto the factory floor and was assaulted by the roaring white noise of half a million soft drinks cans in production. The plant manager's warning disappeared into the cacophony unheard and unheeded. Chris raced over the factory floor after the fleeing worker. Whitelock dived behind a section of large cylindrical storage tanks emblazoned with unfamiliar labels. Chris followed through the obstacles, squeezing between a 'Cation Tank' and an 'Anion Tank'. He tried to keep the flash of yellow jacket in view. The deafening noise around him made it impossible to coordinate his fellow officers into any kind of controlled pursuit.

The bright yellow tracer changed direction and Whitelock bolted up a metal staircase to a mezzanine level, twenty five feet above the factory floor. Chris, a few seconds behind, slipped on the painted floor and overshot the foot of the stairs, losing more time in the chase. When he reached the top he couldn't see where his target had gone. The level contained conveyor belts, hundreds of meters of them, criss-crossing the factory area carrying thousands of tin cans through the manufacturing process. This close to the roof, the oppressive heat sapped his energy and the chemical smell of paint, lacquer and solvents gagged in the back of his throat. Ducking down slightly, Chris was able to see through a gap in the tracks and caught sight of a lurid yellow jacket. He rushed over to it, bashing his shoulders and head on steel support pillars and cross-members. When he reached the point where he'd seen Whitelock last all he found was the safety jacket, hanging limp on a handrail.

'Shed your skin, eh?' Chris thought. 'Well, I'll catch you, snake. See if I don't.'

A shadow flickered across him and he whirled around. Whitelock stood before him, spittle at the corners of his panting mouth. He lifted himself up on a cross-piece and swung his heavy boots into Chris's chest, punting the detective onto a track laden with partially painted cans. Chris scrabbled around amid the production line, trying to regain his breath and his balance. Cans spilled left and right over the edges of the track onto the floor far below.

Whitelock was escaping along another track, his route slowed by a sea of cans that leapt into the air like waves ahead of his kicking feet and cascaded onto the elevated floor. He looked back and laughed at Chris's attempts to right himself. Sirens bellowed out after the machinery's alarm system registered an obstruction on the track. The conveyor at Chris's feet stopped and he was able to resume the chase.

The alarms had alerted the other workers. Three men in white paper overalls, working on a sterile area of the production line, stared slack-jawed at the pursuit. Chris caught one of the workers' eye and pointed to the fleeing Whitelock, silently pleading for him to waylay the absconder. The worker reached out an arm and hooked it around Whitlock's leg sending him flat onto his face. Chris arrived just as he was pulling himself to his knees, snarling at the other workers. Chris stamped onto Whitelock's back. The man was pushed once more into the rough plastic of the conveyor belt.

'You're nicked, scumbag,' Chris spat into Whitelock's ear above the din, encircling an arm around the man's throat and lifting his head from the track. 'And this is for Sally,' he swung his fist in an arc and smashed it into the prone man's nose. Blood spurted from the wound and, barely heard, Whitelock screamed in pain and pushed up, rolling himself and Raine off the conveyor onto the thick mesh mezzanine floor. The man's strength caught Chris by surprise and he lost grip of his captive's neck. Whitelock began to run along the conveyor again. He reached the end of the line and positioned himself for a jump across a gap in the mezzanine floor to another section of the factory.

'Stop! You'll never make it,' Chris shouted. Deaf to his warning, Whitelock leaped. 'No!' Chris wailed.

131

Tony Whitelock's flailing fingertips scrabbled briefly against the edge of the opposite level. Gravity overcame his tenuous grip and dragged him into the void. Chris threw himself to the floor, his face pressing against the mesh. He stared through the gaps, helpless to the falling man's silent scream. In paralysed disbelief he watched Whitelock crash onto the concrete below.

Crighton and Alden, accompanied by the plant manager ran over the factory floor below to where Whitelock lay. The production line had stopped, bringing the noise down to a bearable level. Sirens continued to ring out but Chris could hear the plant manager yelling at Crighton, berating him for allowing his officer to enter the factory unauthorised.

'You're accountable for this,' he shouted, pointing at the prone figure of Tony Whitelock.

Crighton was ignoring him, checking Whitelock for signs of life. He whipped out his phone to call in an ambulance. Turning his head upwards, he met Chris's questioning look with a scowl. Chris groaned and rolled onto his sweat soaked back.

CHAPTER 13

'What the fuck were you thinking, Raine?'

Chris had been ordered straight into Crighton's office as soon as he returned to the station. Alden had followed the ambulance to Kettering General hospital and was stationed on guard in case Whitelock regained consciousness. The emergency medical team had informed them the chances of that happening in the next few days were slim. The intra-cranial trauma Whitelock's head received in the fall had increased the pressure his brain. The medics were forced to put him into an induced coma to reduce the risk of a haemorrhage occurring.

'The only solid lead we had in this case is lying in a hospital bed, pumped full of drugs and as good as dead to us,' Crighton said.

Chris shrank into his chair. Crighton rarely swore but judging by the anger in his voice, Chris expected more profanities to come.

'I saw him running, Sir, and training took over,' he explained.

'Police training?' Crighton quizzed. 'Or Army?'

Chris couldn't answer him truthfully so simply shrugged. He'd seen Whitelock's look of recognition at the factory and something inside his head automatically clicked on. He couldn't explain it other than in the way a hunter pursues its prey. He doubted Crighton would understand or sympathise.

'Whitelock could have lead us directly to who's behind this murder, and possibly to Molly Gowland,' Crighton continued. He shook his head. 'Without him we're back to shooting in the dark.'

He's right, Chris thought. I've screwed this up good and proper. A glance out of Crighton's office window revealed Sally Whitelock at her computer. Her

133

glare when Chris had walked through the station was seared in his memory. Now, biting her nails and absently shuffling through the papers on her desk, he thought she was probably as useless to the case as he felt he was.

'You should be straight onto suspension while this situation's investigated.'

Chris made to object but kept quiet. Something about Crighton's manner told him to wait.

'But we don't have the manpower to be able to do that,' Crighton stood and looked out at Sally. 'Sally will have to go on compassionate leave, now. Damn.'

Chris's spirits dropped another notch. He should have been happy to be kept on the case but Crighton's demeanour suggested he would have preferred Sally on the team over Chris.

'Sir, I couldn't have known he'd risk his life so easily.'

'You've obviously no experience in a factory, son. It can be a dangerous place if you're not on the ball. You shouldn't have gone in there without my say so.'

'He was getting away, Sir,' Chris said in exasperation. At least Crighton has stopped swearing, he thought. I might be off the hook.

A knock sounded on the door and Sally walked in, unbeckoned.

'Guv, I've got the copies of the work that English Heritage authorised with the Council and Simon Hearst,' she said, waving a sheaf of fax papers.

'Sally, you should go home,' Crighton said, concern edging his words.

'I know,' came her blunt reply. 'I think I'd rather stay, if that's OK?'

Crighton frowned, flicking a glance at Chris.

Chris's heart skipped and his stomach turned. Shit, this is it, he thought. I'm out of it.

'That's very admirable, Sally,' Crighton interjected. 'But you can see my concern. I need people to have their mind on the job. Are you sure you can commit?'

'I've got nothing else to do, Guv,' she replied. Crighton alternated his gaze between her and Chris.

'Looks like we have the staff after all, lad.'

Chris's stomach sank again. His future lay ahead like a desert. Days of pacing his living room, daytime TV and drinking too much to alleviate the boredom.

'What's the matter?' Sally asked.

'The lad's going to have to go on suspension while we investigate his involvement in your husband's accident.'

'What? That wasn't Chris's fault.'

'We don't know that yet.'

'Paul, it's obvious Chris didn't push Tony. He didn't force him to jump. What is there to investigate?'

'But I thought you'd want to see things done officially.'

Chris watched Crighton's look of confusion and saw the threat of suspension for what it was, a way to appease Sally over her husband's injuries.

'Guv, you know DC Raine is one of the best officers we have in the station. We need him on the case.'

Both men reddened. Crighton because he'd been caught out in a misplaced act of compassion. Chris, surprised at the praise. He felt a shift in the balance of his fate. The atmosphere changed in the room as the tension ebbed away.

'You can still work with Raine?' Crighton asked.

'I don't see why not,' she said in a matter of fact voice. 'He already knows my relationship with my husband.'

'That's partly what I'm worried about.'

'No need to, Sir. If it wasn't for Chris I would still be under Tony's influence. I would have gone on compassionate. But he's has helped me a lot recently,' she turned to Chris. 'I don't blame you for what happened to Tony. In fact, I think it's done me a favour. I can see him for what he is now. I should be at his side, God knows he's going to be in a tough place if he wakes up.' She shook her head. 'But no, if he lives he'll have to face the consequences on his own.'

Crighton coughed and looked around the room, anywhere but directly at his two officers. Chris broke the silence:

'Did you find anything in the faxes?'

Sally nodded, grateful of the change of subject. 'I haven't had time to go through them thoroughly yet. His handwriting isn't the tidiest in the world.'

'Yeah, I remember that from Friday.'

'See if the official over at English Heritage can help you with it,' Crighton suggested, relieved to be back into shop talk.

'Fat chance. Duncan is the consummate bureaucrat. I think he would ask for a warrant just to give us the time,' Chris said.

'I've seen you in action, Sally. If anyone can persuade him, you can,' Crighton smiled. 'Come on then, Raine, lets take a look at this quarry.'

Chris mouthed his thanks to Sally on their way out.

Chris noted that Stokes's quarry looked much less sinister in daylight. The gates to Superior Masonry and Stone were open so he drove his car straight into the yard. The Transit hadn't returned. It wasn't likely to now. A few cars were parked up, though. They drove to the opposite side of the yard and were met by a man who emerged from one of the work sheds. He pulled a white dust mask down from his nose and bent down to the driver's window.

Crighton waved his badge at him. 'Is the boss around?', he asked.

'Foreman's in the office over there,' the man said, pointing to a Portakabin and retreating back into his shed, casting a look at the officers as he went.

The Portakabin was sparsely furnished. Table, metal-legged spindly chairs, a scab of linoleum on the floor. The foreman, a well-built man in his fifties looked up from behind an ancient PC as the officers entered his office. A long, bushy moustache twitched around on his top lip as he spoke into a telephone receiver.

'I call you later,' he said into the receiver. 'I know. Something came up. I've got to go.' He hung up and turned his attention to to Crighton.

'Police?' he asked.

'Polish?' Crighton, noting the accent, lifted his warrant card again.

'Slovakia,' the man replied, lifting his chin in pride.

'Expecting us?'

'After the raid yesterday, I think no,' he said. 'I told the police everything I know.'

'We don't know that for sure, Sir,' Crighton sat down in front of the foreman's desk and Chris helped himself to one of the chairs lining the side of the office. 'I sent that team in after reliable information was collected about firearms being on this site. I didn't expect them to question you about anything else.'

'What else you want? I told the other policeman I don't know about guns here. They find nothing.' The man's shrug suggested that as far as he was concerned that was an end to it.

'How many people do you have working here?' Crighton asked.

'Ten, maybe.'

'You don't know for sure?'

'Some casual. Seven full time.'

'Who owns the company?'

'Two or three owners.'

'Does John Stoke ever come here?'

'Ask him yourself.'

Crighton frowned at the foreman's cheek. 'What's that supposed to mean?' he asked.

'He just arrived.'

They all turned to the window. A Jaguar had rolled up in the yard. They watched John Stoke exit the vehicle and walk over to the Portakabin.

'Inspector,' Stoke appeared surprised when he opened the office door.

Crighton gave a shark's smile. 'You've saved me a journey. I was going to look you up later.'

'What brings you here?'

'I'm sure you heard of the raid here yesterday.'

'I did. I can assure you no one from this firm would have any involvement with guns.'

'Hmm. Why are you here?'

'I'm checking up on the site, making sure we can still do business after the interruption.'

'You employ a lot of Eastern Europeans, don't you.'

'I'm not sure. My site management teams deal with the employees.'

'You'll know if their Visa's are all in order though?'

'My managers assure me they are. I can't be accountable for all of them. We have a lot of staff turnover.'

Crighton stood and brought his face close to Stoke's. 'Oh, but you will be accountable, as a company director.'

Stoke stood his ground.

'Is there anything else?' he asked, unflustered by Crighton's closeness.

'Yes. There is. I need you to tell me where you were on these days.' He opened his notebook. On the page were the dates where the initials J.S appeared in Hearst's diary two years past. 'Can you account for your movements?' Stoke looked at the page held out in front of him, huffed and stepped back. He reached for his briefcase and extracted a diary.

'This is this year's diary,' he said, flicking through it. 'I don't keep a hold of any previous ones. Unless it's a recurring meeting, I can't help you.'

'No secretary? No-one who can check for you?'

Stoke glowered at him and dialled a number on his mobile.

138

'Sharon, it's John. I'm over at Superior. Can I get to my emails and calendar from here?' He smiled as Sharon told him what to do. 'OK,' he snapped. With a wave of a hand Imrich was ousted from his perch. Stoke sat down in his place and, following his assistant's instructions, logged onto a remote email session. Pulling up his calendar, he invited Crighton to look.

'Planning meeting, Council,' he said answering to the first date. He continued, 'Property evaluation in London. Golf. Site visit with purchaser, Cambridge. Trade fair, Lincoln. Golf.' He looked up. 'Do these have any relevance to you, Inspector?' he sighed, clearly happy that he had Crighton on the defensive.

'Apparently not,' Crighton said, raising his eyebrows at Chris. 'I assume you can get someone to vouch for each of the visits?'

Stoke pointed to the screen. 'Of course I can. Sharon logs all of my appointments at Head Office.'

Crighton seemed to get the point. Stoke had rattled off alibi's at high speed and Chris was sure he'd be able to back them up.

'Mind if we look around?'

Stoke's look matched Crighton's cheery grin. 'Be my guest. Imrich, find someone to supervise the policemen.'

Chris was last out of the door, letting it swing slowly home on its spring. Stoke's voice escaped through the crack and when he looked back through the office window, Chris saw the man holding his mobile phone to his ear, mouth working hard berating whoever was on the other end of the call.

They toured the quarry sheds, Chris once again taking note of a large table saw lining one side of the workspace. The sixty centimetre diamond blade was busy cutting through large blocks of limestone fed in from one end by a worker. The shriek of the saw blade jarred against Chris's nerves when he imagined this might have been the last thing Simon Hearst had ever heard.

'Do you have a log of when the saw blades are changed on these?' Chris asked their guide, indicating the table saw. The look of incomprehension he received in response told him the guy wasn't an English speaker. Was it a tactic by the foreman to help avoid awkward questions?

He scrutinized the workers they passed, hoping to recognise one of the guards from his previous visit. It had been too dark that night to get a proper look at them and he had to be honest, he didn't expect them to still be around.

They walked to the work shed where Chris had seen the man leaving the underground room. The central area of the floor in this building except was made from old wooden railway sleepers, lined up side by side and recessed into the ground. The outer edge was concrete.

'The trapdoor to the silo has been blocked off, Guv, look,' He pointed to a pile of wooden pallets holding plastic sacks of decorative gravel, their labels displaying the brand of a DIY chain. The goods were located a few feet away from the shed's wall, out of place to be naturally stored there.

'No other reason to store them there,' Crighton agreed. 'Can you move these?' he asked the worker. Again the only response they got was a confused frown and a shrug of the guise's shoulders.

'Raine, get someone who speaks English, would you?'

Chris started walking out of the shed but the guide grabbed his arm, pointing to Crighton and pulling him back into the shed.

'Doesn't want us splitting up, eh?' Crighton said. He flashed his warrant card to the worker and pointed forcefully at Chris. The worker seemed to understand and didn't obstruct Chris's second attempt to leave.

A few minutes later he reappeared with Imrich, the foreman, who dismissed the worker with an annoyed stream of what Chris could only guess was Slovakian.

'Why do you have pallets covering the trapdoor

to the room below?' Crighton asked.

'I don't know about door.' Imrich said.

'Move these pallets.'

'You have warrant?'

'Do I need one?' Crighton's tone suggested his patience was wearing thin.

'No. I move,' Imrich ceded. He walked to a nearby forklift and switched it on.

'I see he knew exactly which ones to move,' Chris whispered to Crighton as they watched the hatch being revealed. 'You do know about door,' he said quietly, mimicking the Slovak.

They lifted the heavy wooden hatch from the entrance and the detectives descended a rusty ladder into a subterranean storage area, their torches picking out details in the dark room aided by a shaft of light from the entry hole.

The storage room had most likely been used as a silage bunker when the place had still been a functioning farm. The floor was dry, and there were drain holes at one end, probably leading to the pipe Chris had crawled along. He shivered in the underground cold at the thought of his escape. It was one thing facing an enemy when he was in the Army, gun against gun, but unarmed as he had been the other night, the only sensible course of action had been to run.

Outdoor sounds drifted through the trapdoor above, muted and distant. In one corner he could see imprints of the sacks that had been taken away. The bags must have laid on a plastic liner because no residue of their contents lay around. Looking upwards they could see the ceiling was supported by angled iron crossbeams, themselves welded to iron uprights Torchlight sent their shadows leaping around the opposite walls. Lengths of chain had been welded to some of the uprights. Chris directed the beam of his torch along the links of one of the chains. The last link had a fresh grinding mark on it where something had been cut off. The two men shared a look.

'Why do you think these have been cut, Chris?' Crighton asked.

'Well I don't want to jump to conclusions, but. . .' a sudden bang cut off Chris's reply. Both men whirled around and saw that the square of daylight had disappeared from the entrance hole.

'Hey,' Crighton shouted. 'Open up!'

A scraping sound above suggested the pallets were being replaced over the doorway.

Panic rose in Chris's stomach, knotting itself upwards and squeezing the air from his lungs. He choked back the urge to cry out too. In the torchlight he could see Crighton race up the ladder, his face twisted with anger, fists beating on the trapdoor.

'Hey! Hey! Open the door!' Crighton shouted. He pushed upwards but the door didn't budge.

Chris battled to keep calm and reached for his phone. The tiny screen lit up but the little antenna icon displayed no bars. No signal.

'Sir, come down,' he begged. 'Let me get up there.'

'No, no, I need to get their attention,' Crighton's panicked voice rose an octave.

'Sir, let me see if I can get a signal on my phone. We can call in support.'

'No. Let me try my radio,' Crighton appeared to be getting a grip of himself. He tried to contact the station. No answer.

The men swapped places, Chris moved his phone as close to the door as possible. One bar popped into existence on the screen, stayed there for a few seconds then disappeared.

'Anything?' Crighton asked.

'Not enough for a call. I'll try to send a text to Sally. She'll get support over here.'

He tapped his message into the phone and pressed send. The transmitting icon stayed on the screen longer than normal.

'Come on,' Chris whispered. 'Get gone.'

The icon disappeared and the screen displayed a message: 'Sending failed. Resend at 17:02'

Chris groaned and tried to send the message manually again. Again the phone responded, 'Sending failed. Resend at 17:04'.

He rested the phone on a ledge and returned to the bottom of the ladder.

'The text might get through if the signal comes back in strong enough,' he explained. 'Why did they block the door? They know we're in here?'

'I don't know, son. Stoke is bound to know that we'll get backup. Maybe he's messing with us.'

Chris thought about this. 'Maybe he wants us out of the way for a while.'

'Hmm.'

'Seriously, Guv I heard him on the phone to someone in the office. He was having a right go at them. Telling them to get over here as soon as possible.'

'When was that?' Crighton asked, interest picking up.

'Just before we started looking around.'

'So you think they warned him to distract us?'

'Yeah. I only heard his half the conversation. I thought he just wanted them over here for someone to shout at.'

'OK. Switch your torch off. We need to save the batteries.' Chris did as he was asked, leaving a solitary beam of light emanating from Crighton's. In the quiet, dead air of the storage room the distant sounds of quarry activity filtered through to them. A louder rumble vibrated through the thick ceiling, as though a large truck, or lorry had arrived and parked outside.

'You were going to tell me what you thought about these chains.' Crighton aimed his torch back to the end link of one of them.

Chris took a deep breath of the cool, musty air and was reminded of his first night in Afghanistan eight years previously. Having expected it to be baking hot out there, the evening temperatures had surprised him by

143

dropped to near freezing.

'Over in Afghanistan, the compound we were based in was a captured Taliban headquarters. In one of the buildings there were prison cells. They were in a pretty disgusting state, even though they were empty. One thing that sticks in my mind are the chained manacles, fixed to the walls.'

'Uh-huh.'

'You said you thought Stoke might have links to a drugs cartel.' Chris licked his lips, uncertain to air his thoughts in case Crighton thought him prejudiced.

'I do. Go on, lad,' Crighton encouraged him.

'Well, there are a lot of foreign workers here at this quarry. It's common for drugs traffickers have a hand in other activities - prostitution and people smuggling. This would be an ideal place to hole up their 'merchandise' before moving them on. Out of the way, in the country. Foreign workers might help with the language barrier and cover up anything suspicious.' Chris paused, waiting for a verdict on his assumption.

'I think you might be right, Chris,' Crighton said. 'It's a shame we can't do anything about it right now.'

'Let me have your torch a second, Guv,' Chris asked. Crighton handed it over and watched Chris investigate the floor.

Chris searched around the base of each pillar, the torch illuminating only a small patch of ground at a time. He found nothing of interest on the floor.

'What are you looking for?'

'Any trace of human evidence. Scratches, words, anything really.'

'Be lucky to find anything with that torch, lad.'

Chris was reluctant to give up. By pulling one of the chains taut, he found it ran almost to the edge of the room. Had he been secured to it he would easily reach the wall. The narrow shaft of light played across it.

'It's no good, Guv,' Chris said, surrendering the torch back to his boss. 'You're right, there's not enough light from that to do a proper search.'

Again they heard the rumble of a truck through the ceiling, the sound receding into the distance.

'Damn, what's going on up there?' Crighton cursed. 'When I get my hands on Stoke...'

Small flashes of light briefly strobed over the surroundings before stabilizing and illuminating the floor with a pool of weak light. The sound of footsteps grew closer and Molly Gowland's world grew bright as the cupboard door was wrenched open. She raised her arms and shielded her eyes, her wrists red and chafed from the cord bindings.

Her captor stood at the door and shuffled another person into her prison. Dressed in filthy clothes the boy looked about sixteen, with bare, dirt blackened feet and sparse whiskers on his grubby face. Tied and gagged in the same manner as Molly, he grunted with muffled animal sounds. His wild eyes swivelled around, taking in his new surroundings. Molly retched at the stink emanating from her new cell mate and pleaded through her gag to be set free. Fearful eyes beseeched the man at the door to spare her from the ordeal, but they met a cold, dispassionate stare that darkened then disappeared as the door swung shut.

She wept and struggled to distance herself in the cramped cell from the scrabbling, shuffling form who had joined her. Through the door, the man barked into a phone.

'Are you ready for Wednesday? Good. I have two packages to go, now.'

The boy in her cupboard continued to try to make himself comfortable. Molly heard the clang of a mop bucket toppling over and gasped as she felt cold water seeping around her. Her sobs grew louder and she leaned on the door wondering if she'd ever be free of discomfort and fear again.

'No, I pay you one and half times the price. You don't drive twice so you don't charge twice.'

Why, Dad? Mum? Why didn't you care?

'That's better. This is a good price for you.' He laughed. 'Yes, and me. Dovidenia.'

The light under the door clicked off the cell was plunged into darkness and, to her astonishment, she could hear the boy snoring.

CHAPTER 14

'Stoke had an alibi for all of those dates,' Crighton mused in the darkness.

The two men were sitting with their backs resting against a wall. The background noise of the quarry had begun to diminish and the officers realised the site was beginning to wind down for the day. Chris wondered if he was going to spend another night at the quarry.

'He didn't seem bothered by it,' Chris agreed. 'It got me thinking. If he's not the J.S in Hearst's diary, I've an idea who it could be.'

'Oh?'

'Yeah. When we made our notes, we had trouble reading Hearst's writing and his spelling was really bad.'

'And?'

'What if he's spelled the person's name wrong and put the wrong initials in there.'

'Bit of a stretch isn't it?'

'I know, but the other initials in the diary were for Diane Ellis. He was a womaniser, remember. I wonder if he had an affair with Mrs. Stoke, Gemma, and didn't know how to spell her name.'

'You think he wrote J.S for Jemma Stoke?'

'It's possible,' Chris offered. 'He'd have John Stoke on his mind if he was seeing his wife. That might have triggered the mistake.'

'And you think Stoke found out about the affair and finished Hearst off?'

'Judging by Geoff Ellis's reaction to his wife carrying on with Hearst, it's easy to see how it could send a man over the edge.'

A short musical tune trilled into the darkness. Both men looked up, confused by the sound.

'It's my phone,' Chris yelped, spotting the lit screen at the top of the ladder and climbing to retrieve it. He'd not recognized the unfamiliar jingle. He checked the phone to see whether it was an incoming call or a text.

'Support on way' the screen read.

'It's from Sally,' he said. 'At least we'll be out of here soon.' He sent silent thanks to her, grateful that the signal had come in strongly enough to swap the texts.

At that moment they heard a scraping sound above. The trapdoor lifted out of it's recess and a flood of light pierced the gloom.

'That was quick,' Chris said, covering his eyes from the uniformed officer's flash-light that appeared at the entrance.

'We got a call from CID Kettering about fifteen minutes ago,' the uniform replied. 'Said there were a couple of plain-clothes lost in the quarry.'

'Not lost, trapped,' Crighton spat, scowling at the man. He lifted himself out of the room. Stoke stood nearby with his foreman at his side.

'What the hell do you think you're doing, Stoke? Trapping us in there.' he demanded.

'I don't understand, Inspector, I thought you'd left,' Stoke said, a knowing smile slipping quickly away from his face.

'Rubbish. Our car is still parked over there,' Crighton pointed a shaking finger to Chris's Focus. 'You knew we were down there, and you instructed your men to shut us in.'

'Now come on, Inspector, I had no idea you were in there until this policeman arrived.'

'Not good enough. You're under arrest for obstructing the police. Raine, take the foreman and pick up any CCTV footage they have of this site. Then arrest him too.'

Chris led the foreman across the yard to the office, where fluorescent lights burned brightly in the twilight.

'Where do you keep the CCTV tapes?' he asked Imrich, the foreman.

'In here.' Imrich opened a cupboard in the Portakabin and ejected the tape from a video recorder.

'Have you got any more? from last week, maybe?' Chris asked, taking the tape and hoping to get hold of one that showed his visit on Saturday.

'No. Only one. On loop,' Imrich explained.

Yeah, sure, thought Chris, noticing several empty video cases in the cupboard. 'Where are the cameras?'

'At gate. That is all,' the foreman replied.

'Come on, then. You heard the Inspector,' Chris said and ran through the arrest procedure as he lead Imrich to the marked police car waiting in the yard.

'Raine, I'll ride with PC Taylor and these two,' Crighton indicated Stoke and the foreman. 'I'll see you over at Kettering first thing.' He drew Chris close to him, away from the others.

'Listen, there's not much I can hold Stoke in custody for at the moment. I'm going to keep him in the cells overnight to teach him a lesson. I want to take a drive over to his house in the morning, before we release him. Have a chat with Mrs. Stoke whilst her husband's out of the way.'

Chris nodded, pleased to find his boss respected his opinion.

'Meet me over there at about eight. If J.S is really G.S, then we've got a motive. Let's see if another of your theories holds water.'

Chris stepped out of his shower cubicle, grabbed a towel from the rail and rubbed vigorously at his hair. He remembered doing the same for Sally a few days ago, and the can of worms he'd opened up with it. Was she really OK now? Tough cookie if so.

Crighton's reluctance to charge Stoke with anything stronger than obstruction worried Chris. Stoke had business interests that were in opposition to Hearst. He had the means to inflict the injuries that Hearst had suffered, and he'd been in the pub the night the Cartwrights boat had been left empty. All that was left was motive. If Hearst had been carrying on with Stoke's wife, then the case against him grew stronger.

Maybe that's why Crighton wanted to speak to Mrs. Stoke again. Ascertain a reason to charge him with murder. It didn't get them any closer to Molly Gowland, though, and that jarred against Chris's nerves. If only he'd been less impulsive, Tony Whitelock would be in custody now instead of in a hospital bed, unconscious.

Chris had to admit that his suspicions over Stoke were all circumstantial. There were others in the frame for Hearst's murder but, as far as Chris could see, none of them had a reason for taking his daughter too. Polson's argument with Hearst was purely business, he had no motive for kidnap. And the Ellis's and Cartwrights didn't seem the types to go around abducting children, either.

The problem was that none of them, including Stoke, could have predicted Hearst would have his daughter thrust upon him at such short notice. But who would have the conviction to follow through their plans once they knew she was in the picture?

Chris finished drying himself, his belly grumbling. The doorbell rang and a moment later a hand rapped on the wood. Someone's in a hurry, he thought. After a spray of deodorant and a delve into a drawer for t-shirt and jeans, he rushed downstairs.

'Really?' Sally asked, when he opened the door to her

'Eh?'

'You are the Stig?' she pointed to the slogan on his T-shirt.

He gave her a sheepish grin and took the plastic bag she held out to him.

'Couldn't face sitting at home alone,' she said. 'Thought you might like Chinese.'

She'd caked the foundation on again but he but he could still make out the swelling around her face, her left eye remained almost closed. She followed him into his living room and made herself at home while he dished out the food.

'I've got no wine,' he called through from the kitchen. 'You want a beer?'

'Not with the pain killers, thanks,' She replied. 'Coffee would be good though. Could I have a glass of water too?'

Chris kicked himself. Mr. tactful. 'What have they put you on?' he asked, finding an un-chipped mug at the back of the cupboard and blowing the dust out of it.

'Zydol,' she called back. 'They're really good but you're not supposed to have alcohol with them. Given me a raging thirst, though. It's a toss up whether to take the pills or sink a bottle of something.'

'Alcohol isn't the answer.' Chris placed a can of lager and pint glass on the coffee table next to her mug and glass of water. 'Ignore the hypocrisy,' he grinned and returned to the kitchen for food.

'Common problem for coppers.'

'Hypocrisy or the booze?' He passed her the plate of Chinese and cracked the can anyway. 'Zydol, that's Tramadol, isn't it?'

Sally rummaged about in her handbag for the pill bottle and read the medical description.

'Yeah,' she said, passing the bottle to him. 'How did you know that?'

'Army medics course,' he said, scanning the prescription label. 'Watch yourself with them, they can be addictive. I was worried about you the other day. Drinking wine in working hours. No wonder you slipped at the weir.'

Sally shrugged. 'I'd have been OK if I hadn't been sent out with wonder-kid.'

'Eh?'

'You know you're the Guv's blue eyed boy, don't you?' She seemed surprised by Chris's confused look. 'He expects a lot from you. I'd have been under much less pressure if Soap had been with me.'

'I see,' he said, although he didn't. She'd changed the subject easily, deflecting his comment about her drinking. He believed Crighton was fairly critical of him,

151

judging by how close he'd come to suspending him.

'At least we got a result with those lawn mowers.'

'Ah, yes,' Sally put her tray down. And reached for her handbag.

'What's this?' Chris asked, taking the photograph she lifted out.

'I started clearing Tony's things out tonight,' she ignored Chris's glance. 'It's definitely over,' she stressed. 'Anyway, I found this in his stuff. School photo. Look at the second row, near the end.'

He examined the gangly youths. Nearly all the girls were hanging onto late eighties styles. Big hair pumped up with mousse, with the odd forward-looking girl displaying long, free-flowing curls. The boys mostly sported lank curtains draped over their eyes, trying to imitate Kurt Cobain or Keanu Reeves. Chris checked the names listed at the bottom of the cardboard frame. He noticed Whitelock's name and located him on the picture. He stood with a cocky stance, appearing confident with this school mates around him, unaware of the truth just around the corner. Mates drifting off to university and careers further afield. Marriages, families and mortgages. No time to keep up with old alliances.

Chris looked at the lad standing next to Whitelock. Round framed, owl-like glasses shielded the boy's face slightly but Chris still felt a flicker of recognition. He traced back to the roll-call at the bottom. James Cook. Now living on a canal boat. No glasses, bad teeth and with a van full of stolen lawnmowers.

'Wow. What does this mean?'

'One thing at least. If they're still in contact with each other, our trail to the stolen documents may not be as cold as we think.'

'Did Tony ever talk about Cook?'

'I don't think so. I don't remember.'

Forks clacked on crockery, both of them working out how to approach this new angle in the investigation. Chris took a few sups of lager and tried to work out the possibilities.

Sally interrupted his thoughts. 'You want to come with me to question Cook?'

'I'll be at Elton first thing, with the Guv We're going to see Gemma Stoke, ' he said. He explained his suspicions about Hearst's womanising expanding further afield than Oundle and Ashton.

'Good idea,' Sally agreed.

'You want to take Soap with you?'

'I suppose I could,' she took the photo back, flicking at the corner of the ageing cardboard. 'I want a thinker though, not just backup. He'll be only just off shift from the hospital, and tired.'

Chris expected the station would soon send a uniform to take over monitoring Whitelock's condition.

'Any improvement on Tony?'

'He's been stabilised but he's still unconscious. Doesn't matter to me,' she sniffed, dismissing the subject once again. 'Got any music?'

Chris dipped into his pocket and tossed her his iPod. 'Bose is over there.' He pointed to the sound dock in a corner of the room.

'Funny, you don't get to see people's music collection much these days,' Sally commented, scanning through his playlists.

'All my CD's went in the loft a few months ago. They were cluttering the place up. Lucky really. It would only have been more to tidy up after the break-in.'

Did the SOCO's make a mess?' She surveyed his recently tidied room. No sign of the break in remained.

'No, they did a good job. The contract carpenter even put a dab of paint on the door frame.'

'A bit young for Jazz and Blues aren't you?' she asked, struggling to find something she liked on his iPod.

'My dad was into it.'

'Kids normally rebel against their parent's tastes.'

'Guess I'm not normal, then.' Chris felt embarrassed to have his music preferences held up to criticism. 'If you've got a player it should connect to the Bose. Your choice.'

'No, it's OK. It's not all rubbish,' Sally said, settling on a Jamiroquai album.

They finished their meal, the strains of acid jazz filling the silence.

'Did you see action in Afghanistan?' Sally pointed at the photo on the wall of Chris's troop.

Chris was in the kitchen, clearing the plates. He paused from filling the dishwasher. 'Enough that I don't like to talk about it,' he replied, thirsty for another beer.

'Sorry I asked.'

'No, it's OK,' he collared another can from the fridge and returned to the living room to top up his glass, noticing her examining his photo. 'I suppose I shouldn't have it up there, really. Conversation always turns around to it.'

'It can't have been all bad. They look a happy squad.'

'Troop,' he corrected. 'Gotta put a face on for your public, haven't you,' he said and immediately wished he hadn't.

Sally didn't appear to notice the connection to her make-up. 'Got any more photos?'

Chris rummaged through a drawer for a photo envelope. All his recent pictures were on his laptop, but these had been taken before digital photo storage had taken over from ink on paper. He thought about the images stored on his laptop. Must get some of those printed out, he thought. He didn't know what he'd do if the hard drive went belly up.

Sally lifted her bag from the sofa cushion to make room for him. 'That's Gaz, Sweeny, Jeff, Brogey,' he said, pointing out old pals in the photo resting in the cup of his hands.

'Sweeny?'

'Mike Todd, 'Sweeny',' he explained.

'And Brogey?'

'Just Brogan. John.' The simple nicknaming seemed juvenile to him now. There had never been any reasoning behind squaddie nicknames as far as he knew.

154

If your name was synonymous with someone famous you ended up with that, if not, it was generally suffixed with an 'ey' or something similar.

Her forearm brushed his when she took a picture from the collection.

'You can see it just behind the eyes,' she whispered.

'The worry?' He knew what she meant. All his mates shared the same look. Outward bravado, comic poses. But in every one of their eyes was that look of apprehension, each of them waiting for a call into unknown dangers.

'Yeah.' She returned the photo and repeated the contact on his skin, sending a tremor darting through his nerve-endings. 'It must be a different world out there.'

'You mark your days off of your chuff chart, do your time, come home,' he stated.

'Chuff chart, what's that?'

'It's a sort of reverse calendar that you put up at the start of whatever tour you're on. On it, you mark your last day, and any other important ones between the start and finish.'

Chris pointed to one of the photo's. Sally noticed the background behind his mates. Collapsible camp beds, sleeping bags, army kit draped over a chair, an SA-80 rifle lying on a bed. On the back wall, a hand-drawn tally chart had been taped up, most of the numbers crossed out. Comic caricatures of the troopers were sketched around the edge, speech bubbles noting something daft one or another had said during the tour. At the bottom, underneath the last day, a small photo of a Hercules C-130 transport plane had been taped to the paper. 'Count down the days till you're chuffed to be going home.'

'I thought all you squaddies ever thought about was fighting. Why the count down?'

'Not everyone signs up expecting to go to war. Some do, of course, but the first experience of action normally puts paid to any gung-ho feelings.'

'Oh,' she said, surprised. 'My old boyfriend used

to be full of it.'

'Did he ever go out there?' meaning Afghanistan.

'No,' she said quietly. 'It was all bravado?' Chris twisted a wry smile. 'It must be so difficult,' She said, reaching out and squeezing his shoulder gently.

'You get used to it, eventually,' he said, words sticking in his throat, head thick with anticipation. 'Usually a few days before your tour's due to end.'

The trace of a smile flickered over Sally's mouth. She understands, he thought. Working in the police, living with a bully. She shares the same feelings, needs reassurance. Discarded photos slipped through his fingers, ignored. He felt drawn to her.

'Things will work out for you,' he said. Leaning over, seeking his own comfort, he kissed her. His mouth encountered the hard scab on her split lip, hiding under lipstick.

For a brief moment he felt her respond but then she gently pushed him away. 'I'm sorry, Chris.'

His head reeled. 'Did I hurt you?' He thought of her bruises.

'Only a little. No, it's Tony,' she said, fumbling in her bag for a tissue. 'I, can't.'

Chris scooped up his pictures and tucked them back into their envelope. He returned them to the drawer, slammed it shut and stood in the corner of the room, hand brushing through his hair.

'You can't what?' he asked, unable to hide the aggravation in his voice.

Sally stared at him, lines creasing her brow. 'Chris, this isn't easy for me, you know?'

'What isn't, leading me on?'

'No. I didn't mean. . . I'm not leading you on. I thought. . . Tony. I thought I could shut him off. I can't. . .' She stood and turned to the door. 'I'd better go. I'm sorry, Chris. I thought I'd be able to. . .'

Chris watched her leave, anger and frustration giving way to self pity once he'd had a chance to calm down. He stomped around the room, clearing the last remnants of dinner away. He consigned the last half-can of beer to the sink, its effects unwelcome and the sour flavour unappealing.

Thoughts jumped around his head, chiding, chastising, berating him. How could you have been so stupid to think she really fancied you? For starters, it was you that sent her husband to Casualty today. She just playing with you, has been all week. Why invite her over anyway? Should've steered clear, idiot. Damaged goods. Literally. Hang on. Damaged goods. Think about it, man. Damaged by the beatings she'd received by her husband, but also to her self esteem through his mental bullying. Don't blame her. Don't blame yourself. Just two souls thrown together through circumstance.

Chris wondered at how fragile, and yet, how strong relationships could be. After trying so hard to keep hers alive under such pressure, Sally had tried to cut Tony off completely only to fail at the first hurdle. But she'd acted too soon, of course. Or you did, Chris, he told himself. Keep your mind on the job, man.

Hearst floated into Chris's consciousness and he tried to build a mental picture the man. Had he ever experienced such qualms about his relationships? Or was he simply on the hunt all the time, looking for the next conquest. Did he ever seek out something more meaningful, more permanent before his life was cut short? His house hadn't shown any personality, no soft touches. The shape and build of the place was the only stamp of identity it displayed. Judged by his house, that bare cold harbour, he'd found no lasting comfort. And did he ever care about the damage he left behind? Diane Ellis and her brittle marriage, for example. Chris found it difficult to sympathise with the man and his untimely death.

He looked inward and scoffed at his own criticism. You're no better, trying it on with a married woman yourself.

No, that's different, isn't it? He tried to rationalize his earlier intentions. The connection he and Sally had made, and the intensity of feeling she'd unwittingly released from him had been overwhelming, and he was convinced she had wanted to take it further. Hadn't she?

Now all he had to do was go into work and face her again.

CHAPTER 15

A thin layer of hard frost on his car's windscreen welcomed Chris the following morning. Scraping the film of ice with a credit card took longer than expected but the fresh air helped clear his head from the lack of sleep and what felt like a hangover, despite his low alcohol count. He fiddled with the car stereo on the journey to Elton, flicking back through a CD to find something to cheer him up. He wished he had his own rewind button so he could revisit the previous night and erase it. Inviting Sally over last night had to be up there as one of the biggest mistakes of his life. The morning sun pierced the car's windscreen and he had to duck about, trying to shield his eyes. The sun visor gave little protection from the dazzling light and he felt as though under a kind of celestial judgement, his headache growing worse. He vowed to steer clear of Sally Whitelock. If only.

'Stoke's lawyer will have told her he's in custody,' Crighton said. They stood at Stoke's front porch. 'Funny how when you bring someone in, you can tell who's going to phone family and who will want to speak with their lawyer,' he continued. 'Try as he might, there was no way Stoke was getting out last night. I expect he thought a quick call to his lawyer would have us doffing our caps as he walked free.'

Chris imagined the Guv dodging Stoke's lawyer at the station the previous night. If he wanted to keep Stoke in for the full twenty four hours allowed without charge he'd have to avoid the lawyer's demands. As it was, Chris had noticed Crighton had already ignored two calls to his mobile in the short time they'd been together at Elton.

'Are you going to charge him with anything?'

'Not yet. I wanted him out of the way so we could

talk to Mrs. Stoke.' Crighton rang the bell for a second time. ' And cheer up, will you? Misery guts.'

'Hope she's in,' Chris remarked, trying to lighten his mood. Mrs. Stoke was in no rush to answer the door. Crighton checked his watch. Eight o'clock.

'Wouldn't expect the wealthy to be up and out this early,' he commented.

A female voice carried over to them from the horse paddock that lined the drive. 'Yoo-oo.' The men turned to see Mrs. Stoke open the paddock gate and approach the house, slinking along in boots and jodhpurs, a white blouse tucked neatly beneath a black coat. The whole ensemble was topped off with her long blonde hair pinned beneath a riding hat.

Only eight o'clock, thought Chris, but dressed to perfection and with immaculate make-up. And neither the Guv nor he had noticed her on their way in. Chris had been too busy checking out the workshops on the other side of the drive during his approach.

'Good morning, officers,' she said. 'If you wish to speak to my husband you'll have to ...' she halted when she saw Crighton's look. 'Ah, but you already know that, don't you.' She stepped up to the door.

'I'm sorry ma'am. It was unavoidable. I'm sure he'll be back with you later today,' Crighton tried to reassure her. 'Just a formality, really.'

'You'd better come in.'

'Thank you, Mrs. Stoke,' Crighton said, forgetting to ask her to call him Inspector. They stepped over the threshold and followed the mixed aroma of perfume and horse into the house. Stoke's wife led them through the house to an expansive kitchen. Chris stole a glance through a door to a lounge as he passed. The room was decorated with stylish and elegant furniture, reminding him of the Guv's comment the other night. The place certainly did reek of money.

The kitchen was no less expensively furnished, with a rural farmhouse style, although Chris couldn't imagine Mrs. Stoke as the type to skin a rabbit on the immaculate oak table.

'I expect you're here to ask me about John,' Gemma Stoke guessed. She prepared a pot of tea while she spoke. A kettle had been simmering on a range cooker which threw heat into the kitchen. Chris took a cup proffered by Mrs. Stoke, sweating in his overcoat. The china cup rattled in its saucer. Unused to such delicate crockery, he had trouble lifting the small cup. His finger and thumb threatened to snap the fine handle clean off.

Mrs. Stoke seemed amused at the the officer's discomfort but didn't comment.

'Actually, Mrs. Stoke, I'd like to ask you a few questions about yourself, if you don't mind?' Crighton said.

'Me? Oh, I see,' she indicated for them both to sit at the oak kitchen table. Chris took the opportunity to remove his coat.

'How can I help?'

'How long have you been married to John Stoke, ma'am?' Crighton started.

'Ten years this May,' she answered, smiling.

'Quite an age difference between you, isn't it?'

'Eleven years. Not such an issue these days,' the smile remained. 'I was twenty nine when we married. John was forty.'

'Hmm.'

Chris could tell that Crighton's approval wouldn't be earned so readily.

'How did you meet?' Chris asked, curious how the age difference was overcome. Crighton probably thinks she was his secretary, he thought.

'I was his first wife's carer,' Gemma answered, the casual smile slipping slightly.

'Carer?' Crighton butted in.

'Yes,' Gemma stood and retrieved a photo from a shelf on the kitchen dresser. 'That's her. She died eleven years ago. Cervical cancer.'

Both detectives sat awkwardly in the silence that

followed. Staring at the fading photograph and wondering why it would still be prominent in the house. Chris remembered seeing a larger one in the lounge, and yet another in the study on their previous visit.

'I looked after her at home during her last months.'

'And John asked you to marry him after she'd passed away?'

'Not straight away,' Gemma snapped. 'He loved her. He was distraught when he lost her.' She replaced the picture and poured herself a glass of water, swallowing two paracetamol tablets with the drink. 'I looked in on him regularly after she passed away. I was worried he'd do something stupid.'

'And one thing led to another?' Crighton asked.

'I suppose they did.' She brushed his suggestive tone away. 'Anyway, we found we had a lot in common and we married the following year,' she said, offering the minimum of information, indicating the matter was closed. 'I don't see what this has got to with your investigation?'

'Which investigation would that be, ma'am?'

'Oh, er, I don't know,' she stammered. 'I just thought you must be investigating something if you keep coming around here.'

Crighton made a show of reading through his notes. Chris took the hint and kept quiet too, using the technique to put Gemma Stoke on edge. Given the opportunity, most people had a tendency to let their mouths run-on to fill the silence. Gemma appeared more self composed than most, though and seemed content to let the silence hold. She sipped her tea, her slender fingers neatly holding the cup and saucer.

'Do you ever go to the Chequered Skipper pub in Ashton?' Crighton asked, immediately eliciting a change in Gemma's posture. Her shoulders dropped almost imperceptibly, Chris barely noticed the movement. But the light disappeared from her eyes and her cheeks sank as sadness seeped into her face. Noticing the change,

Chris had the unusual feeling of being unhappy to see that a hunch was about to be proven.

'Only very occasionally,' she said, her voice flat. 'To the restaurant.' She lifted the inflection on the last word, then tried to hide her emotions by pulling it down again. 'The food's rather good, for a pub.'

'Why don't you tell us about him?' Crighton asked, nodding in encouragement.

'I'm sorry?'

'Simon.'

Gemma shook her head, the line of questioning had changed tack and she seemed to be having trouble keeping up.

'The man they found on the boat?' she asked.

'Simon Hearst, yes,' Crighton confirmed.

'I don't know what you mean? What about him?'

'Did you know him?'

'No,' she said, fidgeting on her chair. She's a terrible liar, Chris thought. 'I saw it in the paper on Saturday.'

The local newspapers had started to grate on Chris's nerves. With very little forthcoming since Hearst's name had been formally been released to the press, their speculation had reached ridiculous levels. This morning's local paper had led with their own appeal for witnesses, suggesting the police were unable to progress the case.

'Mrs. Stoke, let's not beat about the bush,' Crighton said, his voice firming. 'We've been investigating Simon's murder this week. We found links in his diary to a number of women, including yourself.'

That was stretching the truth, Chris thought. But too much? He wasn't sure.

Gemma began to protest but saw Crighton's look and held her tongue. She began weeping.

Crighton nodded for her to go on. She reached for a handkerchief tucked up her sleeve, pulling herself together.

'We met in 2008, at the Stone Show in London,'

she said in a resigned tone.

Chris had to suppress a laugh. For all the seriousness of the conversation, he'd been caught off guard by her confession. Who meets a lover at a 'Stone Show'?

'The Stone Show?' Crighton threw Chris a warning look. He was playing this straight.

'Yes. The Natural Stone Show, to give it it's formal title. It's held at Excel every other year,' she explained. 'John always goes, and sometimes I tag along. I can't see the attraction in stone, like the other delegates do,' she said, trying to distance herself from the notion that she'd be interested in the industry. 'But I like to support John. He picks up business and contacts there.'

'And you pick up, what? lovers?' Crighton dragged the conversation back on his thread.

'Crude, officer,' she looked down her nose at him. 'Simon sought me out, actually.'

'Did he?' Crighton pretended to be admonished.

'Yes,' she patted her hair softly. 'He was quite charming. Vulnerable. A bit of a Hugh Grant. It was his first visit, too,' she recalled. 'He'd been invited by the Stone Federation. They were having a big push in the industry to encourage more members.'

Chris was getting interested now. He'd initially dismissed the show as being, niche, almost ridiculous. But thinking more about it, stone working would have a collective organization, with operational guidelines and standards like any other industry.

'He said he'd noticed I was wandering around alone. John was in a meeting with a potential machinery supplier. Simon told me I looked as bemused by it all as he was. He'd not long started out in stone masonry.'

Chris could imagine Hearst stalking Mrs. Stoke around the arena. He'd have been bowled over by her looks, watching who she was talking to, seeing if she was accompanied and, true to his character, waiting for a time to move in.

'So, weren't you surprised when you found that

164

he lived nearby?'

'Not really. There are quite a few quarries around here. I've met a some of the owners with John, so I didn't really give it a thought.'

'And you saw each other again when you returned?'

'I didn't want to, initially, but he was quite persistent, and quite adorable.' She sniffed into her handkerchief. 'We grew close.'

'And when did the relationship end?' Chris asked. Crighton looked surprised.

'About six months ago,' Gemma said, straightening her back. 'He lost interest. I thought it might have been another woman but he insisted it was just the end of the road for us.'

Crighton raised an eyebrow at Chris.

'You've not mentioned your husband in all this, ma'am,' he said. 'I'm sure he wouldn't have taken kindly to the situation. Did he know?'

Gemma shook her head, 'I know what you're thinking, officer. He didn't know about us, but it wouldn't have made a difference. We've not been,' she hesitated, 'intimate.'

'Because he still holds a candle for his first wife?' Chris asked.

'No. It's more delicate than that,' she said.

Chris looked blankly at her. Crighton was scribbling in his notebook.

'Delicate?' he repeated her word, trying to understand what she was saying.

Crighton looked up. 'Would you say that your marriage has been platonic all along?' he offered. Chris was getting more confused.

'Platonic is appropriate, I suppose.'

'Room and board, with domestic and business assistance?'

'You could put it like that,' she said, thin lipped. Her hair flicked and she stared at the ceiling. 'But, while he was happy with the situation. . .'

'You got bored,' Crighton chipped in.

'Not bored, officer. John is an amazing man and I enjoy being with him. But I needed to feel wanted, desired.' She glared at Crighton's disapproving face through wet eyes. 'Doesn't any woman?'

Crighton shrugged, his opinion of extra-marital affairs unspoken. Chris felt on safer ground now. Whatever the reason Stoke and his wife weren't sleeping together, at least she was being honest with them. And it raised the perfect motive for Stoke to want Hearst dead.

'Do you think your husband might have found out about the affair?' Crighton asked.

'Oh.' The realization hit Gemma. 'You don't think John could have. . .' she stopped, unable to finish the sentence.

'It's a very strong reason, ma'am. Any man would get upset.'

'But he's never had a problem in the past,' she insisted.

'You've been unfaithful more than once?'

'It's not a question of being faithful,' she retorted. 'I've told you, our marriage is celibate. We have an, understanding. Have had for years, now.'

'He knows you see other men?'

'Yes.'

This put a spoke into Crighton's wheel, stopping his interrogation dead. His mouth flapped open and closed wordlessly.

'Did your husband know Mr. Hearst?' Chris took over to give his boss a chance to compose himself. Crighton's traditional outlook of marriage had taken a knock by the looks of it.

'No.'

'Are you sure? He never had any business dealings with him?'

'Absolutely not. We spoke a lot about John's work, but Simon never did business with him.'

'We will have to tell John about this when we speak to him,' Chris warned. Maybe the threat of exposing her affair to Stoke would trip her up, make her change her story.

'I'd rather you didn't,' she said, raising his hopes slightly. She immediately dashed them. 'But I can't stop you. John wouldn't do anything so brutal. He's a gentle man and, like I say, he's never had a problem with it.'

'Well, thank you for your candour, ma'am,' Crighton said, standing. 'And thank you for the tea. We'll let you get on.'

Gemma escorted them to the front door and Chris took a few steps down the drive. Crighton stood at his driver side door, about to enter his car.

'Would it be possible to take a look around your workshops, Mrs. Stoke?' Chris asked.

'I'm afraid you'll have to wait until John's here to do that,' she answered. 'He has the keys.' She left the detectives on the drive and closed the door.

Chris trudged back to the cars.

'How did you guess Hearst had finished the affair?' Crighton asked.

'Well, she seems sad he's dead, but not distraught,' Chris replied, using Gemma's own word. 'I reckon she's got a bruised heart, but it's definitely not broken.'

'You think she was on to Hearst's womanising? I wonder if her heart was bruised enough to want retribution.'

'Don't know, Sir, but she'd need help, wouldn't she? No way she'd be able to cart a man's corpse aboard that boat.'

'John Stoke?'

'Would he be a willing accomplice? More to the point, could he have been the instigator?'

'She told us he'd not have been bothered by an extra marital affair,' Crighton still didn't seem to be able to get his head around this.

'That's hard to believe, Sir.'

'Hmm,' Crighton agreed. Best we ask him, ourselves, eh?'

Chris drove down London Road into the town. Kettering Police station's narrow, three storey frontage belied the depth and size of the building. Its red bricks stood dull in contrast to the squat, wide Magistrates Courts next door whose bronze tinted windows glowed as though on fire under the bright sun. The towns Registry office finished off the row. All three buildings were interconnected, a little island of authority floating amongst the town's commercial and religious centre. Across the road sat the impressive, crenellated twin towers of the United Reformed Church, sharing the street with a welfare rights charity.

The unexpected warmth of the early spring day energised all those who walked along London Road. Dark winter coats had been shed and the bright colours of new spring fashions were on display. Mums pushed their offspring along in buggies, light raincoats stored underneath in case the weather turned. Past the Registry Office, left, then left again, along Church Walk and Chris was faced with the wide, dark blue security gate of the shared car park. Crighton had arrived ahead of him and was waving his tag against the electronic lock on the gate. Luckily the Magistrates Court wasn't busy. Chris was able to find a space in the small lot and didn't have to resort to the municipal car park down the road. No reserved spaces here for a humble DC.

'Make a brew, Raine. I'll see you up there,' Crighton called across the car park and disappeared into the station's rear entrance. Chris followed him up the stairs, stopping at the tea area to start the brew, then on to fire up his ageing workstation while the kettle boiled.

In the CID section, Sally Whitelock stood with her back towards him, staring at the incident room's whiteboard. Photographs and maps festooned the board's surface. Sally used a marker to annotate a section with notes. She turned as he entered the office. Chris felt his throat constrict, threatening to choke him.

'Brew?' Was all he cough out.

Sally gave a washed-out smile. 'Please.' She turned back to the board, engrossed in her notes. Chris returned to the brew station, cursing his luck. She was supposed to be at Oundle with Soap today, wasn't she? Shit, this meant Soap hadn't been relieved from hospital guard duty. Or if he had, then he'd gone straight home. Nothing for it lad, he told himself, spooning coffee into mugs. Just get on with the job.

When he returned, Sally and Crighton were looking at the school photo of Tony Whitelock and Jim Cook she'd pinned to the whiteboard. They were deep in conversation, discussing the picture. Sally had perched an old fashioned 14-inch television on her desk. It sat off-centre, the back resting on a pile of paperwork which threatened to send the box sliding off the edge. Its bulbous, curved screen showed a picture on pause from a video tape whirring in the built-in player. Lines of static fuzzed across the screen, obliterating much of the scene but Chris could still make out the entrance to Superior Masonry and Stone. A seven and a half tonne truck appeared to be leaving the site.

'Take a look at the tape, with Sally,' Crighton said, taking his mug from the tray. 'I'm going to give Stoke's lawyer a call, get him over here for questioning with Stoke.'

Chris nodded and settled down next to Sally. He handed her the coffee and stabilised the TV. 'Are we OK?' he asked, when Crighton was out of earshot.

'Yeah, we're good. Too soon, Chris,' she said. 'Some other time, eh? See if you can make that number out on the truck.'

Chris played the tape back a few times. The film was made up of single shots separated at 10 second intervals. The camera had barely picked up the truck arriving on site, and almost missed it leaving.

'So that's the only shot we've got with the number plate on, then?' he asked, looking at a three-quarter side shot of the truck entering the site. 'That's hardly a security camera, is it?' Sally nodded her agreement.

'I think I can make out the first part of the number, but the second is too blurred,' she said.

'It's a MAN truck,' Chris pointed to the logo on the grille. If we can find the variant, we'll have a better chance of narrowing down the number.'

'Well done, truck spotter,' Crighton had arrived back at his shoulder. 'Keep digging and see what you can find. Sally, I want you downstairs with me to interview Stoke. His lawyer is in town. He'll be here shortly.'

Chris groaned. Without Soap around to pick up the routine jobs he'd been relegated to desk jockey. He checked his cheap replacement phone and the woeful camera on it. Would it be good enough for what he had in mind?

CHAPTER 16

'My client wishes to protest in the strongest possible way to the methods Northamptonshire Police believe they can employ to harass and impede his business.' Stoke's lawyer, a pudgy faced man with thinning, lank black hair began haranguing Crighton the moment he switched the tapes on to record. John Stoke sat upright in the interview room alongside his brief. Unshaven and still in the clothes he'd been wearing on arrest, he held an air of dignity the blustering official seemed unable of replicating.

Not a good start, thought Crighton. His raised hand stopped the lawyer's diatribe before he could continue. The man sat poised, open mouthed, tongue pressed against his top teeth ready to launch into another attack.

'How about a cup of - coffee?' he guessed, earning a nod from Stoke. 'Sally, would you ask uniform to oblige, please?' Crighton's manners had elevated a notch from upstairs.

'We won't keep you too long, I hope,' he reassured the men before him. 'DS Sally Whitelock is leaving the room,' he said, for the benefit of the tape. 'Hopefully we can clear this up and you'll be back to, whatever it is you do, shortly.'

'This isn't good enough,' the lawyer butted in. 'You've held my client on a very weak charge, for way over the allowed time limits. . .'

'You'd be wise to get yourself better counsel, Mr Stoke,' Crighton began. 'He should know you can be kept here for 24 hours without formal charge.'

'Where are the Inspector's reviews, at six hours and at fifteen hours?' the lawyer exclaimed triumphantly, slapping his note pad with thick fingers. 'My client should be released with immediate effect.'

171

'Well, Mr.' Crighton looked down at his notes. 'Caplan?'

Caplan smirked and nodded, pleased at his ingenuity of bringing up the Police and Criminal Evidence Act guidelines.

'Well, Mr. Caplan I think you'll find we have executed both reviews in accordance with PACE,' Crighton smiled back. He calmly looked at the ring binder containing Stoke's arrest and detention sheets. 'My colleague, Inspector James Murfit conducted the reviews at midnight-fifteen and this morning at nine-fifteen.'

'Aha, why was I not told of the six hour review, then?'

'Sir, the duty solicitor attended that review,' Caplan's face sagged, 'because you could not be located. Mr Stoke tried to contact you last night, to no avail.' Crighton gave Caplan the full benefit of his shark's smile.

This left Caplan flustered. He leafed through his copy of the charge sheets, screwing up the corners and ripping a page in his hurry. He found the reports, two thin sheets of carbon paper almost fused together, at the back.

'Ah, I see,' he said, deflated. 'They've become stuck together. My apologies Mr. Stoke.'

Stoke stared at him with disdain. 'You, sit quiet,' he instructed, poking a finger at Caplan. 'And don't speak unless I tell you,'

The lawyer nodded, mute.

Crighton updated the tapes again when Sally returned to the interview room. She threw a questioning look to Crighton in the awkward atmosphere.

'Mr. Stoke has just been establishing the parameters of his legal representation,' Crighton explained. He lifted a cup and slurped. 'Not bad. Won't be to your standards, of course, Mr Stoke. Your wife makes a decent brew of tea, though, eh?'

Stoke's interest shifted to Crighton and a little of his arrogance disappeared. 'You've been to my house?'

'Just this morning.' Crighton savoured the

moment. Always good to start an interview with the upper hand, especially when it was gifted so readily. 'But we'll get to that later. I want to know why you trapped me and my officer in that room yesterday.'

'As I said, Inspector, I had no idea you were down there. I thought you'd left.'

'My officer's vehicle was still in the car park.'

'I wasn't to know that. I arrived at the quarry after you, remember.'

'Your foreman knew.'

'He didn't close the hatch. It was one of the workers. Imrich thought you were touring the facility.'

'A likely story,' Crighton felt he was losing the advantage. He had no proof of who'd locked them in, nor on whose orders.

'It's the simple truth.' Stoke reached for his own coffee and drank. He noticed Sally for the first time.

'What happened to you?' he asked, indicating her swollen eye. She'd was still sporting signs of the beating, unable to hide the fact only one eye was working properly.

'None of your concern, Sir,' she replied. 'Police matter.'

Stoke gave her a long wink. She couldn't work out whether he was imitating her lop-sided look or sending a message. Did he know how it really happened?

'Why don't you tell me about your quarry business,' Crighton changed the subject.

'My client is not obliged to tell you anything,' Caplan interrupted.

'I won't tell you again. Shut up,' Stoke snarled at his lawyer. 'I'll decide what I want to talk about.' He fixed Crighton with a stare. 'This idiot is right though, Inspector. Unless you wish to charge me you have no right to keep me here.'

Stoke took a swallow off coffee, enjoying Crighton's discomfort.

Crighton leafed through the charge sheets. It was true, he didn't have much to charge the man with. He balanced the choices. The DCI would have something to say about such a weak charge when the team was supposed to be on a murder hunt.

'Very well. Interview terminated at 09:53' Crighton clicked off the tapes. ' You are free to go, but I'd appreciate it if you'd stay and answer a few questions. I'll only be chasing you up later anyway.'

Stoke relaxed in his chair. 'You. Get lost,' he told his brief.

The lawyer shuffled his papers together. 'I'm sorry, Mr. Stoke. The firm shouldn't have sent me,' he protested under his breath, 'I do conveyancing, not criminal.' He stomped out of the room.

'Your Lawyers can't think much of you if they don't send a criminal lawyer as representation,' he said.

Stoke flicked the insult away. 'They probably can't believe I've been taken in,' he suggested. 'Maybe they thought it was a property matter.'

Crighton jotted down some notes, his fountain pen scraping in the quiet air between the men.

'You been in property long?' Crighton asked

'I did a lot of work with a friend in the late eighties, early nineties, selling holiday homes in the Adriatic.'

'Italy?'

'Yugoslavia. Before it split-up,' he shrugged. 'The Bosnian war made me leave. Nearly broke me. Since then I've been working in the UK.'

'Hence the conveyancing solicitor?' Sally suggested.

Stoke smiled in agreement. 'I'll be having words with his boss,' he said.

'Did you have any associates back then?'

'Graham Yarwood,' Stoke answered, losing the smile.

Crighton stopped writing. 'Ah,' Crighton said. 'Perhaps he could have done a better job today than Caplan, eh?'

'Probably. You know he was a solicitor, then?'

174

Crighton nodded. Stoke continued. 'He helped with the deeds on the holiday homes. Our relationship is purely social these days, since he retired,' Stoke scratched at his overgrown stubble. 'Golf and the odd drink.'

'Nothing to do with Superior Masonry, then?' Crighton asked.

'No.'

'Who are the other owners?' Sally asked.

'Just one other. Theodore Black.'

'Theodore Black,' Crighton mused. 'Where have I heard that name before?' He turned to Sally.

'Aiden James incident in Barton Seagrave, Sir,' she murmured.

Crighton's eyes clouded over. 'Yes. that one.' Crighton dropped his pen, silenced.

Sally stepped in. 'We spoke to the Estate Agents about that house. They told us you dealt with the lease personally. Why was that?'

Stoke thought for a minute. 'As I remember it, I acted as guarantor for Black. He had some workers that needed accommodation. But I don't see the problem, the occupiers came out of your investigation clean, didn't they?'

'All but the one who murdered my officer,' Crighton exploded, slamming his palm on the table.

Stoke stiffened, the sudden outburst rocking the atmosphere in the room.

'What can I say, Inspector? You have my sympathies. It was a mistake to act as guarantor. I didn't know the men personally.'

Crighton swallowed his retort. He needed to calm down. The murder of his Sergeant continued to eat at him. He pointed out a word on his notes to Sally and indicated for her to continue questioning.

'Let's talk about Simon Hearst,' she suggested.

'That's twice you've asked me about him,' still leaning forward, Stoke tapped the table with the edge of his palm. 'I already told you I don't know the man.' He tapped again, emphasising his point.

175

Sally continued, ignoring the man's protest. 'When we went through Simon Hearst's diary we came up with a number of dates with the initials J.S. written on them.'

'I've been through this with the Inspector,' he insisted, exasperated. 'I've already accounted for those dates.'

'If you'll let me finish, Sir,' Sally continued. 'Hearst's spelling was particularly bad. So, when we eliminated you from that line of enquiry, we got to thinking that JS might be GS,' this earned a blank look from Stoke. 'As in, Gemma,' she prompted.

Stoke leaned back in his chair, his glance flickering between Sally and Crighton.

Got you, thought Crighton. This could be the moment we crack the case. A confession, even though not on tape, would be the start of cleaning up the investigation. He waited, expecting anger and indignation to stream from Stoke.

Instead, Stoke threw his head back and laughed, a gurgling chuckle that scratched Crighton's nerves. The detectives exchanged glances. OK, this isn't exactly what I expected, Crighton thought.

'So that's why I've been here all night?' Stoke asked. 'To give you free rein at questioning my wife? I hope she put you right.'

'She's admitted to the affair, if that's what you mean,' Sally bristled. 'Must be a hard thing to take, finding out your wife's unfaithful.'

'Hard being the operative word, officer,' Stoke continued chuckling.

'I'm sorry?'

'The Inspector knows what I mean, lass,' he said and winked again, more theatrically this time.

'That's Detective Sergeant to you, Stoke,' Crighton said, trying to reclaim their authority on the conversation.

'Whatever, Inspector. The truth is,' he addressed Sally directly, 'we have an open marriage as far as sex is concerned. I'm what they call Erectile Dysfunctional these days. Impotent.'

Stoke's words had the desired impact. Although Sally reacted impassively, Crighton's sensibilities had taken a knock. He hadn't expected such directness in front of a woman.

'That'll do, Stoke,' Crighton reproved.

'Surprised Inspector?' Stoke goaded. 'If Pelé can be open about it then that's good enough for me.'

'We get the picture.' Crighton recalled the recent TV campaign spearheaded by the worlds most famous footballer, for treatment of impotence, or E.D. as it was now being branded. Gemma Stoke's claim that the news wouldn't be an issue for Stoke was bearing up. 'Your wife said as much, herself.'

He tried to concentrate and get back on track, to rid his mind of the image of Aiden James in the mortuary. Slashed throat, blue lips, white skin. His young life snuffed out for being in the wrong place at the wrong time.

Why didn't he follow his orders that day?

'This is what I find difficult to accept though, Stoke,' he said, testing the story's credibility. 'How can you be so calm about a business rival having such an intimate contact with your wife?'

'You're the ones saying my wife had the affair. This is the first I've heard of it, and, since he's dead how can I be bothered about any threat to my business. If anything it'll boost sales with less competition around. And no, Sergeant,' he turned his focus to Sally, 'before you accuse me, I did not kill this man to boost my own sales. That would be idiotic.'

'We've not said you killed him, Mr. Stoke,' Sally responded. A claim of police harassment along with a claim of false arrest wouldn't be well received by the DCI. 'We'd have charged you by now if we thought that.' At least, we would if we had a shred of evidence, she added silently.

Crighton stared at his notes. He hadn't wanted to

believe it, but the Stokes's descriptions of their relationship appeared to have some credence. He had no option but to cut the interview short. Seven days on from the discovery of the murder and their most likely suspect was about to walk out of the station unimpeded.

'Thanks Sally,' Crighton said as they watched Stoke leave. 'I thought we had a motive to pin on him, there. Seems the world moves in a different direction these days.' He shook his head in disbelief.

'It's OK, Paul,' Sally said, gently. 'Not everyone has the same morals as Hearst and Mrs. Stoke. There's plenty of circumstantial evidence to point to Stoke as the murderer.'

'I know, Sally but none of that makes a jot of difference without anything concrete to back it up,' Crighton collected his papers up from the desk. 'I still have to question the foreman, Imrich,' he said. 'Have you got anything to do?'

'I'll take Raine over to Barnwell and have a word with Jim Cook. Maybe he can shed some light on Tony's actions. The leads haven't all dried up.'

'I hope not,' Crighton said, his mouth turned down at the corners.

'Paul, don't take it to heart,' she rested a hand on his arm. 'I know you're hurting from losing Aiden. We all are. Try not to let it get to you, though.'

Crighton shrugged off Sally's concern. 'Just let me know what happens at Barnwell, eh?'

CHAPTER 17

The good thing about modern technology, Chris thought, was that even budget gear was able to produce stunning results. A couple of photographs of the truck on the video screen had been sent in a usable resolution from his budget mobile phone to a friend. A lorry driver by trade, Bryon had replied within ten minutes with the model of the truck, a MAN TGL 7.150 box-body.

Chris opened up a remote terminal programme on his computer and logged into the Police National Computer. Here he re-submitted his search of the partial numberplate he and Sally had gleaned from the screen along with the extra information. The initial search with the partial had resulted in five thousand registrations in the UK. Chris was able to reduce this to one hundred vehicles once the truck model was put into the search. Relieved at only having to chase up a hundred owners, Chris set to work categorizing them them. A quick scan down the list soon had him tapping away on his keyboard, creating a report on the search results.

Sally arrived in the CID area as Chris was putting the finishing touches to his report and forwarding it to his colleagues in an email.

'Guv's in with the quarry foreman,' she announced.

'How did it go with Stoke?' Chris asked.

'Not good. He didn't seem the slightest bit bothered about his wife carrying on with another man. Still claims he didn't know Hearst. Guv can't get his head around the Stoke's sex life, or lack of it.'

Chris took this in. 'You've gotta wonder though, haven't you?' he said. 'I thought people of their age had a more conservative attitude to sex.'

'You're thinking of people who grew up pre-fifties, Chris. The baby-boomers and their offspring are as

179

liberated as anyone, if not more so. No AIDS around in the sixties and seventies.'

'Still, I thought we had him on that motive.'

'Even if he's lying, his alibis are being backed up by his wife's story. We have to move on from that unless something sends us back.'

'Yeah, I guess so. It's possible Hearst was topped at his quarry too, but the Guv won't send forensics in again.'

'He'd need something more compelling before that happens. It's fair to send them to Hearst's quarry, what with him being the victim and owner, but they can't go running to every circular saw in the county.'

'Should I chase up this truck lead further?'

Sally leaned over his shoulder. He experienced the same spark of connection he'd felt the previous night, but the harsh strip lights and the office, cluttered with office furniture and computers, helped to temper his emotions. He could feel a definite aura of professional restraint between them, something that had been missing in the comfort of his own house.

'OK,' she said, scanning through his report on the screen. 'Good work, Chris. Don't know where it's going to lead us, though. Let's see what the Guv wants to do about it. For now, can you drive me over to Oundle? I'm going to Jim Cook's barge.'

'Did you know the Cartwrights are going to get their boat back this afternoon?'

'I hadn't heard.'

'Two o'clock. My mate in forensics told me while you were in the interview with Stoke. While we're over there should we drop in on them? We could ask Mrs. Cartwright about her relationship with Hearst.'

'Good idea.'

Chris navigated his Focus along the route to Oundle. The single carriageway A43 made for slow progress. Lorries using the route to get between Northampton and Peterborough regularly clogged the artery throughout the day, but even this was preferable to the coronary inducing jams on the A14. At least on this road they were moving.

'About last night,' Chris began. They were on the outskirts of town, just past the domestic allotments on the right and getting into the the the flow of traffic.

'Less said about that, the better,' Sally said, trying to suppress the subject.

'Hear me out, please?'

'OK, about last night.'

'Well, all yesterday you were determined to get Tony out of your life. I thought last night we, um, shared a moment.'

Sally interrupted. 'Don't go all James Blunt on me, please,' she scrabbled about in her handbag, looking for something to do.

'It's difficult to find the right words.' He brushed off another interruption, Sally pointing at a van entering their road from the right. 'Look, the job's tough enough that we close our emotions off to the public. Lets not fall into that trap with each other. I meant I think we engaged together, shared an understanding.'

Sally relented. 'I wish circumstances were different, Chris, but there's Tony.'

'I can handle Tony.'

'We've seen the results of that,' that earned her a grimace. 'Sorry, cheap shot.'

'It's what he might to do when he's out of hospital that worries me,' Chris said. 'I've been thinking. Stoke and his missus seem to have an open relationship. Her sleeping with another bloke wasn't strong enough reason for him wanting the guy dead. In fact he's completely indifferent about it.'

'What's that got to do with Tony?'

'Well, he's had a go at you already. Would he take it further?'

'Look what happened on Friday, when he thought we were having an affair. He beat me up, remember. He didn't go for you. Tony's a coward, Chris. If he thought there was no future for us, I'm more worried he'd do something daft like jump of a bridge.'

'So you still have feelings for him?'

'It's hard to just close the door on someone, sometimes no matter what they've done, I don't want to send him over the edge.'

'I'd just like to know where I stand.'

'I can't answer that, yet, Chris. I'm sorry.'

Chris swallowed his reply. He realised his feelings were running away from him again and studied the road ahead.

Shit, shit, shit. That's twice you've been caught out you idiot, he scolded himself. Couldn't let it lie after last night could you. Took advantage of her when she was vulnerable instead of supporting her.

The route snaked its way across the rolling countryside, blurring ahead of the speeding car. Chris, too busy chiding himself, didn't notice his erratic driving.

Trousers do the thinking for you, do they? What was it, did your pride take a hit? Couldn't stand being knocked back and had to go in for another shot? Idiot.

'I'll give the station a call, shall I?' Sally said. 'Tell them where to send the ambulance.'

'What?' he snapped.

'Slow down a bit, can't you?'

'Oh.' He eased off the accelerator.

'Pull in there,' Sally pointed to a service station. 'We'll grab a sandwich.'

Relieved for the break, Chris parked up. He took the opportunity to fill the car up while Sally browsed the sandwich counter in the service station. The few minutes alone helped him calm down and pull himself together. He was surprised at how quickly he'd let Sally get under his skin. Was it the physical attraction that got to him, or was the urge to protect her playing on his machismo? He couldn't work it out. They'd played out the acts of posturing and point scoring, had circled one another like courting birds. All the time Chris had kept the barrier of her marriage in mind, stopping him from taking things further. Once that had been banished he realised he should have slowed things down, made sure they were ready for each other. The first time they'd had a meeting of minds he'd blown his chance with adolescent lust.

Just concentrate on the job, he told himself. When this case is over, think about asking for a transfer.

He was reminded of Soap's revelation that he'd been considered for the Sergeants board. Chris wondered whether he should apply anyway. It would mean a posting away from Kettering and Sally Whitelock. Kill two birds with one stone.

Sally stood in the queue among suited reps in sharp shirts and workmen with dried plaster and silicone sealant smeared on their joggers. She looked out of the window at Chris, petrol pump in his hand.

Why did you have to make things so complicated, she thought. A little bit of office flirting wasn't supposed to lead to this. Or was it just little bit of flirting? Chris Raine had something intriguing about him that she couldn't put her finger on. He'd recounted his experience in Afghanistan with frankness and a lack of bravado that had touched her. Why did men have to take things so quickly, move in too soon?

She thought of Tony lying comatose in hospital. Poor, shy, Tony. Her heart hardened. She vowed never to give him another chance to abuse her trust, abuse her body.

'That's you, love,' one of the workmen nudged her elbow.

Startled, she looked at the man in confusion. He pointed to the vacant till ahead of her.

'Thanks,' she smiled at the man and moved forward to pay.

Chris parked in the layby near the static moorings and they tucked into their pre-packed sandwiches. Chris swallowed a mouthful of cheese and pickle.

'Recognise that car?' he asked, pointing to another Ford Focus sharing the parking spot with them, a distinctive dent in its tailgate.

'Hazel Moran, Kettering Gazette,' Sally answered.

'Thought so. No prizes for guessing where she is. Shall we go and spoil her party?'

'Not yet. She'll only go back later. Finish your lunch.'

The ground descended steeply from the road along a stony track that led to the narrowboat moorings. Barely wider than a path, it was hemmed in by gorse and hawthorn bushes which gave a restricted view along the short but twisting route. Birds tweeted urgently among the branches. Wrens out-sang all others with loud, melodic voices, a portent for warmer weather to come. Around a tight bend they came across Hazel Moran on her way back to her car.

Although surprised to see the detectives, she quickly rallied. 'Ah, here comes the police swimming team,' she said. 'Off for another dip?'

'Been pestering our suspect, Hazel?' Sally asked, ignored the taunt.

'Just doing my job, DS Whitelock,' Moran replied. Her smirk almost a permanent feature, giving her the appearance of always having a nugget of information hidden away. 'Mr Cook was very concerned to hear about his old school pal.'

Where does she get it from? Sally thought. We've not long made the connection between Tony and Cook and here she is, already ahead of us and having spoken to Cook.

'What are you talking about?' Sally feigned ignorance, testing Moran to see how much detail she'd managed to extract from Cook.

'His mate is the one clinging to life in hospital,' Moran took the bait. 'The one with a police guard by his bed. Got to be a reason for that,' she said, eyes twinkling. Sally met the smug look. Moran had revealed she had sources in unlikely places. In this case it was probably a porter or a junior nurse, happy to receive a financial tip for a tip off.

'That's quick work, finding his friend so easily,' Sally commented. She'd been unsettled at Moran having the jump on them and had a disturbing feeling of confirmation that she really didn't know her husband.

'It wasn't too difficult,' Moran said. 'I was at school with both of them. The canning plant gave me Whitelock's name and I just followed up the school records and did my research.' Moran hesitated. She scrutinized Sally. 'Something, incidentally, I think I've probably not done thoroughly enough, Mrs. Whitelock?'

'Well done,' Sally retorted, annoyed but unsurprised Moran had made the connection. Whitelock wasn't that common a name. 'You should be a detective.'

Moran snorted.

'Funny, really,' she said. 'He was never keen on authority at school. Now I wonder, why would the husband of a Police Detective Sergeant be evading her colleagues?' She looked from one detective to the other, their stony stares giving nothing away. 'And from the description the factory workers gave me, you'll be the one who assaulted him,' she said, her gaze settling on Chris.

'Whitelock injured himself during a police pursuit,' he replied. 'If it gets reported as anything else, we'll be having words with you.'

'Did Cook tell you anything?' Sally asked, changing the subject

'I always protect my sources, Sergeant.'

Chris stepped forward, closer to Moran. 'You haven't forgotten we're also looking for a missing ten year old girl?' he said. 'I'm sure you wouldn't want to impede our progress in finding her.'

'Whatever appears in my story could come from numerous sources. I'm sure you can appreciate that.'

Sally joined Chris, crowding Moran in the narrow lane. 'We know you've been to visit Cook. Anything you write that connects Cook with Tony will be of police interest.' She leaned in close to Moran.

Sally could tell she'd hit a nerve. Moran met her

stare for a few seconds then blinked rapidly.

'You know how it is, people have a habit of opening up to the press more readily than the police,' she grumbled.

Moran seemed to be wrestling with some inner voice telling her to keep quiet. Her journalistic instinct found itself in conflict with her exposed position. 'They see their chance of getting their name in print and their mouths run away from them.' Moran's mouth showed no such impulse. 'And they think they don't have to worry about the shadow of prosecution for some minor misdemeanour.'

'Don't worry, we'll make sure he doesn't find out we got it from you,' Sally pressed. 'What did he say?'

Moran huffed, reluctant to betray her source. Eyes darting around as though looking for an escape. But Sally was right. Anything she revealed in her story that was of police interest could land her in a cell explaining why she withheld evidence.

'All I can say is you should ask Jim about his other school mates.'

Sally tucked her hand in a pocket and found her notebook. 'Let's have their names, then,' she said, pen poised.

'Sorry, that's all I'm saying.' Moran edged past the two detectives. Sally let her go, resisting the urge to grill the reporter about her husband. She was desperate to ask her what he'd been like as a boy. Wondered if she knew whether he'd been a bully back then, or had even been bullied. Had there been signs of what he'd one day become in those early years of his life? But to ask her would be to invite public exposure. Moran was right, people opened up to journalists unwittingly. Sally couldn't risk revealing the embarrassing details of her relationship to a reporter. She stood mute and allowed Moran to leave.

An exposed patch of muddy ground was the only reminder that Cook's Transit van had ever occupied the meagre scrap of land next to his narrowboat.

'D'you mind?' Chris asked Sally and nodded towards the boat.

'Be my guest,' Sally said, preoccupied with how much Moran knew of Tony's early life. She was happy to let Chris take the lead while she unscrambled her thoughts.

Chris walked the gangplank and knocked on the boat's small double doors. A dog barked inside. Chris threw a glance at Sally and waited for Cook to come to the door. When he didn't open up, Chris returned to the bank and called out.

'We know you're here, Cook,' he shouted. The dog's bark intensified. 'It's the police. Open the door.'

He watched the boat rock, as a silhouette dashed from one end to the other and back again. Eventually Cook opened the doors.

'I wasn't expecting anyone,' he slurred. 'I was asleep.'

'Sure you were, Cook,' Sally called over from the bank. 'Is your dog under control?'

'She's all right,' Cook said. He moped down the gangplank, arms straight with hands stuffed deep in the pockets of his dirty, skinny jeans. 'What do you want? I've already reported to the station this week.'

'We're not here to check your bail conditions, Cook,' Chris said. Not so cocky now, he thought.

'Looks like you'll be in for a stretch for those lawnmowers.'

Cook shrugged.

'Our uniformed colleagues searched your boat.'

Cook showed no sign of concern. Chris knew he would already have checked and found out the police had taken a small quantity of cannabis taped under a drawer in the galley.

'I'll bet they didn't have to look far to find that little stash. Loads of hiding places on one of these things,' he said, remembering his search of the Cartwrights boat the previous week, 'let alone the vegetation along the bank, eh?'

'You can look all you want.' Cook stood aside from the gang plank.

Instead of accepting the invite, Chris turned and began walking around the perimeter of Cooks allotted mooring space. 'Was Tony into drugs?' He called from a spot along a line of bushes that faced the river.

Cook ran, almost skipped with his hands stuck in his pockets, over to Chris.

'Keep it down, will you?' he hissed. 'I don't need the neighbours hearing about drugs. They're not into all that.'

'Where you're headed, mate, you won't have to worry about these neighbours,' Chris said.

'I won't get a custodial for those mowers,' Cook sniffed. 'I didn't nick 'em anyway,' he added, too quickly.

'I've been through your records, Cook. You've had too many let-off's already,' Chris made a show of peering into the bush, freeing an aged carrier bag from the grasp of the thorny branches. The bag fell apart in his hands, faded scraps carried away on the light breeze. 'No, you'll be spending some time inside for this one,' he brushed flakes of old plastic from his hands.

'They gotta prove it, yet,' Cooks defiance made a shaky return, convincing no-one. He dragged his hands from his pockets, pulling a crushed pack of cigarettes with them. He lit one of the crooked tabs.

Sally had moved closer to the boat and was peering through one of the windows. Cook's dog resumed its sentry duty, barking at her through the glass.

Cook edged back to his boat and brought the dog, an Alsation, out. The animal jumped onto the roof of the barge and Cook stood at the stern comforting it, kneading the back of its neck with a hand.

'Easy, Jet,' he soothed his pet. Sally stifled a giggle at Cook's inadvertent pun.

'Nice looking dog,' Chris said. 'Who's going to look after it while you're away?'

Cook didn't answer. He just looked more glum

and stared at the river.

'Look, we know Hazel Moran's been here,' Chris said. 'She told you about Tony Whitelock, didn't she?'

'What's that got to do with the mowers?'

'Nothing. We just need to know what he might have told you.'

'Told me nothing. He didn't know about the mowers.'

'You went to school with him?'

'Yeah.'

'And Hazel Moran, too?'

'Different class,' Cook sniffed in dismissal. He could have been referring to classroom or status, but Chris got the impression she'd been out of Cook's circle of friends.

'You keep in touch with any other's from school?'

Cook said nothing.

'Hazel seemed to think so,' Chris pressed.

This earned a smirk from Cook. Chris whispered a few words to Sally. In the silence a cable clanked against the mast of a small wind turbine that fed power to Cook's boat. The smell of cooking drifted over from one of the other boats moored at the riverside.

'You know, we could make things easier for you,' Chris approached Cook again.

'Oh yeah? How?'

'We could arrange for a non-custodial sentence on the mowers.' Chris took a long look at Cook's dog. 'Be a shame to send Jet to a dog home.'

'I told you, I didn't nick 'em,' Cook reiterated, but with less conviction than before.

Chris shook his head. 'That's not going to wash, Cook. Your prints are all over them. Look, we could persuade our boss to change the charge to possession of stolen goods. And if you plead guilty, that would keep you out of jail.'

Cook thought about this. 'Speak to him now,' He demanded.

Chris walked a few feet away, out of earshot, and

made the call. After explaining the situation to Crighton, he returned and passed the phone to Cook. Cook listened for a few minutes, nodding occasionally and checking some of the details with Crighton. He handed the phone back to Chris.

'OK, Sir?' Chris asked on the line.

'Shouldn't be a problem, Raine,' Crighton replied. 'You'd better hope it's worth it.'

Chris finished the call, hoping for the same.

'Let's have it, then, Cook,' he said.

'OK, but you didn't get this from me.' Cook became agitated. He ushered his dog back into the narrowboat, shut the doors and rested his forearms on the roof, head bowed, clasped in his fingers. He stood there for a minute, psyching himself up.

'Me and Tony used to work the fields together, potato picking. Before the Poles came along and took all the jobs.' He lit another cigarette. 'Used to get a bit of blow from a mate who got us the job there. His dad's the gang leader on the farm.'

Chris's expectations deflated. This wasn't the revelation he'd hoped for. A small-time cannabis dealer wasn't likely to send them into the arms of their killer.

'Right?' he said, waiting for more. Sally half-turned away, losing interest.

'That's it. Hazel asked about getting hold of some. Seemed keen when I said we were still in touch.'

'You think she's after cannabis?' Chris couldn't believe his bad luck.

'That's what I thought,' Cook looked confused, his revelation not having the reaction he'd expected.

'And Tony?' Sally asked, wondering what involvement Tony might have had in drugs. She'd never suspected him in the past.

'Tony?'

'What did he tell you about your mate?'

'Nothing,' Cook's frown deepened. 'You asked if I stayed in touch with anyone else from school. We both did.'

This was getting worse. Whatever Cook thought he was divulging, his idea of what was important news was at cross purposes to Chris's.

'And Tony gets his weed from this guy, too?' Sally asked.

'Tony doesn't touch the stuff,' Cook said. 'They're just mates.'

What a waste of time, Chris thought. All the effort and persuasion in getting Cook to open up and the trail goes cold, just like that.

'OK, Cook. I don't know how well this is going to help us reduce your charges, but we'll do what we can,' Chris said, indicating to Sally that they should leave. 'What's your mate's name?'

'Matt Stoke.'

CHAPTER 18

'Who's Matt Stoke?' Crighton asked, his voice issuing from the car's stereo speakers. Chris had connected his phone via bluetooth once he and Sally had reached the car. They'd left Cook contemplating whether his revelation would be worthy of a reprieve.

'That's what we were thinking,' Sally answered from the passenger seat. She and Chris had discussed the possibilities during their walk back to the roadside. 'We think that if he's related to John Stoke then we might have a connection with Tony. Someone told him to get that box from Chris's house and this could be the link.'

'OK,' Crighton's disembodied voice crackled in the car. Chris adjusted his stereo to take some distortion out of the sound. 'Raine, I've got your search results on the truck we heard at the quarry. If it's the one we think it is, there's another Stoke to investigate.'

'Yeah, I saw Richard Stoke on the results, Sir. Could be a relation.'

'I'll follow that up from here. Have you heard about the scene of crime? Forensics are releasing the boat today.'

'Yes, Guv,' Sally replied. 'Chris told me. We're going there now to speak with the Cartwrights.'

'Keep me informed.' Crighton said.

'Did you get anything out of the foreman, Sir?' Chris asked.

'No more than I did out of Stoke. His command of the English language has dried up since last night so we had to get on the phone to the language translation service. You know how painful that is.' Chris knew all right. Once the defendant lost the ability to hide behind language, they generally clammed up. They pretended to misunderstand the questions, forcing numerous repeats and gave little away.

Crighton signed off the call and the stereo reverted to a tune on the radio.

'When we get to the Marina, Chris, can you divert Mr. Cartwright away from his wife?' Sally asked. 'I want to ask her about her affair with Hearst and I want to give her a chance to be open with me.'

'Yeah, good idea,' Chris said. He remembered his visit to the Ellis's at the weekend. If he'd known Geoff Ellis had been home, he'd have approached Mrs. Ellis more cautiously.

They soon arrived at Oundle Marina, only a couple of miles from the permanent moorings. The site manager directed them to where 'Mathilda Way' lay berthed, around the back of an area where second hand boats for sale creaked on their mooring hitches, awaiting new owners.

Innocuous and anonymous among the other boats, Mathilda Way gave no indication of being home to the remnants of a brutal murder barely a week ago. Once more Chris cupped his hands around his eyes and peered into the cabin. Forensics had gone to town on the décor. The wooden panels that lined the cabin had been stripped out around the area of the corpse, along with the carpet. The boat looked as though it was midway through a re-fit.

The man from Forensics hovered around the Marina, eyeing up the craft for sale. Chris had seen him around Jed's lab in Northampton occasionally.

'See anything you like?' Chris asked the man.

'Wouldn't mind one of these,' he said, pointing to a thirty foot river cruiser.

'It might be a river boat,' Chris commented, 'but that's a salty price tag.' he pointed to the spec. sheet pinned to the craft. It displayed a price way outside anything Chris could afford. The forensics man indicated the cheaper offerings.

'Maybe when I'm nearer sixty,' Chris conceded. Even the low end stuff, mid-1970's boats that were barely more than empty shells with flaking paint, were too expensive for Chris to consider even if he were interested.

'Maybe,' the man said. He looked close to retirement. Chris wondered whether the man would survive the round of job cuts heading for the force, whether he'd stay long enough to afford his dream.

And what of me, he thought. What are my dreams?

The last few days had felt like he was just getting by, taking each one as it came. He watched a family of ducks swimming towards the pontoon, probably looking for food. No bread for them today. His thoughts were interrupted by the arrival of the Cartwrights. Sally called him over.

Chris took his cue and invited Alec Cartwright over to the boat with the Forensics officer.

'You should probably wait with Detective Sergeant Whitelock, ma'am,' he suggested to Maureen Cartwright. 'Mr. Cartwright will let you know when it's OK to go in.'

Sally took the woman's arm and led her to the Marina cafeteria. Alec Cartwright looked grateful to be free from his wife.

'It's been difficult, this past week,' he confided to Chris while they waited for the man from Forensics to find the right key to open the boat. 'She won't stop going on about the murder. How we could have been on board when the killer broke in. I've tried telling her he must have waited for us to be away from the boat before coming, but she won't have it.'

Chris held out a hand, offering access to the boat. Cartwright hesitated, shoulders hunched and mouth set in a grim line. He took a deep breath before entering his repatriated domain. Chris followed on to find him standing slack jawed in the middle of the cabin.

'It's a good job Maureen didn't come in,' Cartwright said, scanning the interior. 'What a state.'

'I'm sorry about the mess, Sir,' the Forensics man said. 'It was unavoidable, unfortunately.' He gave a sympathetic shrug.

'I understand,' Cartwright said, running a hand along the bare skin of the boat's outer wall. 'I doubt we'll be coming back after today. We've both lost the enthusiasm for boating. Seeing the boat in this state would break Maureen's heart, I think.'

'I know it's difficult, Sir,' Chris said. 'But can you tell me if there's anything unusual missing.'

Cartwright shot him an angry look. 'Half my boat's missing.' He immediately apologised. 'I'm sorry. You've done all you could for us. It's just, look at it.'

'Have a look through the bookcase, Mr. Cartwright. Are there any books in particular missing?'

'I don't know. I don't think so,' Cartwright took a cursory look through the titles.

Chris examined the book spines. They were mostly romance novels, probably Mrs. Cartwright's. There were a few thrillers by Ken Follett and Robert Harris, some Dickens classics and Defoe's Robinson Crusoe. 'Did you have a copy of The Count of Monte Cristo here?' Chris asked.

Cartwright stared at the books and thought for a minute.

'I've read it,' he said. 'But I'm trying to remember whether I had it here.' He ran a finger along the titles. 'Or did I borrow it from the library?' Chris left him for a minute, lost in his thoughts.

'Make him an offer for the boat,' he whispered to the forensics officer. 'Might get a deal out of him.'

The man considered this, scratching his chin with one of the keys. 'A bit insensitive at this time,' he eventually said. 'I might leave him my card, though.'

'So long as you don't mind it having been home to a corpse,' Chris raised his eyebrows.

'Adds to the character, if you ask me,' the man said, handing the keys and his business card over to Chris. 'I'll let you finish off with Mr. Cartwright. Tell him if he's keen on selling I might be interested.'

Chris saw the man off the boat and returned to Mr. Cartwright.

'I think we did have the book you mentioned,' Alec said. 'Maureen bought a job lot from a second hand book shop in Oundle, when we were fitting the boat out.' He surveyed the stripped-out area once more. 'Why would he take it? Was it important?'

'I'm not sure that it was, Sir,' Chris admitted. He guessed the killer had probably seen the book and taken it on a whim to be used as a final taunt to the victim.

'Are you any nearer to finding him?' Alec asked.

'We've made some progress,' Chris said. Then it hit him. They hadn't chased the Cartwrights up since the dead man had been identified. 'Did you know the Simon Hearst?' he asked.

'Operation Sharvor's only been running for a month but we've already apprehended a number of dangerous people.'

The voice on the other end of Crighton's phone belonged to Detective Inspector Andy Vane, a member of the Serious and Organized Crime Agency.

'We've had Richard Stoke on our radar for a while now, pretty much since the Operation began.'

'What's Op. Sharvor?' Crighton asked.

'It's a joint effort by SOCA, Customs, the UK Borders Agency and, surprisingly, VOSA, the Vehicle and Operators Service Agency,' Vane explained. 'It's working out of Victoria.'

Crighton nodded into the handset. London Victoria coach station was the main hub for passenger services traffic arriving from Europe. He imagined all sorts of illicit efforts were being tracked there by UK officials.

Vane told him about the coaches that rolled up every day, full of foreign hopefuls entering the country with European passports or work visas. Many of the immigrants milling around the luggage bays of their transport carried false documentation. Some collected a more serious cargo from the coach's holds. Contraband cigarettes sparked HMRC interest, the tax-man fighting hard to ensure he got his cut of the revenue due. SOCA was interested in drugs and human trafficking, and VOSA were there to check the road-worthiness of vehicles.

'Richard Stoke is a gang leader at a fruit and veg. farm in the Fens,' Crighton said. He'd checked Chris's estimate and found the two Stoke's were indeed brothers. 'I suppose there are no prizes for guessing which trough he's got his snout in?' Crighton asked, eager to get to the crux of the matter.

'Take your pick,' Vane answered. 'Aside from the vehicle defects, of course. We've observed him taking known smugglers away in his mini-bus, plus any number of workers who just disappear off our paper trail. They're supposed to register with their local tax office when they start working, but Richard Stoke's never seem to.'

'Why haven't you lifted him yet?' Crighton guessed what was coming.

'Every now and then we let enough suspects through so we can follow them. Try to find out the extent of the cartel,' Vane said. 'Of course, it goes against the grain of apprehending villains, but we need them to lead us to their masters.'

'Meaning John Stoke?'

'Could be, Paul. We're getting closer to identifying him as one of the ringleaders,' Vane's tone changed, grew more smooth, conciliatory. 'Paul, we need you to ease off of Stoke and his brother.'

Crighton caught his breath. He had half expected something like this but it still stuck in his craw when the request came.

'What do you mean?' he asked, anger creeping into his voice. 'I've got a manhunt in progress. Did you know the murdered man's daughter was taken at the same time?'

'Yes, Paul. I'm sorry. There's a lot at stake on this operation.'

'A lot at stake? The life of a young British girl is a lot to stake.' Crighton was almost shouting now.

Vane back-pedalled a touch. 'We're not saying

don't bring him in. Just don't let him know we're on to him about any of this. We'll not stop you investigating the murder and kidnap, but you can't connect any of that investigation with our operation.'

'I see. And what if the motivation for the murder is drugs?'

'Simple,' Vanes voice recovered its edge. 'You have to back right off.'

There was a long silence as Crighton digested this.

'You've put me in a tough spot, Andy,' he said.

'I'm sorry, Paul,' Vane said. 'Orders from on high.'

Sally sat across from Maureen Cartwright in Oundle Marina's cafeteria. Two plain teacups rested on thick white saucers on the table between them. The woman behind the counter had recognised her and asked how she was coping with her boat. Maureen had supplied a short summary in return. Sally had listened and saw a woman almost disinterested with life. Lines etched her eyes and forehead, and untended grey hairs glinted through her brown hair in the light. A shapeless woollen cardigan hung from her rounded shoulders.

'What woman wouldn't be flattered,' Maureen was saying. 'I was only forty, but to have a young and handsome man like Simon take an interest in me was such an intriguing surprise.'

Sally waited patiently Maureen to continue.

Only forty, she thought. It seemed an odd thing to say. Sally had seven years to go before reaching that milestone yet she didn't feel a day over twenty-five. But wait, she was already halfway between how old she saw herself and that dreaded age. She suddenly felt the years spinning behind her, almost out of control.

Sally looked at Maureen Cartwright in a different light. By the sounds of it, her life really had started at forty.

'He used to work for us,' Maureen continued. 'Sales.'

'Stone Masonry?' Sally asked.

'What? No. Kitchen furniture. Alec and I had a small business back then.'

'What happened?' Sally prepared herself to hear another sad story of Simon Hearst's womanising.

Mrs. Cartwright stirred her tea, the spoon loose in her hand. 'I was the Company Secretary. Alec managed the manufacturing side of the business and I did the accounts. We brought Simon in to cover sales. It wasn't long before he had me completely under his spell.' She stared into her tea. 'He would make all these silly promises of making me rich and pampered.'

'Sounds like the Simon Hearst I've read about,' Sally commented.

'Yes,' came the flat response. 'I went along with it because life with Alec had hit a rut.' For a moment, a splash of colour rose in Maureen's cheeks and her eyes flashed with energy. 'Simon was young and, invigorating. Of course how could I have known he was only after one thing?'

'The business?' Sally guessed. From Maureen Cartwright's account he'd not had to work too hard for the other.

The life ebbed from Maureen's face again. 'In the background he'd set up his own rival business. Bit by bit, he ran down our company, undercutting our prices.'

'And you didn't notice anything because you were enthralled by him,' Sally concluded. She reached for her tea.

'Worse than that, Sergeant. I actively helped him.'

Sally nearly dropped her cup. 'Why?'

'I've told you, he'd promised me the world. All I had to do was help him win the contracts, then when Alec's business was on its knees, I'd leave him and move in with Simon.'

Once more, Sally had to readjust her appraisal of the woman she shared the table with.

'But you're still with Alec,' she said. Something must have gone wrong with the lovers' pact.

'Simon dropped me like a stone when he'd taken

enough business to survive on his own.'

Sally blew across her cup, sipped the tea and watched Maureen. The woman scanned the cafeteria dispassionately.

'It's been a long time, Sergeant,' she said, all emotion drained from her voice. 'Alec never new about the affair. His head was too deep in design and manufacture. I'd prefer to keep it that way if possible.'

'He must know by now that it was Simon who was killed. The papers are full of the story.'

'He knows,' Maureen conceded. 'He's bitter about what Simon did to us, but thought it was a coincidence that he ended up in our boat.'

'And do you?'

'I don't know. It's been ten years since I last saw Simon. We moved to Peterborough shortly after the business went under. Alec thinks the move was his idea but it didn't take much coercion to get us away from here.'

'You keep returning here, though,' Sally said. 'You kept the boat.'

'Yes, Alec's love. Or it was until this happened.' She began collecting her things together. 'I hope he gets rid of it now. I don't think I could face it, knowing Simon ended up in there.' A morsel of regret flashed across her eyes.

Sally nursed a much stronger drink in the pub at Oundle where she and Chris had decamped to. Chris had settled on a coke and a packet of crisps.

'Seven days,' she said, staring at her glass.

'I know,' Chris said. 'We can't blame ourselves. There's been a lot else going on.'

'Yes, but the Guv questioned the Cartwrights the very day after the murder. How did we miss this?'

'We didn't have an ID on the corpse then, Sally. And when we did get one, the trail took us elsewhere.'

'I suppose so. What do you think to Maureen Cartwright's story?'

'Sounds plausible enough.' Chris ran through his notes again.

'It's shocking that she could run her own business down like that.'

'Seems like Hearst was quite a charmer,' Chris said.

'The marriage must have been in trouble for her to seriously consider a future with Hearst.'

'Yeah, it makes you wonder how the Cartwrights have kept together afterwards, doesn't it?'

'I suppose the rejection from Hearst spurred Maureen on to making the relationship with her husband work. If she didn't have the nerve to make a break alone, that suggests to me she needed to stay with Alec to regain some self-esteem.'

Chris shot a glance at Sally but she wasn't looking at him, possibly ignoring the parallel with her own relationship.

'I guess Maureen Cartwright could've confided in Diane Ellis,' he offered, moving the conversation on. 'That might explain how Geoff Ellis knew about the affair. If Diane passed the news on, that is.'

Sally thought about this. 'So could Ellis and Cartwright have worked together? Killed Hearst and dumped him on the boat?'

'It doesn't add up, Sally. First, their alibi's are tight. They were in the pub on the night Hearst was dumped but, unless all four of them were in on the plot, the husbands wouldn't have been able to get back to the Ellis's house without raising suspicion in the women. And would they be able to keep the women quiet?'

'So maybe all four were involved.' Sally suggested. 'Both women had affairs with Hearst. Both had been humiliated.'

Chris held a crisp in front of him, using it as a pointer, running down his list of notes. The time-line could be made to fit. The logistics of moving the corpse was an easier operation for two men than one. But something stopped him from drawing a conclusion.

201

'Why dump the body on Cartwright's boat?' He thought aloud. 'It just draws suspicion straight to them.'

'Maybe that's why they did it,' Sally suggested. 'Hidden in plain sight. After all, it's taken us a week to join the dots up.'

'Yes, but that's just it. We did join them up. And it just doesn't seem realistic to me.'

'Why not?'

'Maureen Cartwright's affair finished ten years ago. If she'd confided in Diane Ellis, do you think Diane would have had her affair at all?'

'When did Diane go with Hearst?'

Chris checked his notes. 'Three years ago.'

'So, maybe they got talking after Hearst had finished with Diane,' Sally said. She didn't hold much belief in the theory but was happy to play devils advocate to draw out any inconsistencies.

Chris frowned and crunched his crisp. 'Have those two men got it in them to actually behead someone? It's a gruesome way to go and none of them seem the ghoulish type, much less have access to an industrial circular saw.'

'What does Ellis do for a living?' Sally asked.

'Accountant, I think.'

'Hmm,' Sally had to concede the idea of Cartwright and Ellis joining forces to exact revenge on Hearst was beginning to lose its credence, unless one of them cut stone on a grand scale as a hobby. She took a large sip of wine.

'Off the painkillers already?' Chris noted.

Sally nodded. 'Still hurts, though. This is taking the edge off of it.' She raised the glass in a salute.

'Go careful, eh?' he said.

'It's OK, you're driving.'

Chris shrugged. He lifted his car keys from the table. 'We should tell the Guv what we've found.' Sally quickly finished her drink and followed him out to his car.

The drive back to Kettering was quiet. Sally had nodded off and snored softly in the passenger seat. Chris looked over at her and felt a pang of sorrow. Recovering from the beating must be taking its toll out of her physically. A wave of fatigue washed over him, too. Fretting over Sally the previous night had knocked his energy. He drove straight to her house, bypassing the station.

He shook her gently after parking outside her home.

'Sally,' he called, gently rousing her.

'Wzzsst?' She woke slowly and stretched in her seat. 'Sorry. Knackered,' she mumbled. 'We at the station?'

'We're at yours. You should get some sleep,' he suggested. 'Give it a few hours and you'll be able to take some more painkillers. You should do that.'

'Got to do report for Guv' The shroud of sleep lingered around her as she fumbled around the foot-well and managed to corral her handbag.

'I'll do that, Sally. Don't worry. See you tomorrow.' Chris waited until she'd closed her front door before trying to connect with his boss. Crighton's phone went straight to voicemail. He left a brief summary of their visit to Oundle and headed home.

'Don't run away now,' the man snapped into the receiver. 'Jump now and you will alert the Police. I will settle this.'

The man marched back and forth along a well-worn path in his office carpet, the pile crushed and faded from what must have been many similar stressful conversations prior to this.

'I'm telling you, Stoke, I will deal with it. Your brother is helping me and after tomorrow, we need not worry about the girl.'

He paused.

'Do not test me,' he hissed after a listening for a while. 'One way or another, she will be gone. Do not get in my way.'

CHAPTER 19

After he'd got home, Chris had fallen asleep on his sofa watching a wildlife program: Lions and leopards stalking gazelles through the African savannah. A plate of congealing gravy rested on a tray on his lap, the remnants of another hearty contribution from Ida next door. It jumped and clattered back down on his legs when he jerked awake.

He lifted the tray and carried it through to the kitchen. The dream that had woken him replayed through his head. Part of the television program he'd fallen asleep to had got mixed up with his recent experiences at Stoke's quarry. Lions had trapped him in the underground room and were circling the open trap door, waiting for him to expose his head at the opening. Somehow the pipe he'd fled through on his earlier visit had appeared in the room and he'd escaped again, only to find another big cat ready to pounce at the other end. 'A leopard never changes his spots,' the animal said, before it leaped at him.

Chris was in no doubt that Hearst had been a predator. He'd prowled after women all his life. After stalking and capturing them he'd callously stripped away their dignity with no more regard to their feelings than a big cat would have for its kill. Like the animal, his hunger was never sated for long.

The next morning he rose early and decided to walk to Kettering station. He turned his collar up at his door. The early morning grey sky matched the slates on the house opposite. Despite a broken night filled with dreams he walked the ten minutes to the station with renewed vigour.

He aimed straight for the remaining boxes of documents they'd recovered from Hearst's house and began digging for information on the efforts to run down Cartwright's kitchen furniture business.

Luckily Hearst had filed his documentation by year and Chris soon found a trail of contract acquisitions from around the time Maureen Cartwright confessed to having had the affair. He built a picture of Hearst's deeds and by cross-referencing them with a copy of the man's company accounts Chris could see the business grow from 1997 through to the millennium. After that time the contracts seemed to dry up. This would have been shortly after he'd finished the affair with Maureen Cartwright.

Not the entrepreneur you believed you were, eh Hearst? he thought.

Chris unearthed the winding up order for Hearst's business in documentation from 2003. He wondered if the thrill of coercing Maureen Cartwright into relinquishing her contacts and contracts had been the real driving force behind Hearst's actions. At its height, his business had employed ten staff and had a turnover of £4million per year. Profits were impressive too at half a million. But the downturn looked sharp and Hearst had struggled in the last two years of business before closing the company.

DI Crighton arrived at CID looking surprised to see Chris.

'What brought you in so early, Chris?' he asked.

'Morning Sir. After speaking with Mrs. Cartwright, I thought we should have built up a more thorough profile of Hearst's business dealings,' Chris replied. 'If we'd done this earlier maybe we'd have been better placed to quiz the Cartwrights.'

Crighton looked on the computer monitor at the beginnings of Chris's report on Hearst's business dealings.

'How does this get us closer to the killer?' He asked.

Chris shrugged. 'I don't know yet. But something caught my attention last night.' He didn't want to reveal his dream to his boss, so ploughed on with no further explanation. 'If Hearst had used Mrs. Cartwright to steal business from her husband, there's a possibility he'd done it before, or did it again later. A leopard doesn't change it's spots, Guv.'

Crighton gave Chris a strange look. 'Strange idiom to use, son, but I get where you're coming from.'

When the boss referred to him as 'son', Chris found it generally meant he was being indulged. In a good way. He carried on.

'I've just got to 2007. He'd been working for someone else since 2004, a Stonemason in Corby. He started his own business in '07, but I haven't found anything unusual about his contracts.'

'OK son. Let's come back to this a bit later,' Crighton's tone caught Chris's attention. He looked up at his boss. He looked old this morning and a sadness tugged at his jowls.

'Sir?'

'Grab a brew and meet me in my office, lad,' he sighed and turned to go.

Chris knocked on the door a few minutes later. On a nod through the window from Crighton, he entered.

'Cheers,' Crighton said, taking his mug.

'What's up, Sir?' Chris's asked. His mind had been spinning during the last few minutes as to what could be eating the DI. Could Tony Whitelock have died in hospital?

'Sit down lad, I've got a bit of bad news.'

Chris did as he was asked, his curiosity growing by the second.

'DS Whitelock phoned me this morning.'

Oh shit, thought Chris. She's complained about me kissing her the other night.

'Sally has tendered her resignation, effective immediately.' The air thickened in the silence that permeated the room.

Chris regained control of his jaw and worked it

around so he could speak.

'Why, Sir?'

Crighton, lost in his own thoughts, shrugged himself back to life.

'Her husband has regained consciousness at the hospital, and the doctors have given an early prognosis of moderate brain damage,' he explained. 'DS Whitelock has decided that she needs to be with her husband during his recovery. I know,' he said, catching Chris's incredulous look. 'I couldn't believe it either.'

Chris shook his head slowly, the news finally sinking in. So, she's ignoring all our efforts to support her and is going back to him. He could hear the Guv talking but he couldn't tear his thoughts away from what Sally had done.

'. . . at least until we can get someone transferred in,' Crighton was saying.

Chris looked up. 'Sorry, Sir. We do what until we get someone in?'

'I need someone who can run this investigation with me,' Crighton said. 'You're acting Sergeant now.'

'No, no,' Chris said, his head light with trepidation. 'I can't do it.'

'Why not?' Crighton demanded.

'I, er. I mean, we can persuade her to retract, can't we?'

This was terrible. It wasn't how he'd hoped to be promoted. What would Sally say when she found out he was taking her place?

'I've tried, son, trust me,' Crighton said. 'It's not that I don't think you're good enough,' he quickly added. 'I was going to recommend you to the board soon, anyway.'

'Um, thanks Sir.' Chris tried to look surprised and not give away Soap's revelation almost a week ago. 'Maybe I could talk to Sally. I've been working closely with her this week. I think I know what might be on her mind.'

'Oh? What?'

Chris immediately regretted his words. How could he tell the DI that he and Sally had been getting close? Crighton was bound to frown upon it.

'Er, she, er, she feels some misplaced loyalty to him. One minute she says she's through with him, the next she's not so sure. I think she would benefit with some proper counselling, at least before throwing away her career.'

'Well, if you think you can help, you're welcome to try,' Crighton said. 'God knows we need to keep all the experienced staff we can at the moment.' Crighton began sifting through the paperwork on his desk, the conversation over.

Chris stayed in his seat. 'Sir, did you get anywhere with Cook's friend, Matt Stoke?'

Crighton looked up.

'Sorry, rude of me,' he admitted. 'I did update the incident board.' He rose and led Chris out to the whiteboard. 'Matt Stoke's father is Richard Stoke.' He pointed to a new list he'd added on the board. 'Richard Stoke is the owner of the MAN truck we heard at the quarry.' He pointed to an arrow drawn in black marker that connected Richard Stoke to the truck, and another arrow who's destination was the Superior Mason and Stone quarry. A final arrow, in red, led to John Stoke. 'Richard and John Stoke are brothers.'

Chris followed the DI's finger as he traced the connections.

'Cook said that Matt's father employed him and Whitelock at a farm for a while,' he commented.

'Richard Stoke is the Gang Master at a vegetable farm in the fens. He'll have hired the young men to help pick sugar beet or potatoes.'

'Why does a farm truck need to visit a stone quarry?' Chris mused.

'I'm still working on that. He may have known his brother was on site and went to visit him. He could have been sent there to deliver or collect something.'

'While we were stuck underground.'

'Hmm?'

'We both got the feeling we were being held there on purpose. That they hadn't simply forgotten we were on site.' Chris explained. 'You thought Stoke was playing with us, but what if he was holding us to buy some time. To get something off site that could be incriminating?'

'Such as more sacks like the ones you saw being moved previously?'

'Or something that had been chained up in that room.'

'Molly Gowland?' Crighton asked. Chris nodded. It was certainly possible that something had been removed from the site. They'd been trapped underground for over an hour.

Crighton ushered Chris back into his office and leafed through a file amongst the paperwork on his desk.

'Take a look at this,' he said. Chris skimmed over the document. It described the investigation in the the the drugs cartel that Crighton had been working on with the Serious Organised Crime Agency.

'You still think John Stoke has connections with a drugs operation?' Chris asked.

'I do. It's still with SOCA at the moment and I've been ordered to hold back in case I upset the whole investigation,' he took the paper back from Chris and stared at it himself, his lower jaw grinding in frustration.

'That's crazy, Sir. We've got a duty to find her. We should have an alert out for Richard Stoke, his truck, anything that might lead us to her.'

'Settle down, lad' Crighton said. 'Running around like headless chickens isn't going to get us anywhere. SOCA have have also stopped me from interviewing Theodore Black, Stoke's business partner.'

'He runs that Estate Agent's as well, doesn't he?' Chris asked, remembering Joe Alden's visit to the business.

'That's right,' Crighton said. 'We've found out his real name. Ciernik - It's Slovakian for 'black'. I suppose he changed to the English translation to give him more credibility over here.'

'Why is Black so important that he can't be questioned," Chris asked.

Crighton slipped another sheet of paper out of the file. Chris read it through.

'Black, or rather Ciernik, was one of Stoke's contacts in the early '90's, when he was selling holiday homes in Yugoslavia,' Crighton explained. 'SOCA believe Ciernik is heavily involved in the importation of drugs into this area.'

'So why don't they just take him in?' Chris couldn't get his head around his bosses inaction.

'They have to go carefully on these operations, lad. If they spring the trap too early, they may get one or two players, but the rest of the cartel dissolves into the background. SOCA will be working closely with the Met. and Interpol, as well as us and other regional forces. It's frustrating, but the wrong move could bring the whole case crashing down.'

'So why did you question Stoke, yesterday?' Chris asked, confused. 'weren't you worried you'd jeopardise the investigation then?'

Crighton shook his head, and rested on the edge of his desk.

'No, Chris. You have to picture these as different scenarios. Grilling him about his wife's infidelity wouldn't alert him to our investigations about the drugs case, and it allowed us to drop the odd oblique question in about that without raising his suspicions. I don't know if Hearst was involved in the drugs ring, or if Stoke really did know him but when we had the opportunity to quiz Stoke on something unrelated, we took it.'

Chris nodded, trying to keep up.

'Let's say Stoke did kill Hearst out of revenge over the affair,' Crighton explained. 'And we convicted him without connecting it to the other case, we'd have been able to control the situation better. Nailing Stoke with the murder would have taken him out of the picture.'

'He'd be able to communicate from prison though, wouldn't he? It happens all the time. Smuggled mobile phones, prison visits used to pass on orders,' Chris said.

'True,' Crighton agreed. 'But the cartel would still be unaware that we were watching them. And with Stoke's influence severely limited, we'd expect others in the cartel to make some unusual moves - make up for the absence of Stoke's skills. It could even help us identify previously unknown players.'

Chris understood Crighton's logic. It made him feel like a very small cog in the machine. Having not been party to the overall investigation, and having been distracted by Sally, he was brought down to earth with a bump.

'Did you tell Sally any of this?' he asked.

'Not much. I didn't want it influencing her approach to the the murder investigation. It's only since you've started making connections with the businesses that I felt I needed to tell you more.'

'But what we've dug up only comes down to infidelity. Even that's shaky. There's no drugs connection in any of Hearst's accounts that I've seen,' Chris was confused once again.

'Stoke's accounts seem clean, too. At least those that we've been able get from Companies House. I've opened up the security on the files so you can access them on the Server. Doesn't mean there isn't a connection, Chris,' Crighton emphasised. 'I need you to be on your guard from now on. If you see any link to drugs you've got to back off and let me know,' he paused to let the order sink in. 'Send Alden in when he gets here, will you?'

Crighton shifted from his perch on the edge of the desk.

'Sir?'

Crighton looked up from his chair, expectation in his gaze.

'Do you suppose Stoke might have had Hearst

killed? Had a contract out on him?' Chris asked.

'It's possible,' Crighton agreed. 'So far, we don't really know how far Stoke's influence reaches. If he is responsible for Hearst's death, he may have used henchmen, or he may have worked alone. He looks strong enough.'

Chris dipped his head and removed himself from the office. He returned to his desk via Sally's. Her workspace was strewn with papers and empty cups. Just like her car, he thought. What a tip. He rifled through the documents in her drawers and on the desktop. The scope of the cases she had been working on brought home to him how busy his workload was about to become. If he was to take over all her work it would mean a few late nights catching up with it all.

'Why did you have to resign?' he said, the walls of the empty room soaking up his words. The extra work didn't worry him so much as whether Sally had done the right thing by leaving so abruptly. He concentrated on retrieving any paperwork she might have that concerned the murder.

A few minutes later he was seated back at his own desk working feverishly through a sheaf of fax papers, shaking his head in disbelief. Hearst's agreements with English Heritage had been lying on Sally's desk undisturbed for nearly two days.

All that sweating over the missing box of documents, he thought, and when we get copies of some of them they get overlooked.

Chris had no accounts information to match them up to, as he had with the Cartwright's kitchen furniture business, but he created a spreadsheet on his computer with the details on the faxes - dates, work agreed, quotes, invoices. The majority of work involved repair work to historic buildings. Stately homes, churches, public buildings and the like.

He remembered Hearst's foreman telling him the quarry had been supplying English Heritage listed buildings with stone for around eighteen months. He'd have to check who had been the previous suppliers, but he had an idea where to start looking.

He cross-referenced the chronology of contract approvals with the timespan in which Gemma Stoke had admitted to seeing Hearst. There was no correlation early on in the affair, where Chris guessed Hearst had been embedding his claws into Gemma. But later, once Hearst had earned her trust, Chris imagined there was plenty of scope for him to coerce business information out of her.

But what about the contracts themselves? The Council would approve and distribute grants to applicants, the owners of the buildings. They in turn would engage with local firms to provide the materials and labour. Those firms would have to be authorised by the Council and English Heritage to ensure they delivered the required quality and value for money. How had Hearst managed to persuade the Council that his company was best placed to fulfil the orders?

According to Sally's conversation with Maureen Cartwright, Hearst usually stole her husband's contracts by undercutting his quotes, documents that she'd willingly handed over to Hearst.

In this case, with the Borough Council responsible for authorising grants, even if Gemma Stoke had divulged her husband's tender information to Hearst how had Hearst managed to manipulate the Council to sign them over to him?

Chris guessed that most Councils would be influenced by the lowest price, but they would also have to persuade English Heritage and the buildings' owners that the company was reputable, as well as capable of doing the work. Winning these contracts wouldn't have been as easy as his previous conquest. Chris noticed in the list that the most recent work agreed had been signed off only a few weeks previously. Unlike the Cartwright scam, Hearst had been able to keep his new venture going after the demise of his affair with Gemma Stoke. Chris checked the Council signatory. Steven

Caulfield. Where had he heard that name before?

He looked up when he heard the door at the far end of the CID area open and Joe Alden let himself in. Chris checked his phone's clock. Nine on the dot.

'Checking up on me, Chief?' Joe asked as he sauntered across the room.

'No,' Chris said, embarrassed that he'd been caught out monitoring Joe's arrival time. 'Just surprised how quickly the time's going.'

Joe took his coat off and draped it over his chair.

'Soap, does the name Steven Caulfield ring a bell?'

Joe thought for a minute. 'Wasn't he the Council planner who authorised Hearst's planning permission on his house?'

Chris slapped the table. 'Of course. Cheers Joe.'

'What's he done?' Joe asked.

'I don't know yet, but Hearst might have had him in his pocket,' Chris said. 'Guv wants to see you.'

'What about?'

'You'd best just go in, mate.' Chris couldn't get his mouth around the words to tell Joe he was his new Sergeant. Best he hears it from the Guv, he thought. How much longer would he be able to call Joe 'mate'? His promotion was only an acting rank at the moment, but that would soon change, he was sure. The application papers to formally sign up for the Sergeant's board would soon drop into his pigeon-hole. He'd take the course, then likely be posted to a different station or even a different regional force. Although not unheard of, a newly promoted officer would rarely be able to stay at his current station. There was too much potential for friction with former peers. Jealous colleagues could cause trouble and old mates would invariably be asking for favours from their new senior officer.

Do you really want this? He asked himself.

Chris sighed and picked up his jacket. He didn't want to be around when Alden got out of the Guv's office. Joe would either be insufferably witty or surly with envy. Before Chris left the station he typed a quick email to Crighton and attached the spreadsheet he'd been working on.

CHAPTER 20

A thick smell of disinfectant filled Chris's nose when he passed through the main entrance of Kettering General Hospital into the reception area. A gaggle of people stood at the receptionist's desk arguing with a weary eyed woman sitting at a computer terminal, a black cardigan over her uniform staving off the air-conditioning that kept the atmosphere artificially cool. Chris tried to catch her eye by waving his warrant card, but she wasn't interested. Her eyes remained fixed on the terminal's screen while her fingernails tapped on the keys, all the time fending off the complaints of the irate group who sounded like they were trying to find a family member in the maze of wards.

Chris noticed an open door along from the reception desk and risked a peek through it. He remained unchallenged by the receptionist. Inside the room, a few nurses chatted. He tapped the door, silencing the room. One of the nurses eyed his warrant card and tutted, irritated to be drawn from her conversation.

'Sorry to bother you,' Chris began. 'I'm looking for someone who's probably in intensive care.'

'What's the name?' the nurse asked, walking over to a spare terminal next to the receptionist and logging on.

'Whitelock, Tony,' Chris said, following her. The original receptionist finally acknowledged his presence, throwing him a withering look. The nurse tapped on the keyboard.

'He's in ICU3. I'll have to come with you.'

Chris followed the nurse upstairs and to the end of a corridor. He realised why the nurse had to accompany him when he saw the locked doors blocking their path. The nurse swiped a plastic security key through a reader and they were in. The ICU rooms lined the wall opposite. To his left he could see a family room, doors open. It was occupied by a group of people sitting in mute apprehension. He couldn't tell from their vacant stares whether they waited in hope for good news or resigned anticipation of an inevitable passing.

He looked along the corridor and spotted Whitelock's room immediately. A uniformed officer was placed outside, seated on a plastic chair reading a motorsport magazine. The nurse left him at the door and returned to her post. Chris waved his warrant card at the officer.

'I see we've got uniform on the job, now,' he commented.

'Yeah, I don't think Soap could handle the pressure,' the officer joked.

Chris chuckled along with him. 'Is he in?' he nodded to the door.

'Yeah, but he's going for an CAT scan in a minute,' the uniform said. 'He's out of his coma but isn't in any shape to speak to anyone. Doctors reckon it'll be months before he talks again. Why are you here'

'I was hoping his wife would be here.'

At that moment, the door to ICU3 opened and Sally exited the room, red-eyed and clutching a glass of water.

'Thought I heard you,' she said. 'What are you doing here?'

'I need to speak to you, Sally. I can't believe you've resigned.'

Sally threw a brusque glance at the uniformed officer, then turned to inform the nurse inside that she'd be away for a while.

'I'll see him when he's back from the CAT scan,' she told her.

'Not MRI, then?' Chris asked as Sally marched him along the corridor away from the Intensive Care Unit. Kettering General had an excellent MRI facility on site.

'Not while he's hooked up to all the machines,' she replied, businesslike. 'Too difficult. CT is safer in his

217

condition. They'll do an MRI once he's breathing on his own and they can remove the ventilator and ICP monitor.' She looked at his blank face. 'Inter-Cranial pressure,' she continued the stolid narration. 'They drill a hole into his skull and measure how much pressure the brain is exerting and how well it's being managed with the drugs.'

'I heard he's out of the coma. Is he conscious?' Chris inquired.

'Not properly. They took him out of the induced coma but he's not conscious,' she said. 'He's having regular CAT scans to monitor his progress.'

'Is his brain damage permanent?'

'They say so. They won't know how bad it is for a while, yet.'

Sally led him back downstairs, past the WRVS shop with stuffed toys and get-well balloons filling its windows, to the small cafeteria next door.

The café wasn't busy and they had no trouble finding a quiet corner to talk.

'Are you OK?' Chris asked.

'I think so,' Sally replied, her gaze similar to those he'd seen in the ICU family room, upstairs.

'You sure you've done the right thing?'

'No.'

'You look tired.'

'I'm back on the Tramadol, they've made me a bit drowsy.'

'How many a day?'

She focused on him, her stare hardening. 'I don't know,' she snapped, 'Four? six?'

'OK,' he said, leaning back and raising his hands. 'But that's a big dose, Sally. The prescription was two a day, wasn't it?'

'So? How do you know, anyway?'

'I saw it on the bottle the other night.' He reached out and rested a hand on her shoulder. She flinched and turned away. 'They're 200mg tablets, Sally. Just be careful, eh?'

'I know,' she huffed. 'They help me sleep.'

'They're addictive. You're supposed to cut down the dose as the pain goes, not increase it. Go and see the doctor if you need help sleeping.'

'OK. Stop having a go.'

'I'm worried for you, that's all. I don't want to see you become dependant on them.'

Sally pulled a face.

'I'll be OK.' She rose from the chair and walked to a vending machine. Chris kicked himself for leaning on her so much about the pills.

Somebody has to tell her, he thought. She needs support, and that's going to be difficult if she doesn't come back to work.

Sally returned with a bottle of water and took deep swallows, the plastic crunching as the bottle collapsed in on itself. She watched him over the edge of the bottle.

'Thirsty?' he asked, eyebrows raised. He knew the Tramadol dosage she was taking would increase its side effects.

'Point taken,' Sally breathed heavily. She toyed with bottle, screwing and unscrewing the cap on its thread. 'Anyway, you're not here to give me medical advice. What do you want?'

He searched for the right thing to say. 'We need you back,' he shrugged.

'Tony needs me,' she said, blinking rapidly.

'You said you were finished the other day.'

'I can't just leave him,' she said. 'I still love him.'

'After everything he's done to you?'

'He can't hurt me any more,' she said.

Chris let her words hang between them for a minute. He mulled over what he should take from her statement. There would be little threat of violence in the relationship now, that was a given. She would have the upper hand, but at what cost? A career cut off in its prime. Years of patient care to come. Did she really know what lay ahead of her? She didn't deserve this.

And you put her in this position, Chris, he thought.

They sat in silence. Hospital visitors began milling around them prior to the morning's visiting hours. Dads corralled toddlers away from the toys in the WRVS window and steered them into the café, trying to catch a quick brew before visiting the maternity ward. A couple of worried looking middle-aged women sat down at a table near Chris, their conversation spilling over to him.

'It's good that she's out of Intensive Care, isn't it?' the first said, seeking reassurance from her companion.

'Where have they moved her?' her companion replied.

'High Dependency Unit. But that's got to be a step in the right direction hasn't it?'

'You'd hope so.'

Chris stood and indicated to Sally to follow.

'The place is filling up. We should give the table to someone,' he said, waving at a man who was looking around the room for an empty spot.

Chris and Sally walked outside to the hospitals main entrance. They watched an ambulance unload a stretcher into the Accident and Emergency ward over to their right.

'The Guv made me acting Sergeant,' he said. Sally glanced at him briefly then returned her attention to the ambulance.

'That's what you wanted isn't it?'

'Not like this,' he countered. 'Not in your place. Yeah, I'd like to move up but this seems wrong.'

'You'll be Inspector before you're thirty-five.'

'Maybe. That's not fast track, though. That's not what I'm in for. I'm happy to be time-served.'

Sally smiled. 'Very honourable.'

'I thought we'd be able to work together,' he continued. 'I'm sorry about how this came about, Sally, I really am. I'd happily step back if you want to return.'

She slowly shook her head.

Chris tried again. 'Why don't you take

compassionate leave? See how you think in a few weeks.'

'Guv's already offered me that. I don't think it'd work. Walking out in the middle of an investigation. How would I get any respect when I came back?'

'Nobody's judging you, Sally. Least of all, me.'

The ambulance crew finished dropping off their delivery and and the vehicle swept past the detectives on its way to the next call, sirens wailing and blue lights strobing off of their faces, Chris's flushed with blood, Sally's pale and waxy.

'I'll think about it. I have to see about Tony, first.'

'Just don't throw your career down the pan on a snap decision,' Chris implored. 'Get off the painkillers as soon as you can. I mean that. You're not thinking straight dosed up on Tramadol. Clear your head, then decide.'

'Thanks, Chris. I will.' She turned to go back into the hospital, arms folded, shoulders slumped. 'What's happening at work?' she asked, over her shoulder.

'I found the faxes that English Heritage sent you,' he said. 'Hearst won a whole bunch of contracts at the same time he was seeing Gemma Stoke.'

'Up to his old tricks again, then?' She stopped walking, a spark of interest in her voice.

'I think so. I'm going over to Stoke's. Speak to Gemma. Maybe she'll reveal more about her affair with Hearst.'

'Good luck with that,' Sally said. Fatigue crept back into her eyes and she resumed walking. Chris watched the hospital swallow her up and stood at the entrance for a minute. He hoped she'd heed his advice. She hadn't been taking the Tramadol long. It should be possible to wean herself off them, so long as she sought proper advice on coping with the recent stress. He worried for her though, given her recent track record in asking for help.

He shook his head and crossed the access road to the car park, head up, searching out his car amidst the other visitors. Something caught his eye. A dented tailgate.

Why is Hazel Moran here? he thought.

He returned to the hospital, entering through A&E this time. He'd guessed right. Moran stood in a corner of the waiting room, smart and alert amongst the day's influx of emergency cases. Sad looking people in various states of dress sat on a few lines of plastic chairs, some still in night-clothes and dressing gowns. Moran stood chatting to a man dressed in sports kit: tracksuit and trainers. Chris caught her eye and she extricated herself from the conversation.

'Come to question the victim?' she asked. They stood beneath a bulky television that hung precariously on a wall bracket.

'Victim?' he repeated, baffled.

'That'll be a no, then,' the cadence of her Irish accent taunting him. 'Although maybe victim isn't the right word.'

'What's going on?' he asked.

'Car crash,' Moran said. 'Just waiting for the air ambulance to come in.'

'Thought the paper would send a cub reporter for something like that.' Chris noticed his words had no effect on Moran. She didn't seem to be above taking the small jobs.

'Minor celebrity,' she said, adding credence to her presence there. 'Footballer. Plays for Kettering. That's his coach over there,' she pointed to the track-suited man. 'Seems like the wee lad enjoys racing around the county in his Mercedes. A touch too enthusiastically if this is anything to go by.'

The pair of them had begun to draw attention from the attendant throng of patients. The television above them was switched off, so they became the entertainment for the bored, anxious assembly. Chris ushered Hazel Moran out of the building so they could talk more candidly.

'I hate to ask, but I thought you'd be following the Hearst case?'

222

'You need to speak with your Chief Superintendent about that,' Moran replied. She dipped into her handbag, found a pack of cigarettes and lit one up. Across the open doors another woman, dressed in pyjamas, dressing-gown and slippers was doing the same. Chris wondered at the irony of smokers at a hospital. He'd been treated to the same view outside the maternity ward over from the car-park, when he'd dropped coins into the parking meter. Young, heavily pregnant women shared cigarettes with family and partners, oblivious or ignorant to the damage they were handing down to their potential offspring.

If people are so bothered about their health and well-being, he thought, why smoke? He waved Moran's exhaled smoke away.

Moran had also fished her Blackberry out of her bag and was checking it for emails.

'What's the Chief got to do with anything?' he asked.

'He and my Editor have come to an agreement,' she said. 'We're to tone down our reporting until further notice.'

'Oh,' Chris said, unable to find a suitable comment.

'I can see the instruction hasn't flowed down hill like most shit does,' Moran said, clearly put off by the situation.

Chris regained his composure. 'To be fair, it's us that's investigating. The papers are supposed to restrict their involvement to reporting.'

'You mean lap up your insipid press releases and wait patiently for an announcement? The media doesn't work like that any more, Constable.'

Chris scowled at the reference to his rank. He couldn't bring himself to declare his, admittedly acting, promotion yet. The rank sat uncomfortably in his mind at the moment in a mixture of elation and apprehension.

'The press should work the same as all civilians. Let the police do the investigating.'

'You think it's like the old days? These days even civilians are reporters. Newspapers and TV have to use any means they can to get the story in first.'

'The story has to be accurate, though. Otherwise innocent people get tarred when they're caught up in it.'

'Well, that story's going to have to wait,' Moran said. They'd both picked out the clatter of helicopter blades emerging from the distance. She stubbed her cigarette out and switched off her Blackberry.

'Wait. Do you have to go in straight away?' Chris asked, firing a look over his left shoulder to the direction of the helicopter landing pad. 'It'll be a while before you get any news from the emergency team.'

Moran stopped, her body already turned towards the A&E doors.

'What's up?'

Chris hesitated. He knew he would be breaking the rules by opening up to a journalist, but Moran's revelation about the reporting restrictions gave him confidence.

'Off the record?' he asked, seeking her assurance.

'Now, why would I agree to that?' Again the taunting lilt tripped through her orange lipstick.

He took a deep breath. 'If you can help me, I'll give you the exclusive when the Chief Super lifts the restrictions.'

'What can a little Detective Constable do for me?' she laughed. 'You didn't even know the agreement was in place.'

Chris bristled at her words.

'I'm the feet on the ground,' he countered. 'You don't get closer than that. You might get the facts from the press office at the end of the investigation, but I can give you the detail, the meat of the story.'

Moran considered his proposal. The noise from the air ambulance had grown closer and the helicopter could be heard landing at the back of the hospital.

'OK,' she relented. 'Off the record. What's eating you, DC Raine?'

'Simon Hearst,' he began. 'He had a knack of stealing from under his competitors noses. The latest were English Heritage restorations, issued by the County Council. I need to find out how he did it.'

'How am I supposed to help?'

'Don't you have close contact with the Council? A lot of the reporting in the local papers is about Council business.'

'We do get under their skin. And up their noses,' she accepted. Chris returned her smile, hoping for more. 'You think he might have had a corrupt official working for him?'

'Yeah. I mean, English Heritage aren't going to drop an incumbent supplier just over price are they? They rely on quality and reputation as much as price.'

'I suppose so. I wouldn't know.'

'Any thoughts on how he'd do it?'

Moran looked quizzically at Chris. 'You don't have much experience in this area, do you,' she stated.

He shrugged and gave an apologetic smile. The Army hadn't furnished him with much in the way of business sense. They stood whilst Moran thought, the air growing quiet after the helicopter's engines were cut and its blades slowed down.

'Of course you'll have considered bribery?' She sighed heavily at his dumb response. 'Well, there's that. You should check his bank transactions.'

'We've been through those. I think we'd have flagged something like that up,' Chris said, although he wasn't sure. He made a note to ask Joe Alden to look through them again later.

'Then there's intimidation, he could have coerced someone to sign them over. And don't forget good old nepotism,' she added.

'Nepotism?'

'Favours for relatives or friends?' she elaborated. 'Do you know what family he had? Did he have friends in high places?'

Chris tried not to show his surprise. No nepotism

225

for Hearst, but maybe for someone else.

'I don't think so,' he said. 'He didn't have any family in the area and his friends were very thin on the ground. I'll keep it in mind though, thanks,' he said. 'I think you're wanted.' He pointed at the doors to A&E where the football coach waited expectantly.

'Don't forget,' Moran said, 'When you wind up the case, you come to me.'

Chris nodded and smiled his reassurance. 'No problem.'

CHAPTER 21

Chris phoned Joe Alden from his car, en-route to Elton and Gemma Stoke.

'All right, Sergeant Rainey day,' Soap said by way of hello.

'Thanks Soap, I think we can keep to first names for now, don't you?' Chris said, raising a fist in celebration, inwardly cheering.

'No problem. What can I do for you O' master,' Soap continued the charade.

'I'm trying to find how Hearst could have persuaded that Council Official, Steven Caulfield, to sign over a bunch of English Heritage contracts to him.'

'Oh yeah, that was the last thing we spoke about before you sloped off.'

'Sorry. I thought the news was best coming from the Guv,' Chris said.

'S'alright, I already said it was going to happen,' Soap said, no trace of irony detectable in his voice. 'Anyway, what do you need?'

'Can you run through Hearst's bank records, see if he paid Caulfield in the period since he won those contracts? The dates are on a spreadsheet on the server.'

'Could've paid him cash,' Joe noted. He sifted through the murder case folder on the station's computer system. 'Got the file.'

'Can you check anyway? Maybe see if there are any regular cash withdrawals in that period?'

'OK, boss. What you up to?'

'I'm going to see Gemma Stoke again. I think she could be involved.'

'Sure you're not just going for a letch?' Joe chuckled. 'Later Rainey.'

'See you later.' Chris hung up the call and focussed on how he would approach Gemma Stoke.

In Elton he left his car parked on the main road and walked along the gravel driveway to Stoke's house. He could see a silver Range Rover parked at the top of the drive, next to the paddock gates. A horse in the paddock watched his progress. When he reached the workshops that lay opposite, he veered from the drive and sidled along the long single story building. He peered through the windows. A car rested in the first room. Hidden under a cover, the contours of its classic body shape stood out in relief through the dusty shroud. Chris moved on to the next workshop. The windows of this one were covered and when he tried the door he found it locked. The final room exposed nothing more than a few work tools lining the wall and a large pile of sawn logs occupying a wall near the outer door. In the gloom he could make out a connecting door to the middle room. He considered checking it out but decided he should ask first.

Chris returned to the drive just as the front door opened, revealing Gemma Stoke pushing her arms through the sleeves of a coat. She waited, monitoring his approach to the house.

'Your visits could be better co-ordinated, officer' she said. 'I can't stay.'

'Sorry, ma'am,' Chris said. 'I don't think I'll take much of your time.'

Gemma indicated for him to continue. Her hand remained on the door handle.

Chris took the hint. 'Mrs. Stoke, before you started seeing Simon Hearst, did you know how well his stone business was doing?'

Gemma pulled the door shut and began walking to the Range Rover.

'His business didn't concern me, Officer. I was only interested in Simon.' She whirled around when she reached the vehicle, tears brimming in her eyes. 'Look, it's bad enough losing him without everyone digging up the memories.'

'Everyone?' Chris asked, confused.

'You. My husband. The papers.'

'The papers? Who's been in touch from the press?'

'Kettering Gazette,' she said. 'Look, unless you have reason to stop me, I am busy.'

Chris baulked, wondering whether he should detain her. She was acting irrationally, but was that enough to bring her in? He chanced a final approach before deciding.

'Mrs. Stoke. Before you go, what's your maiden name, please?'

'Caulfield, why?'

'You have family working in the Council?'

'Yes. My brother, Steven.' she gave him a puzzled look.

'What's his position there, do you know?'

'He's a Conservation Officer, working in the Planning department.'

'Did you introduce him to Mr. Hearst?'

'No,' her frown grew deeper.

'Did you persuade your brother to sign work over to Simon?'

'No. I told you, I had no interest in Simon's business. What's all this about?'

'It's just routine,' Chris tried to reassure her. 'Thank you, ma'am, and I apologise for interrupting you without calling ahead.'

Gemma Stoke opened her mouth, a half-question forming an 'O' on her lips. The question remained unasked and she turned to climb into the Range Rover. She drove off without a backward glance.

Chris stood alone in front of the house and watched her leave. The horse in the paddock, spooked by the speed of her vehicle, raced around its enclosure kicking up clods of mud. Chris took a slow walk back down the drive fuming, phone clamped to his ear. What did Moran think she was doing, chasing up the Stokes? Didn't they have an agreement?

'Joe,' he growled, when the call was answered. 'I need you to get me Hazel Moran's mobile number. She's the journalist who was looking for me in the pub last week. All freckles and Irish wit.'

'You on the prowl again, Rainey?' Joe asked.

'Do you ever give up? Text it to me when you have it. Another thing,' he added. 'I've just spoken to Gemma Stoke. Steven Caulfield is her brother. I'm going over to see him now. Can you let the Guv know? Cheers.'

He'd arrived at the roadside by the time he'd finished the call and he sat in his car, waiting for Joe's text.

Gemma Stoke was lying to him. She knew about the link between Hearst and her brother, he was sure. Her reaction had been enough to convince him of that.

A few minutes later his phone pinged with a text from Joe. 'yr new girlfriends no.' it said, followed by Moran's mobile number.

'Hazel Moran,' she picked up the call.

'What are you playing at?' he demanded.

Moran chuckled at the end of the line. 'DC Raine, I presume?'

'There is no agreement between the Chief Super and your boss, is there,' he said, feeling foolish that he'd been taken in by her. 'That's why you're still chasing the Stokes up, isn't it?'

'For your information, Constable, there is a reporting restriction,' she countered his accusation and cut his prepared tirade off before he could begin.

'What?' he blustered. 'So why did you phone the Stokes?'

'I've not spoken to them since the agreement was put in place.'

'When was that?'

'This morning.'

'When did you call them?'

'Yesterday evening. One of our reporters recognised her husband coming out of the police station. I spoke to Mrs. Stoke but didn't get anything of use from her.'

Chris let out a long breath and realised he'd been too hasty. Moran would now be alert. With Stoke still under suspicion, she'd be able to narrow her own scope of investigation, potentially jeopardising the case if she decided to ignore her Editor's orders.

'Relax, Constable Raine,' her cool, conciliatory voice issued from his car stereo. 'I'm not going to break our deal. Just make sure you don't.'

'I won't,' he said. 'And it's Sergeant Raine, if you don't mind.' He kicked himself as soon as he'd said it.

'Woo, Sergeant, eh?' came the sarcastic reply. 'Am I permitted to report that?'

'Er, no,' he back-pedalled, embarrassed by his over-eagerness to impress. 'It's acting rank at the moment. But it'll be permanent before long.'

'OK, Sergeant,' she said, playing along with him. 'Let me know when we can start reporting again, won't you?'

Chris ended the call and returned to Kettering, driving on autopilot. Why had he been so keen to emphasise his new, temporary, promotion? Was it because Moran had been winding him up so much? After downplaying the promotion to appease Sally, and with Moran constantly referring to him as Constable, he'd not been able to stop himself from blurting it out. Again he wished he had a rewind button to erase his embarrassment.

He pulled up in the car park off London Road, a couple of hundred yards down from the police station. The Council offices fronted the adjacent Bowling Green Road with an impressive red-brick façade and tall white-framed windows, but the less-grand, main customer entrance opened on electric sliding doors to the rear, next to the car park.

The roof of the police station was visible from here and Chris thought about why he'd rushed over to Elton before coming to see Caulfield at the Council offices. The look on Gemma Stoke's face alone had justified the trip. She knew that Hearst had gleaned those contracts from her brother, he was sure. Hearst had been using his old tactics to build another company, but had he bitten off more than he could chew with Stoke?

Chris showed his badge to the receptionist and asked to see the Conservation Officer.

'Do you have an appointment?' came her waspish reply.

'It's a police matter,' he replied. 'I need to see him as soon as possible.'

'Our staff are very busy you know, officer. We can't just interrupt them willy-nilly. He may be in an important meeting.'

'I appreciate that, ma'am,' Chris said with as much charm as he could muster through gritted teeth. 'Could you check for me, please?' he smiled.

'I'll see if he's available,' she grumbled.

A few minutes later Caulfield, a thin, nervous looking man in his mid-thirties, arrived in the foyer. The man's resemblance to Gemma Stoke struck Chris so much he was able to recognise him and intervene before Caulfield reached the desk.

'Mr. Caulfield, I'm Detective Sergeant Raine, Northants Police,' he introduced himself. He noticed the receptionists scowl at being unable to impede him further and hoped she hadn't noticed that his warrant card still displayed 'Detective Constable'.

He shook Caulfield's outstretched, clammy hand.

'Hello Sergeant. How can I help?' Caulfield replied. He didn't appear to be in a hurry, but looked anxious, wringing his hands and looking everywhere but at Chris.

'Is there somewhere we can go?' Chris asked.

'Um, OK,' Caulfield checked his watch. 'It's almost time for my break anyway.' He led Chris out of the building and around, through an alley at the side, onto Bowling Green Road. They walked past the imposing front face of the offices, the union flag fluttering in the gentle breeze on its pole, the large double oak doors closed to the public. Next door lay an ornamental garden, neatly manicured and planted with spring flowers. Caulfield chose a bench to sit on and turned to Chris.

'I'm investigating the murder of Simon Hearst,' Chris said.

The man stared at the ground. Traffic hummed past on the adjoining street.

'I've been checking out his business background,' Chris continued. 'You signed over a lot of English Heritage work to him over last couple of years.'

'A lot of work passes through my office,' Caulfield said. 'If it was English Heritage and in this Borough, I'll have dealt with it, yes.'

'You're a Conservation Officer, right?'

'That's right.'

'What does a Conservation Officer do?' Chris asked. He only had a vague idea of Caulfield's role.

'On the whole it's the preservation and care of the historic environment in the Borough, but it has many facets.'

'And sourcing and allocating grants to craftsmen falls in its remit?'

'Yes.'

'You also signed off Hearst's planning permission to build his house in Oundle,' Caulfield's eyes widened in surprise. 'How does a Conservation Officer get involved in regular planning?'

'Um, I sometimes stand in for the normal Planning Officer when he's on holiday or off sick,' Caulfield stood. 'I really must be getting back,' he said.

'Sit down Mr. Caulfield,' Chris ordered. 'Unless you want to continue this in your office.'

Caulfield sat. Chris had guessed he'd been brought outside so Caulfield's colleagues wouldn't overhear their conversation. Caulfield had just confirmed that.

'So, you knew Hearst.'

233

Caulfield sighed and nodded, eyes still fixed on the grass at his feet.

'You knew he was having an affair with your sister?' Chris asked.

Another nod.

'And what? Did your sister persuade you to sign to Hearst?'

'No! She knew nothing about it,' Caulfield jumped to his sister's defence.

'Then tell me.'

'Tell you what? What are you asking me?'

'How he got that work.' Chris's tone hardened.

'He applied for it, just as anyone else would,' Caulfield insisted, fidgeting on the wooden bench.

'What, just like that? A whole raft of quotes that just happened to undercut the incumbents best price?' Chris shook his head. 'I've looked through the dates on the agreements and Hearst appears on the scene from nowhere, suddenly winning grant after grant.' He let the words sink in. Caulfield sat in miserable silence. 'There's no way Hearst could win such an amount of work in one block. Someone would have had to fill him in on what applications were being submitted and how much they were likely to go for. Someone on the inside.'

Caulfield wriggled again in his seat.

'So Steven, either you start talking or I put you in a cell until you do,' Chris jerked a thumb over his shoulder across the car park behind them. 'It's not far.'

Caulfield's gaze followed the direction of Chris's thumb and shuddered. For a few moments he continued to stare at the police station. Chris could see his expression changing through various levels of misery and fear as he wrestled with what he should say.

'OK,' he whispered. 'But you've got to believe me, I didn't want to do any of it.'

'Any of what?' Chris said. 'You need to tell me, Steven.'

'Hearst blackmailed me,' Caulfield announced. Once he'd let it out, he seemed to relax. Free from the burden of his secret, he gained confidence. 'I need that to be noted. I could lose my job over this.'

'Mr. Caulfield, a man has lost his life, and a young girl is currently missing,' Chris reminded him. 'Probably because of this.' He found himself irritated by Caulfield's selfishness.

'Yes, I know. But he treated me very badly,' Caulfield maintained his defence, indifferent to Chris's comment.

'I'm getting tired of asking this. How?' Chris asked, thinking he was going to have to carry out his threat and arrest the shivering specimen in front of him.

'He found out about Gemma's previous – relationships – other men that she'd seen behind her husband's back. He threatened to tell John if I didn't help him.'

'So you passed Stoke's grants over to Hearst?'

Caulfield tipped his head in a nod.

'I didn't want John to know. Gemma's been so much more stable since she's been with him.'

'Stable?'

Another nod. 'She's had – emotional – problems in the past,' Caulfield said. 'When she became a carer she settled down a lot. And after John's wife died, well, they seemed to help each other through the bereavement.'

'You didn't think to warn your sister of Hearst's threats?'

'Didn't you hear me? I didn't want to put her through the pain, I had no idea how she might react. I tried to tell her in a round-about way to stop seeing Hearst, that he wasn't good for her, but she ignored me.'

Chris took the words in. He'd have to check out Gemma Stoke's 'emotional' problems. He turned his attention back to Caulfield.

'Did English Heritage question this change of supplier?'

'They took the usual precautions. Simon was registered as an authorised IHBC supplier.' Caulfield stopped at Chris's questioning look. 'Institute of Historic

Building Conservation,' he explained.

'Was it only John Stoke's business that you handed to Hearst?'

'Mostly,' Caulfield answered. 'There were the odd one or two others that were easily passed on. Businesses that were running out of the quality of stone required and that Hearst's quarry could produce.'

'And what did Stoke think of all this?'

'It took him a long while to cotton on. Aside from the initial bulk of orders I was just drip-feeding the business to Hearst. John was livid when his allocation of contracts dried up. He demanded to know who I'd signed the grants over to. I'd given him preferential treatment in the first place,' Caulfield stalled, realising what he'd said, but it was too late.

'Hmm, you're going to have to give me more than that, Steven, if you're going to survive this,' Chris said.

'Survive it?' Caulfield stammered.

'Your job,' Chris clarified.

'Look, I did all I could to not get taken in by either of them. Hearst was easily twenty-five percent cheaper than John, anyway. I told John as much, but it didn't seem to solve anything.'

'When did John Stoke find out?'

'About a month ago.'

Fits in with the time-line, Chris thought. 'You'll have to make a formal statement to the effect, you know,' he said.

Caulfield nodded. He looked fearful. Of what? Was he worried Stoke would bump him off? Had Stoke killed Hearst because of the double-cross?

'How much were the grants worth?' he asked.

'I don't know exactly. A lot of work passes my desk. Around £100,000 to £150,000 each year at a guess. Less, once Hearst took over.'

Enough to kill someone over? Chris wondered. He had a couple of final points for Caulfield to clear up.

'Did Hearst make you sign the planning consent on his house?'

236

Caulfield took a moment to answer. 'Sorry. Had to think about that,' he said. 'Yes. He told me to run it through while my colleague in Planning was on holiday.'

'And you didn't know that the Stokes marriage was platonic? That John already knew about Gemma's indiscretions?'

'What?' Caulfield exclaimed. 'So Hearst blackmailed me for nothing? Bastard,' he cursed. He shrank into himself, hugging his waist.

Chris walked over the large car park to the police station, leaving Caulfield to his self-centred misery.

The CID area was deserted. Chris powered on his computer and tried to call DI Crighton whilst the system booted up. The Guv's phone went straight to voicemail.

'Sir, call me when you can, please,' Chris spoke to the machine. 'I've seen Caulfield and he's confirmed Hearst conspired to take business from Stoke. Both he and Gemma Stoke deny her involvement but I think she knows more than she's letting on.' He tapped his logon details into the computer and continued with the voice message. 'Caulfield believes he's telling the truth. The man's a drip. Hearst was blackmailing him. There was no reason for Gemma Stoke to get directly involved with the council, if she had access to Stoke's business documents. She probably passed his quotes over to Hearst to allow him to bid at a lower price.'

Chris hung up and searched the Server for the files on Stoke. Crighton had amassed a fair number of documents and Chris had a quick scan through them. He took another look at the drugs case document that he'd seen earlier and read through a summary of Operation Sharvor, the investigation of crime passing through London's Victoria coach station.

By mid afternoon, the echo of his lonely key tapping and mouse clicking was getting on his nerves. He had covered all the available information on Stoke and had collated a comparison between Hearst's contracts and the accounts declared by Stoke to Companies House. One thing was clear. Caulfield's claim that Hearst's costs were twenty-five percent cheaper than Stoke's didn't match up with Stokes accounts. The difference between the two men's prices were closer to fifty percent. Added to that, Stoke's accounts showed unusually high running costs at all of his businesses, from employee wage rates to utility costs. The extent of the anomalies could only be attributed to money laundering. Stoke must be involved in the drugs cartel as Crighton suspected. Chris needed to share the discovery and tried Crighton's number again. Straight to voicemail. He left another message then called Joe Alden.

'Soap, do you know where the Guv is?'

'Meeting with the DCI, Sarge,' Joe answered, already comfortable with Chris's new rank.

'Where are you?'

'Back on stag at the Hospital.'

'Any news on Whitelock?'

'Nothing interesting. Sally's gone home though. She looks dog tired, Chris.'

'Yeah, I saw her earlier. Wish she'd change her mind about resigning.'

'Me too. Getting fed up with standing in for uniform here all the time while you go swanning off interviewing gorgeous women.'

'Sorry, mate. Someone's gotta do it,' Chris chuckled.

CHAPTER 22

The river Nene's slow, muddy progress mesmerised Chris as he stood on its bank pondering the case. Chris had come to Oundle to clear his head while he waited for Crighton to return his calls. The SOCO's tent had been dismantled and taken away from the scene of crime but a square of light coloured grass betrayed its position and confirmed that warmer days were inbound. Transfixed by the water's easy flow his mind floated with it, unravelling and opening up, freeing itself from his feelings for Sally.

Now he'd made a solid connection between Hearst and Stoke, and had begun to expose Stoke's fraud, he knew the case would be taken away from the Kettering team. The Serious and Organised Crime Agency would want to assume full control. The team's work would be acknowledged, which was some consolation. But they would miss out on the real satisfaction of nailing Stoke and his associates for the brutal murder of someone on their patch.

What could have tempted Stoke into drug running? Greed, probably, Chris thought. His property development business looked healthy enough, even without the inflated profits that Chris had unearthed in his accounts.

What kind of greed takes a man to another level? Had Stoke been given an incentive from his early life in the Adriatic? Maybe he had contacts and finance avenues in the Balkans. He'd told the Guv the experience had virtually bankrupted him, though, so he'd probably want to distance himself from that episode of his life.

So perhaps he'd been coerced into it? By Theodore Black, perhaps, or maybe even Graham Yarwood, his one time solicitor?

And what of Hearst? How had he become

embroiled in the situation? Was it really a chance meeting with Gemma Stoke at the stone exhibition that led him to resurrect his old practices, or had he planned that too; earmarking the Stokes for attention, then concocting the encounter with Gemma?

Chris's gaze lifted and he watched three red kites sailing the thermal currents that ascended from a freshly ploughed field on the opposite bank. Similar to the buzzard, the large birds of prey soared in large circles. Unlike their cousins, kites were carrion as well as hunters. These scavengers weren't picky over how fresh their food was, always on the lookout for an easy meal. Much like Hearst, Chris smiled wryly.

Dusk was beginning to draw in and Crighton still hadn't surfaced. Chris chanced a call to the DCI's office.

'DI Crighton left about two hours ago,' the Chief's assistant told him.

'Is the Chief Inspector in?' Chris asked.

'He is. I'll see if he's busy,' there was a pause. 'I'll put you through.'

'Acting Sergeant Raine,' the DCI's warm voice carried across the cell network. 'I've been hearing good things about you.'

'Thanks Sir,' Chris replied, 'I'm sorry to bother you. I left a voicemail earlier for DI Crighton to call me, but I haven't heard from him.'

'That's unusual,' the DCI said. 'He left here a while ago. Perhaps his phone battery has run flat. He told me he had some questions for John Stoke this afternoon. Maybe that's where he's headed.'

'Thanks, Sir. I'll see if I can find him,' Chris rang off, worried.

He rang the station. Crighton hadn't checked in with his destination. Had he gone to Stokes home office or to the quarry? After all his lecturing, Crighton had failed to follow the rules himself.

The kites had tightened their circle of flight and had dropped in height. Occasionally one or another would swoop to the rivers edge on Chris's side, about thirty feet downstream. Had an angler left some bait or part of a catch on the bank side? Chris began to walk that way, curious to see what occupied the birds' attention.

Should he follow the Guv and tell him of the information he'd gleaned from Stoke's files? The case was running perilously close to the Serious and Organised Crime Agency investigation and they couldn't afford to slip up with an inappropriate question now.

The path back to his car beckoned but he continued past it to the spot where the birds had become more animated, their keening cries piercing the air. It's not far, he thought. I'll be back on the road in no time. Whatever they've seen it's got them agitated.

Below the birds Chris couldn't quite make out the object in the water, a few feet from the bank and surrounded by reeds. He moved in closer, shooing the kites away. The reeds blocked his view. He looked around for something to sweep them away with and found a dead branch lying at the water's edge. Green algae covered its bark and the branch slipped in his grasp. He wiped the branch and his hands on the grass, then tried again. With wide, sweeping arcs Chris cleared a swathe of reeds out of the way. His efforts revealed a body, half submerged and partly covered with foliage.

'Oh no!' he gasped. 'Is it Molly Gowland? Are we too late?'

He thrashed in the water with the branch, clearing the tangled vegetation from the corpse. 'No,' he thought. 'Too big to be a young girl. And dressed in a business suit.'

In the disturbed water the body rolled over, face up. Its pallid, waxy skin was surrounded by a halo of short greying hair floating in the brown water. A ragged grey cut bisected the throat, all blood washed away. One of the body's limp legs kicked out a slow rhythmic beat, tugged at by the slow current. An eye had been pecked out and there were beak marks around the other, but the cadaver was still recognisable.

Chris sat down heavily onto the grass, shocked at

the discovery of John Stoke's corpse. Breathing heavily he punched a call through to the station.

'Get someone over to Oundle as soon as possible,' he said, panting out his orders to the desk sergeant. 'John Stoke has been killed.' He described the scene and the location of the corpse. 'And get a team over to Stoke's quarry too. I think DI Crighton's in danger.'

Sally stirred on her lounge sofa. The back of her head pounded with thick beats and she had a stale taste in her mouth. She sat up and suppressed an impulse to heave. Through the half-sleep she heard her phone chirping from the depths of her handbag. She dragged the bag across the floor. As it drew closer the rattle of pills within almost tempted her to ignore the call and reach for the painkillers.

'Chris,' she mumbled into the handset. 'What do you want.' Her voice rasped and tickled out a dry cough. She stood and stumbled to the kitchen, searching for a fresh glass of water while she listened.

'Sally, I need your help,' Chris said, spilling details in a panicked rush. 'The Guv's gone missing and I'm sure he's in trouble. I need you. Now. The DCI says he's meeting Stoke, but Stoke's dead and if I don't find him soon something bad's going to happen, I'm sure of it. And we don't have anyone free on the team. Soap's at the Hospital.'

'Hold on, Chris,' Sally halted him. She gulped a mouthful of water, clearing her throat. Her headache threatened to crack her skull and she was having trouble keeping up with his tumbling explanation. 'Slow down a bit. What's that about the Guv?'

'He's supposed to be seeing Stoke but I've just found Stoke dead.'

'Dead?'

'Throat slit and dumped in the river. I've just discovered him a few yards from where we found Hearst.'

'Where was the Guv?'

'I don't know,' Chris moaned. 'He hasn't reported in on the station log.'

'What do you want me to do?' Sally's brain started sparking into life. The two white tablets that had somehow appeared in her palm were tossed into the sink and the bottle discarded in the bin. Something began to settle in her mind, muscling the headache to one side.

'Can you relieve Soap at the Hospital?' Chris's ragged breathing crackled through the speaker. 'I need him at Stoke's quarry. I've got uniform coming in from Oundle, but we need our team there, too. I'll be getting on the road as soon as I can.'

'I can't stand guard on my own husband,' Sally replied. She'd made her mind up at last. Something would have to be done about Tony's care, but she wouldn't desert her colleagues. Right now she needed to be part of the team. 'I'll come over.'

'No, Sally,' Chris brought her up short. 'You're not ready for this yet. You have to sort yourself out first. Send Joe. It's for the best.'

She paused, staring at the painkillers starting to soften in the sink. Contemplated scooping them out. 'OK. I understand, Chris. I'll go now.' Sally turned from the dissolving pills and shrugged into her coat, slipping her shoes on at the door. She picked up her car keys but stayed on the line. 'I wonder, Chris. Why Stoke? And why dump him there?'

'I don't know, Sally,' she could hear Chris getting into his car, and did the same, waiting while the phones switched over to their Bluetooth connections.

'Are you there? Chris asked.

'Yeah.'

Chris picked up the thread as he pulled out onto the road and gunned the motor. 'I saw Gemma Stoke at home, lunchtime. She was in a hurry to leave.'

'She's not the type to be able to drop a body off in a river, Chris.'

243

'I know, but after speaking with her brother, I'm convinced she was conspiring with Hearst. They were going to bring her husbands company down. Maybe she's paid someone to finish Stoke off.' Chris rolled the thought around his head.

'Who? She wouldn't find a hitman in the yellow pages, would she. What contacts could she have?'

'You're right, I suppose. Her brother said she was emotionally unstable when she was young. Maybe she got caught up in a bad crowd back then?'

'And I suppose she got back in touch through Linked-In, or Facebook?'

Chris gave a harsh laugh. It was a preposterous assumption, he had to admit. Thinking about the business contacts web-site, Linked-In, he realised he'd omitted Theodore Black from his thoughts.

'Stoke was in business with Theodore Black,' he said, driving through the early dusk. Leaden skies had accelerated the onset of darkness and rain was on the way. 'They both part-owned the quarry. They were both in property too, weren't they.'

'Stoke told me and the Guv that he started out in holiday home sales in Yugoslavia.'

'That's right,' Chris slapped his steering wheel, 'And Black is Slovakian. His real name is Ciernik'

'You're losing me,' Sally said. 'This headache's killing me. I've not had any painkillers this afternoon.'

'That's good, Sally, Chris enthused. 'Just try some Ibuprofen or Paracetamol, eh? See if you can get through.'

'What's the connection?' She asked.

'Stoke returned to the UK penniless and he probably owed Ciernik, too,' Chris speculated. 'Once Slovakia entered the European Union in 2004, cross-border travel and employment would have been made easier. I reckon that's when Ciernik came after Stoke. He either coerced him into helping with drugs trafficking or Stoke was a willing partner. We've also seen possible evidence of people smuggling, too.'

'But why would Ciernik go as far as to have Stoke killed?'

'Maybe he got wind of Hearst's scam and had him killed, horrifying Stoke. If Ciernik has Molly and Stoke knew about it he might have threatened to go to the police, especially after we'd started questioning him. Ciernik may have snapped, lured Stoke to the river and killed him. If he's involved in human trafficking he'd have a route out of the country to make Molly disappear.''

Chris shivered at his own words. The thought of Molly Gowland slipping through their fingers into the murky world of international people smuggling sparked angry emotions, blurring his thought process and dominating his mind. He'd felt a guilty rush of relief when he identified Stoke's body. Relief that he wasn't staring at the mutilated face of Molly. That brief consolation was being quickly replaced by despair at knowing he still had no control over her fate.

'There's another possibility,' Sally's voice echoed through Chris's car speakers.

'What?'

'Gemma Stoke,' she offered. 'We know she wasn't averse to seeing other men behind her husband's back.'

Chris thought back to Gemma's hurried exit earlier in the day. 'Good point, Sally,' he conceded. 'You think she might have had an affair with Ciernik, as well as Hearst?'

'Uh-huh.'

'Her brother told me she'd had problems early in life. I wonder if she could be complicit in the kidnap,' he said.

'You think she helped Ciernik?'

'I don't know, Sally. I'm just trying to run through all the possibilities. There's one problem if they were working together against Stoke and Hearst.'

'What's that?'

'How would they know the Cartwright's narrowboat would be empty if Stoke wasn't involved?

We don't know whether Ciernik was in the Chequered Skipper the night Hearst's body was dumped. We don't even know what Ciernik looks like. Serious and Organised Crime Agency will, but they've put a block on us questioning him.'

'Shit,' Sally breathed. Chris detected a shift in her voice. She seemed to be gaining interest in the case again.

'Yeah,' he agreed. 'Look, I've got to go, Sally. Thanks a lot for your help.'

'No problem,' she replied.

'And think about coming back to us?' he asked, too late. The line had been cut.

DI Paul Crighton struggled in his bonds. He lay flat on a table, the same as Simon Hearst had so recently, aside for the blindfold and gag. He wished his eyes were masked though, because his concentration was drawn to the jagged teeth of a circular saw-blade suspended above him. In the background he could hear a stream of muffled chatter. The language sounded similar to that used by Stoke's foreman, Imrich.

He tore his eyes from the blade and looked around the room. The window gave no clue to his whereabouts. Blanked off by a sheet of Hessian, nailed to the frame, it blocked off all light. The only illumination came from a dirty, low wattage bulb affixed above one of the room's two doors, its exposed cable trailing loosely along the top of the the brickwork and through a gap into the next room. Piles of junk edged the walls: An old anvil, a few lengths of scaffold tube and rusty paint tins.

The large door scraped open and he took a deep breath, his nose filling with the smell of sawdust and oil. A man entered the room, sliding a mobile phone into a pocket in his suit. Crighton tried to get a look over the man's shoulder but night was approaching fast and he couldn't make anything out past the bare light bulb.

The man turned a key in the mortice lock. Tall and thin. Black hair and a thick five o-clock shadow. Ciernik.

Crighton had seen his picture on the Serious and Organised Crime Agency files.

'The nosey policeman,' Ciernik announced, pacing around the room. 'What to do, what to do,' he muttered.

Crighton strained his head, following the man's progress. He smelled stale tobacco and craved for a cigarette. Twenty years since he'd smoked his last yet here he was, hankering after that bitter nicotine hit. Considering his predicament, he wondered if it had been worth all those weeks of cardboard-like chewing gum and breathing deeply in smoky bars trying to wean himself off the habit.

An electronic chirp halted Ciernik's pacing and he took his phone out to read a text. He grunted and replaced the handset again.

'Your friends are looking for you, policeman,' he said, his Slavic accent tinged with round English vowels. 'But they won't find you.'

'Don't be hasty, Black,' Crighton said, trying to catch the man's eye. 'Don't make things worse for yourself.'

'It is you who is making things worse, nosy policeman,' Ciernik smirked. 'Like Hearst,' he said, pronouncing the name He-arset, instead of Hurst.

Crighton finally locked eyes on his captor. 'What did Hearst do, Ciernik?' he asked

Ciernik jumped at the use of his real name. 'Hearst got too close.'

'Too close to what?'

Ciernik merely smirked again.

'Too close to your racket,' Crighton guessed. The thin orange twine he'd been tied with had begun to cut of his circulation. 'Not content with taking Stoke's wife he went after his business too. Your business.'

Ciernik shrugged, suddenly unwilling to speak.

Crighton had lost most of the feeling in his legs and he was losing his temper. If it's going to end here, he thought, I'm not going out quietly. 'Hearst threatened to expose you, didn't he?'

Ciernik had rested his hands on the saw's release mechanism. The hydraulic arm that the blade was attached to worked on a controlled release. To avoid burning any stone it cut and to keep the blade cool, the arm was designed to drop at a controlled rate, a centimetre at a time.

'Hearst was greedy,' Ciernik snapped. 'He saw our profits didn't match the stone we produced.'

'He wanted in, didn't he?' Crighton said.

Ciernik ignored him and delved in his pockets for a cigarette. The smoke trailed across the table, tantalising Crighton's already strained will. Oh, for one last drag, he thought. Escape seemed impossible, and talking Ciernik around equally as futile.

'But you don't just get 'in' to your crowd, do you,' he pressed on. 'Hearst could have been useful to you.'

Ciernik gave a short bark. 'Ha'.

'No way you'd work with a man you couldn't trust, though,' Crighton continued. 'Who knows what he'd do later on, eh?'

Ciernik nodded thoughtfully. 'A rat is a rat. He will not change. A policeman, though? He may change, no?'

Crighton let the suggestion go, ignoring the attempt at bribery. 'And that's why you placed his head on show? To warn off anyone thinking of doing the same.'

Ciernik laughed, nodding his head in mock humility. 'A show, yes. Like Vlad the Impaler. A hero.'

'What have you done with his daughter?'

'Ah, an unexpected bonus. On her way to the Middle East as we speak. A young white girl will earn good price in certain, markets.'

'You fucking animal.'

'Enough talk, I think,' Ciernik said, flicking his cigarette stub into a corner of the room.

'Don't do it Ciernik!' Crighton cried out, panic rising in his stomach. 'I've got officers on the way. You won't escape.' He thrashed helplessly on the table.

Ciernik laughed. 'There are many ways for a man

like me to disappear,' he gloated. 'In my country there is not so much difficulty in persuading the police to – ignore – you.' He turned the master switch on the table saw. The blade whirred into life, further dimming the weak light briefly and flicking wood chips down onto Crighton's face as it gained speed.

CHAPTER 23

A police car blocked the entrance to Superior Masonry and Stone, parked at an angle across the gates. Shouts carried over the air throughout the facility as uniformed officers rounded up the staff. PC Taylor from Oundle's rural station was organising his team, confining the workers to the foreman's office.

He spotted a car arriving and approached the gate.

'Come through DS Whitelock,' he said. 'We were expecting one of your colleagues.'

'Well, I'm here,' Sally replied, stepping around the parked patrol car. 'Any news on DI Crighton?'

'We've not found him yet, Sarge. There's still half the facility to search, yet.'

'OK, have you looked in the underground room?'

Taylor gave her a withering look. 'First place we looked.'

Her phone showed no signal bars. 'Back of bloody beyond,' she commented. 'Do they have any painkillers here?'

She followed Taylor into the foreman's office and rummaged around in a first aid box, bolted to the wall. 'No bloody paracetamol,' she cursed.

Her headache still throbbed and, for a moment, she wished she'd taken Chris's advice to go to the hospital. That wasn't really an option, though. It would have been wrong to officially take over guarding her husband. If anything were to happen to him without a third party in attendance, she'd be first in the frame in any investigation that followed. Chris was good, she had to admit, but he still had plenty to learn. Come to think of it, where was he?

'Seen DC Raine?' She asked Taylor.

'No Sarge,' he replied. 'We've not looked over there yet,' he pointed to a shed.

'Let's go.'

Sally had a thought and sent Chris a text, the same as he had done when trapped in the underground room. Her message disappeared immediately, the cell-phone signal just strong enough to accept a transmission.

'We're missing something,' she said to Taylor as they walked over to one of the production sheds. The stone-finishing machinery inside lay dormant. Half-hewn blocks of limestone rested on tables, beneath motionless cutting blades. No sign of Crighton. They swept the room anyway, looking for any sign of another cellar or hidden room.

Taylor shrugged. 'Dunno what we're missing,' he said. 'Is DI Crighton even here?'

Typical beat bobby, Sally thought. Good for routine but don't ask them to think outside the box.

'You know what car he drives?' the PC asked. Sally immediately regretted her previous assumption. She rushed out of the shed and over to the darkening yard. There were seven or so cars parked on the concrete in front of the foreman's office, but no blue Passat.

'Shit,' Sally hissed. 'He's not here. Why?'

'Do these people own another quarry?' Taylor asked.

'I don't know.' Sally admitted. She realised how far the case had slipped away from her since yesterday. Ordinarily she'd be in the thick of the action and would have chased up Ciernik as soon as she found out how deeply he was involved. By giving up last night in place of looking after Tony her concentration had shifted focus and she was already out of her depth.

Three days of high strength Tramadol had taken it's toll, too. Her brain felt thick as treacle, refusing to deliver the possibilities that should be driving her forward. It had taken PC Taylor's suggestion to kick-start her thinking process. She stood in the quarry yard, turning around slowly, at a loss for her next move.

Chris edged along the workshops that lined

Stoke's drive the same as he'd done earlier in the day. A chink of light spilled from the edge of the middle workshop window where its cover hadn't quite reached the edge of the pane. His view through the crack revealed nothing but the back of a cardboard box. He stepped back and searched the window frame for any other opportunity to see into the room. There, high up in the middle pane, another splash of light escaped the room. If he stood on tiptoes, close to the window, he could just get an eye to the crack. It was an uncomfortable stretch and his body pressed against the window. He hoped he wasn't silhouetted against the it from inside.

The scene inside the room made him reel back in shock. The Guv was lying prone, tied up on a table saw similar to the one's at Stoke's quarry. This one was older, though, it's yellow paint worn and chipped, and the structure was built with a heavier gauge steel. Stoke must've brought it here from the quarry after it became obsolete, and used it to cut the store of firewood logs in the end room. The wood-cutting blade on its hydraulically supported arm loomed above the Guv's neck, its highly serrated teeth more prominent than the square edged diamond blades that would be used to cut stone. Ciernik stood with his back to the window. Chris could hear the men arguing but it was difficult to make out what they were saying. He heard Crighton cry out and knew he must act quickly. At the moment that Ciernik powered the saw up a shrill beep emitted from Chris's jacket: his phone's text alert.

Ciernik jumped. 'What was that?' he asked. 'I have your phone.' He fished Crighton's phone out of his pocket along with his own. Neither of the screens showed any activity. 'You have another?' he demanded

Crighton couldn't answer. His gaze fixed on the spinning blade above him.

'Someone is here?' Ciernik's puzzled expression changed to anger. His arm reached out to release the holding mechanism on the saw's arm. 'It's too late for you.'

Crighton let out an animal noise. Not quite a scream, more a strangled growl, as he struggled against the tough twine in a final attempt to free himself.

At the end of the workshop building Chris rammed through the end door and stumbled into the first room. The whine of machinery in the next room urged him on. Too late, he thought. You're out of time.

But in the gloom of this unlit room he spied an old electrical junction box, high up on one wall. He leapt for it, fingers grasping at the main circuit breaker, and flicked the heavy switch. The light spilling from underneath the inner door disappeared and the saw's electric whine slowed. Chris's momentum carried him forward, bursting through into the middle room.

Ciernik stumbled around in the darkness. Chris had the advantage, his eyes already accustomed to the shadows. He pounced on Ciernik, sending them both crashing to the ground in a clatter of paint tins and other junk. Ciernik thrashed underneath Chris, both men panting in the frenzied scrap.

Ciernik grabbed at a short length of scaffold pole. He aimed a crack at Chris's head, scoring a glancing blow. Chris chopped at Ciernik's wrist and sent the pole skittering over the floor but Ciernik quickly retaliated, gripping Chris around the throat and squeezing with desperate strength. Chris felt his airway cut off, his energy sapping away with surprising speed. He managed to land two blows on Ciernik's face before his vision clouded over. Ciernik's triumphant grin swam below him, spittle flecked against the edge of the man's lips.

Chris felt himself going under. Through a flashing kaleidoscope of white spots on blackness all he could see was a silhouette of Ciernik's head. Chris drew down on Ciernik and leaned his forearm on the Slovak's throat. In one final push he pressed all his weight down and felt Ciernik's grasp weaken.

The pressure on Chris's neck receded and he

253

gasped a guttural breath. Air rushed into his lungs and gave him strength. He maintained pressure on the man under him, feeling the clinging fingers loosen from his neck. Ciernik pawed at Chris's face, his efforts growing weaker and weaker until he stopped, one hand mid-stroke on Chris's cheek. His eyes rolled back in their sockets, the grin twisted into a grimace and finally slackened in a sad, loose mask.

Chris leaned back and gasped in great gob-fuls of air. Eventually, he sucked up a deep breath and reached into a pocket for a set of cuffs, securing Ciernik by one hand to the saw table.

He staggered to his feet and turned to Crighton's aid. The DI lay prone on the table, his head stretched over to the left in an anguished attempt to escape the spinning blade. He didn't respond to Chris's touch. The saw had bitten at Crighton before the lifeless motor had stopped spinning, ripping at the flesh and sinking its jagged teeth into his neck.

A stillness enveloped the room. Chris's mini-Maglite pierced the darkness and flickered over Crighton's body, resting on a wet stain on his shirt collar. Chris searched for a pulse and was rewarded with a faint, steady beat . Spurred on, he lifted the saw's arm until it clicked into a locked position, then isolated the power supply.

He ripped both sweat stained sleeves from his shirt and rolled one up, pressing the wad against Crighton's wound. The other secured it in place, tied loosely as a scarf around his neck..

On the floor, Ciernik groaned. The cuffs rattled as he attempted to rise. The captive growled and uttered a stream of words in Slovakian that Chris could only guess were obscenities.

'You sit tight,' he ordered. He closed in on Ciernik's bloodshot eyes. 'You'll pay for this, you bastard,' he spat, pushing the Slovak back, flat on the floor.

Ciernik kicked a weak leg out at Chris's feet. Chris

dodged it and stamped on the flailing ankle.

'I won't tell you again, mad dog. Stay still.' Chris felt for his phone but came up short. It must have fallen from his pocket during the fight and skittered off somewhere. He returned to the first room and brought the power back on-line. Bathed in light once more, the middle room looked like the aftermath of a human sacrifice. Crighton had spilled a fair bit of blood, a tell-tale run that followed a channel on the table top and dripped onto the floor.

On bloodstained hands and knees, Chris scrabbled under the piles of junk searching for his phone. The sound of a vehicle crunched the gravel outside. Was this Ciernik's men, summoned to remove the Crighton's corpse? Too late to kill the lights again. Chris crept to the open connecting door between the rooms and slid through, taking the discarded length of scaffold pipe with him.

'Shouldn't have left the Guv there, Chris,' he thought. 'They'll finish the job off for Ciernik, then come looking for you.' Peering through the window of this end room, he spied the car that had pulled up outside. The pole slipped from his fingers and clattered to the floor. He slumped forward, forehead resting on the cold glass.

Sally stepped out of the patrol car and rushed over to the workshops. She rattled the middle door. 'Chris! Chris, are you there?' she called.

Chris tapped on the window and caught her attention, indicated the way in around the corner of the building. She came, with PC Taylor following close behind. Chris pointed in mute exhaustion to the central room, too weary to speak. Sally steadied him and leaned him against a wall where he slid to the ground. She knelt in front of him and cradled his chin, holding his gaze. Her concerned frown blurred and disappeared into blackness. The sound of Taylor request for assistance and the crackling reply echoed in Chris's ears as he passed out.

CHAPTER 24

A box-bodied MAN TGL truck rumbled along the A2 towards Dover, innocuous amongst the other traffic. The driver, Richard Stoke leaned on the steering wheel, his elbows propping up his chin.

'Come on John, answer,' he growled into the mobile phone pushed against his ear. The lorry veered into the centre lane and a car sounded a long beep on its horn. Richard lifted a middle finger and returned the warning with a blast of his air horn.

'Fuck it,' he cursed, redialling and resuming his position on the wheel.

'Gemma?' he barked. 'Richard. Where's John?'

'I don't know,' came the reply.

'What do you mean you don't know? Where are you?'

'Theo told me to meet him in Peterborough. I'm at his house there, now.'

'Shagging around again? Dunno how John puts up with it.' Richard had suspected Gemma was seeing Black behind his brother's back. 'Tell Black this is the last run I'm doing for him. John's not happy about it and nor am I. Whatever love triangle you three have got going is nothing to do with me, but I'm not risking my neck again for him.'

'I don't know what it is you're doing for Theo, Richard, and I don't care. You'll have to straighten it with him yourself.'

'Yeah, cheers.' Richard Stoke stabbed at the red button on his phone and tossed the handset onto the dashboard. 'Slag,' he concluded.

'Theodore Ciernik is saying nothing.' Sally announced as she arrived in the CID office from the cells.

'Where's DI Murfit?' Chris looked up from his

desk. The Inspector had accompanied Sally on Ciernik's initial interview in Crighton's absence.

'Gone back to Northampton. We're stuck.' Sally slumped into her chair.

'Guv's stable,' Chris said. 'Joe went to see him after he was relieved at Tony's door.'

'Is he awake?'

'Tony? I don't know.'

'No, the Guv,' Sally scowled.

Chris tapped at his keyboard. 'He managed to pass on what Ciernik told him. Said Molly was on her way to the Middle East.'

'Shit.'

'I've been going through the documents again. Guv told me that SOCA held him off from arresting Ciernik.' He pointed at the screen. 'I've got their number here.'

Sally squinted at the screen. 'This headache is getting worse. I can hardly see that. Just tell me.'

'We should call the Guv's contact, DI Vane. Tell him we've arrested Ciernik and we need their co-operation. Ciernik's cover is blown anyway. There's nothing stopping us from investigating further, and we've got to if we're to do Molly Gowland any justice.'

'OK Chris, you go for it. I can't overrule you anyway.'

'Are you still resigning?'

'Don't know yet. But at the moment I've no authority.' She stared around the room, jaded eyes drinking in the dead atmosphere in the office and the incident board with its multicoloured lines tracing connections and identities. Chris wondered if she'd ever shake herself out of the trance of despair she seemed to be wallowing in.

'I'm here for you, you know that?' he tried to reassure her.

She gave him a wan smile. 'Thanks.'

The customs officer held his hand up to stop

Richard Stoke's truck. He indicated to a large corrugated iron shed that stood to one side of the row of Customs barriers. Stoke drove slowly into a marked bay and cut the engine.

'Problem?' he asked.

'You've got a loose crash rail.' The customs officer pointed to the left side of the truck.

Stoke jumped down from the cab and walked around. One of the horizontal metal rails fixed between the front and rear wheels flapped loosely on its mount.

'Sorry. I'll get it tightened.' He reached under the truck and opened the tool chest affixed to the chassis.

The customs officer looked closer at the truck.

'You've fitted an extra fuel tank?'

Stoke straightened and approached the officer, a large spanner in his hand. He walked past and began tightening the bolts holding the crash bar onto the truck.

'Extra range,' he explained. 'Three hundred litres. Costs a bomb to fill up. Cheaper to fill up on the continent,' he chuckled.

The customs officer laughed along. 'I'm not surprised,' he agreed. 'All OK? Drive safe, sir.'

Stoke packed his tools away and returned to the cab.

'Sir, wait,' Chris implored, trying to inject some urgency into his weary voice. 'DI Crighton is in hospital, injured. We have Ciernik. I'm convinced Richard Stoke is involved and has been persuaded to take Molly Gowland out of the country. You've got to put a stop on the ports.'

He tried to see if Sally looked as incredulous as he felt, but she sat with her elbows on the table, her face hidden in her hands.

'I'll decide what steps we take, young man.' Vane's arrogance leapt from the speaker-phone on the desk.

'At least do a search. See whether he's passed through a border point.'

'This is a bigger operation than you can

comprehend.' Vane's obstinacy persisted. 'Your DI has been updated and that's all you need to know.'

Chris couldn't understand how the SOCA officer could be so detached from the situation. A human tragedy was now unfolding. All because Chris and his team had been so hamstrung by the lack of knowledge early in the operation, the stubbornness of their prime suspect and now the belligerence of an official who thought himself better than everyone else.

'Listen, Sir, I don't care how big your operation is. If anything happens to that young girl, I'm going to personally make sure you can't hide behind your department. I've seen how much you've suppressed DI Crighton in his enquiries and, to me, there's enough evidence to show you've jeopardised her chances of being rescued.'

Chris's angry response had jolted Sally upright. She dropped her hands to the table and looking at Chris with curious respect.

'Don't threaten me, constable,' Vane retaliated, his voice betraying uncertainty. 'I'll have you out of your job before you can think...'

The line went dead

'Try not to take it personally,' Sally said.

'I can't. There's a girl's life at stake.'

'You'll face worse than this in your career, Chris. You have to try to disassociate your feelings from it. Look, you'll be Sergeant soon enough and won't be able to get so emotional in front of your own men.'

'I suppose,' Chris said quietly. He knew the call would soon come. The posting order that would see him established in another region, with a new team and with new responsibilities. He didn't relish the idea.

Consciousness crept back to Molly Gowland in small painful jolts. Dark. Hard to breathe. Cramp screaming through her legs. She tried to stretch but was bound so tightly she could barely move. She could hear a constant deep rumble that sent a dull throbbing vibration through the container that held her. Small holes in the lid allowed light and an oily smell in.

Her last memory had been of the foreign man pushing a needle into her unresisting arm. That had been back at the house, still tied up in the cupboard that she'd shared with the smelly boy. He'd been injected first and carried out unconscious. When her turn had come she resisted the urge to struggle. She'd learned from numerous slaps in the previous week not to fight back at the man with the dark, cold eyes.

Where she was now she had no idea. The diet of chocolate bars and water had left her feeling sick. Combined with the after effects of whatever had been used to put her to sleep, her treatment in the previous week had crushed her spirit and she could only wish for release from this latest captivity. To what fate it would lead her, she no longer cared. The noise and vibrations around her diminished and she wondered whether this was the end of her nightmare or if it was just the beginning.

Chris woke to the sound of his phone signalling a text inbound. He looked around the office. Alone. Sally had departed whilst he slept at his desk. A post-it note on his monitor read: 'Good luck Chris.' So, she'd finally made her mind up. Would he see her again? It probably didn't matter any more.

He looked at his phone. The text that had roused him had come in at 6:26 a.m. 'Don't forget our agreement' Why was Hazel Moran reminding him of his obligation? She couldn't have heard about Ciernik's arrest already, surely.

He started looking for the web browser on his phone, quickly realising the basic device didn't boast such a luxury. Remembering the Guv had a radio in his office, he skirted desks and the incident board to gain access to his bosses room. The office was cold this early. Another cold harbour, Chris thought looking around.

Shelter, but no warmth. No support and no sustenance.

The radio clicked on to the dying bars of a song. 'Don't stop believing,' repeated to fade, followed by the 6:30 news jingle.

'Police turned a cross-channel ferry back to Dover last night after an order from the Serious Crimes Agency. A sixteen year old boy, missing since 2006, was found tied up and hidden in the back of a truck.' Chris's heart sank. The announcer continued. 'Ian Holloway had disappeared from Stoke on Trent aged twelve. Police had believed he may have been sleeping rough in London since then.'

Chris slumped in his bosses chair. Moran's text must have originated after Ciernik's capture, then. No news of Molly.

'To their surprise, Police also discovered the recently disappeared ten year old girl, Molly Gowland, hidden inside a false fuel tank. A man has been been arrested and linked to the murder of the girls father, Simon Hearst.'

The rest of the news program continued on the periphery of Chris's consciousness. He left the radio playing to itself and left Crighton's office. Feelings of pride and relief swam through him and Sally's warning echoed through his head. How could he not get emotionally involved when the results brought such relief and pride?

He stared at the incident board with its names, photographs and connecting lines. The the tally that had to be counted. The lost and damaged lives, the broken relationships and debts owed. All of these sat alongside the triumph and achievement he felt and he realised he needed to harden himself to both if he was to succeed.

'Is that what you want?' he asked himself. Looking around the empty office, he wasn't so sure.

2702689R00143

Printed in Great Britain
by Amazon.co.uk, Ltd.,
Marston Gate.